ALLOWANCE FOR A TEENAGE HOOKER

RB PAHL

ISBN
978-1-961250-61-1 (Paperback)
978-1-961250-62-8 (eBook)

Allowance For A Teenage Hooker

PROLOGUE

Sandy made it out the back door and was sticking to the shadows alongside the building. She'd had enough. Called on to turn a trick in her room for the fourth time tonight was enough. She wasn't going to wait for a fifth. She was sore, and her face burned from one of the johns getting his jollies by slapping her silly when he climaxed. She could see the parking lot in the back and it was empty.

Emboldened, she struck out straight for the tree shadows on the far side of the driveway.

"Gwine somewhere?" A deep voice asked.

"Shit!" she shouted and bolted to run. A man who played linebacker in college tackled her on the neighbor's lawn. With a large man on each arm, she was brought before the "House Mother", AKA Black Willa.

"Girl," The heavy woman said, "Yo knows the penalty for leavin' without payin' up your bill..."

She struggled to no avail. "I've paid my god-damned bill, especially tonight! Four johns and one of them a beater? I think I've done my fucking share!"

"Not quite girlfrien," the woman grunted and slugged Sandy in the stomach repeatedly for what seemed like an eternity. "Yo gots two more johns tonight. These two nice bros who heping you to da car in the parking lo..."

Sandy screamed before a meaty hand clamped over her mouth. With an incredibly deep chill, she realized that she would never see sunrise again. Her bladder released its contents.

It was nearly an effortless lift for the two black "guards". In truth, they were enforcers, and they had just enforced the supreme punishment for the pretty teenaged girl with copper hair. She wasn't pretty now.

Her crime was trying to leave the house. By the time the two goons finished raping her; finished kicking and stomping her; she was unrecognizable as to her identity, and almost unrecognizable as to being human.

She was bloody, limp, dead meat to wrap in an old carpet. They tossed the roll into the trunk of their car and drove away, heading for Fort Point under the Golden Gate Bridge. Fort Point was as good as any place to dump the body. It was close to the place where the tidal waters moved the fastest, and at this time, just turning to an outbound tide.

They prepared the roll per Willa's instructions. Add enough weight to counteract the air entrapped in the carpet; allow the body to sink, slowly. It might take perhaps twenty-five to forty pounds.

They did their work efficiently, as they had done this before. The necessary materials were at hand. Tightly wrap the ends with duct tape, so the carpet wouldn't unroll for quite a while, if ever. Finally drill a one-inch hole through the carpet right into her viscera. Place a one inch perforated plastic pipe in the hole, so that body gasses would escape into the depths, take a couple a tape wraps around the girth, just for good measure, and the girl would rest in Davy Jones locker forever.

If they did the job correctly, the roll would have a slight negative buoyancy, but not enough to make it sink and stay on the bottom of the bay under the rushing current. It would tumble and bounce along the bottom until it came to a really deep place, or the current ran out of strength. Then it would drift into a depression in the bottom where even a moderate surface current couldn't move it. Any trapped air would dissolve into the seawater, and in about ten hours, the body could be five miles offshore, and in it's final resting place.

They consulted their watches, because the body had to be dumped at a certain time to take the most advantage of the millions of tons of water moving to the west at speeds up to five knots. When it was time, they carried her down the riprap to the water's edge and threw her as far into the black bay as possible, which was about ten feet. Even a foot or more out into the water would make a difference.

"She's history," one of them said.

"Yeah. A giant, human sushi-roll for bottom-feeders," the other said.

"Time for a long pull on that bourbon bottle."

"Amen, Brother."

CHAPTER ONE

I stood at my office window, not really seeing what I was looking at. A common enough thing for frightened people. Visibility was about a mile in one direction, and a quarter mile in the other where an ugly black rain cell was moving in. When I looked up at the overcast I could see a dull gray low-to-the-ground scud skittering to the east, cleansing the air with its steady drizzle. The only good thing about the sporadic showers was that it was shining and repainting the yellowish World War Two style warehouse buildings across the tarry dirt parking lot.

My mood was as dark as the weather. A month ago, I hung out a shingle claiming that I was a Confidential Researcher. It's been a whole month and the phone hasn't rung once… well, that's not entirely true.

I've received (according to my detailed cell-phone log) three sales calls from computers, one obscene call (note to the guy who called: If you've lost my number, it's 555-415-7245), and five dunning calls from a department store in San Francisco. It was the only one left I owed money.

My cell phone rang like an old-fashioned phone, startling the daylights out of me.

"Tracy Cunningham."

"Miss Cunningham, my name is Bradford. Charles Bradford. I was given your number by a mutual friend."

Didn't think I had any friends.

"Who?"

"Your Madam. Nora Pincolini."

"Eff off! I'm not in that line of work anymore, you sorry sonofabitch!" I slammed the phone down a bit sharply.

Sheese! It isn't even lunchtime yet!

What's a Confidential Researcher? She's a person who wants to be a Private Investigator but doesn't have the guts to have a background check run. I'll explain.

A few weeks ago everything was fine in my life. I was safe. I was an investigator for the Peerless Insurance Company, the third such company I'd worked for in six years. I was twenty-five, single, and knocking down pretty decent money. I had an apartment overlooking the Marina in San Francisco, a rather expensive pad, especially for my salary. Over fifty percent of my base wage went for rent. The question was, "How could I afford such digs?"

Simple.

I supplemented my income at night. If that makes you think I might have been something like a professional party-girl, a ball of fluff, a bed bunny intended to decorate a man's arm in public and provide an age-old form of aerobic exercise in the privacy of a bedroom, you're right.

My phone rang again.

"Wait a second!" the voice shouted before I got my greeting out. "I'm not calling to get laid!"

"Mister, if you're lying, I'm going to call a cop friend of mine... a BIG cop friend of mine."

"Girlfriend," he said with disgust, "I have all the doxies I can handle at my fingertips. I don't need to relieve my tensions with a under-built, overpriced ex-hooker."

The only part I could agree with was the 'underbuilt' crack.

I had to take a chance that he was sincere. I wasn't in a position to choose my cases.

"What can I do for you?" I asked.

"First of all, tell me where the hell your office is! I've been all over this town looking for you."

"It's rather hard to find," I chuckled, "How about I meet you at the Ginnaker?"

"Fine. How soon?"

"I'll be there in fifteen minutes."

"I'll be the one guzzling beer."

I ran through the rain to Maggie. Maggie is my beautiful MG-TF 1500, a college graduation present from Dad. Maggie and I have this agreement. She doesn't let me down and I won't push her off a cliff. Most of the time it works...

The last time she refused to cooperate with me was the day I was late for work, got caught talking trash to a nighttime client and got myself canned. So I blame Maggie for that bad day. It was her fault. Completely! Even though I hate 'em, if I'd had a gun, I would have jammed it up her tail pipe and shot her black little distributor out.

I dodged potholes on a muddy, graveled roadbed alongside the old railroad tracks until I got to asphalt-paved streets.

We motored on down to the Ginnaker, a well-known restaurant in Sausalito's downtown tourist section. The name was a play on words, combining Gin and Spinnaker. Not too many people know there really is a sail called a Ginnaker. It was a cross between a Genoa and a Spinnaker, like that stupid-looking thing Dennis Conners flew off the bow-sprit of that equally ridiculous Catamaran in the America's Cup back in the eighties. But that started a trend, and now when the new America Cuppers race, they use these kind of foresails.

I entered the classy restaurant, stopping in the foyer to take off my raincoat and make sure I looked presentable. I was wearing neatly pressed aqua slacks that were tastefully snug, and a white Angora sweater. A quick brushing primp of my hair, a check to make sure there was nothing green and slimy wedged between my teeth, and I decided it was as good as it was going to get.

I walked into the polished room with and old Brunswick-styled bar and smiled a hello to Dennis, a good bartender and one of my few platonic male friends. He was a pro, not acknowledging that he knew me or knew what I was drinking unless I told him.

The guy at the end of the mahogany bar drinking a Budweiser straight from a long-necked bottle had to be Bradford. And I knew he'd asked Dennis if he knew me.

A pair of super deductions, right? Not really. Dennis tilted his head in my direction when I walked in, and there was just one customer in the place because it was only eleven in the morning. Somewhere in the restaurant, there was the cyclical hum of a floor polisher.

Bradford was dressed in an expensive dark brown suit, accompanied by a classic white-on-white shirt, French cuffs, garish gold and fake ruby cuff-links, a red silk tie, and expensive-looking shoes. He wasn't very big, maybe five-ten.

He was somewhat stocky, and my practiced eye… trained by the paranoia of being a small woman who once made a living meeting unknown men at night… told me he was powerful in a physical sense. Dark haired, he looked like he was in his mid-forties to early fifties.

I stood next to him and smiling, held my hand out to shake his. "Mr. Bradford? I'm Tracy Cunningham."

"Glad to meet you." His eyes gave me the requisite cursory once-over, just slow enough to tell me he was boorish, sullen, and ill-mannered and that was being charitable about it."

What's it going to be, Miss Cunningham?" Dennis asked formally.

"Black coffee, please." I turned back to Bradford and stared at an imaginary spot between his eyes. "Step into my office?"

He picked up his beer and napkin, following me to a table next to the window with a great view of the silver surface of the bay. There was no activity on the water. No sailboats, just a distant freighter to the east.

"Nice office."

"The rent is great, too."

He sat up a little and faced me. "Speaking of which, how much do you charge?"

"For what?"

"For investigating, of course."

"I have to be honest, Mr. Bradford. I'm not a licensed P.I."

Why not?"

"Seems to me that if you went to Nora, you know my background."

"A little bit, yes."

"That's why."

"Are you any good? As an investigator, I mean."

"I don't know. I charge two hundred a day plus expenses. I'd like a five-day retainer… in advance." I couldn't be sure, but I thought I saw a slight upturn of the corners of his mouth. "That's all?"

"Mr. Bradford, I'm brand new in this business. I'm working alone and I don't know how good or bad I'm going to be. If it turns out that I'm good, then you'll probably be the only person to get my services at this price."

"And if not?"

"There's always the Golden Gate Bridge."

"Huh?"

"Forget it."

"I'm your first client?"

"Yes, sir."

"At least you're honest," he said, flicking his eyes downward again. It didn't take a genius to know what they were focused on when they stopped. I had been conscious of a slight chill waft of air in the room and I suppose my body had reacted. "And I take back that crack about you being under-built. You're slender, but I wouldn't say underbuilt."

I decided to consider that wasn't a come-on, just a statement of fact. Besides, I couldn't just slap him and walk out, could I? I needed a job too badly.

"Thanks," I said. "Mind telling me why you went to Nora, of all people?"

"I was in the hopes that she knew something about the girl I'm looking for. She didn't, but she said that one of her top girls was trying her wings as a quasi-private eye. You tell me. Why did Nora recommend you?" He sat back a little and his eyes studied mine.

"I worked for the Eden Connection part time. My daytime job was investigating for various insurance companies."

"That's your legitimate background?"

"That and a degree in Criminology from UCLA, with a minor in Criminalistics."

"That's a little more like it. Any experiences with missing people?"

"Some. I've found guys who were trying to pull life insurance scams when others... male investigators... had tossed in the towel."

He suppressed a smile at my wisecrack. "Any other experience?"

I was beginning to get impatient. I thought the investigator was supposed to ask the questions. "No. Want to tell me what this is all about?"

"Can you find someone for me?"

"Depends."

"On what?"

"I don't know," I snapped. "Just depends."

"You have a bit of a chip on your shoulder, don't you?"

"Do I? I didn't notice."

The distant freighter was near enough to see that it had a green hull.

He took something from his coat pocket. "I'm trying to find this girl."

He handed me a black and white wallet-sized studio portrait of a pretty teenager with flowing dark hair. I looked it over it and checked the reverse side. Under a simple "Love, Steph" was his name, address, and phone number. If it was the same, her home address was on Belvedere Island.

"Who is she?"

"My daughter. Her name is Stephanie Bradford."

"How old is she?"

"Almost fifteen there. Seventeen, now."

"A kid."

"Legally, yes. Otherwise, no."

"What's that mean?"

"She's been out of my home and control for a couple of years."

"With her mother?"

"No."

"Who, then?"

"On her own."

"So she's an emancipated teen?"

"I suppose."

"When was the last time you saw her?"

"Two years ago."

"And you're just getting around to tracking her now?"

"Yes."

"Why?"

"That's my affair."

"You don't want to find her very badly, do you?"

"Why?"

"Why hire someone like me... someone who has no track record? Obviously you aren't poor, unless that suit is the only thing of class you own. You can afford a lot better than me."

"True. But I was thinking that if anyone in the city would know where to look, it'd be you."

"Why?" "Shit, girl. Do I have to spell it out? How in the hell is a fifteen-year-old girl on her own going to earn her way? You're an ex-whore, right? Who best can find a girl who's undoubtedly whoring herself?

"Do you want the job or not?"

I bit my tongue. I hate the word "Whore". As much as I wanted to spit in his eye, I figured now was not the time to explain that the class of escorts I once was wouldn't know too much about teen-hookers or where they'd hang out.

"I want it."

"Good. Can you start now?"

"I start the moment you give me a check."

Without another word he wrote me a check for a thousand dollars. I looked at it with a feeling of relief." If you find her quickly, say in a week or two, there'll be a thousand dollar bonus in it for you."

Before I did something stupid like hugging him to say thanks, I said, "Want to give me some clues about where I can find her?"

"The last time I saw her, her ass going out the door. December, two years ago. I got two calls from Cincinnati. One the month after she left and one about a year ago. They were 'I'm all right' calls. Not even from her. It was from some sort of runaway child hot line number."

"And the last you heard from her was...?"

"I've been hearing rumors that she relocated back here about six months ago."

"That's it?"

"They were pretty reliable rumors. She's someplace in the Bay area."

That narrowed it down to about twenty or thirty cities. "Great... Where did she go to school?"

"Lincoln High in San Rafael."

"If you lived in Belvedere, how come she went to school in San Rafael?"

"They're the only ones who would take her."

"Anything else?"

"Shit, kid, if I knew more I wouldn't need you, would I?"

"I guess not. Where's her mother?"

"Beats hell out of me. The last time I saw her ass, she was heading out the door. A couple a years or so earlier than the girl."

"You get that view a lot, don't you?"

"Seems like it."

"You're gonna get it again."

While I was behind the foyer screen putting on my coat, I overheard Bradford say to Dennis, "No tits, but she's got a great little bucket. Bet she screws like a mink in heat. Come to think of it, she'd have to, to be one a Nora's top girls. That's a very expensive stable, you know."

"Don't know 'bout that. But I'll give you this: Trace's ass is the nicest I've ever seen on a little woman." I'm going to have to remember to give Denny a bigger tip next time I'm in. Bradford can keep his eyes and wagers to himself.

If I stand up straight and stretch a little, I'm five two, weigh a hundred and ten, plus or minus three pounds, have shoulder-length blonde hair and sky blue eyes. If the truth were to be known, I'm down to one oh three because I've been hoarding my meager funds by eating once a day. That's not enough for a person who eats like a lumberjack and has the metabolism to burn it off without getting overweight.

That's why I'm so frightened. I've been at this investigating thing for a month, and my income has been zip.

I'm told that I have a reasonably good figure. I can't quite fill a B, but a freshly washed A-cup makes my eyes cross. Luckily, I can just go without. The best part of my shape is from my belly button down. In that zone, I'm as close to a perfect ten as a shrimp can be.

No brag, just fact.

I've always been good at investigating. As a child I was always curious about things. Which is a way to say I was quite nosy, which earned me more than one black eye and a few skinned knuckles.

I graduated from the University of California at Los Angeles a few years ago in Criminology. I am the only child of a widower who happens to be one of the Lord High Mucky-Mucks in the Los Angeles Police Department.

My father is the only son of a well known and much loved, now deceased, Police Captain. So I have plenty of background to make investigating the sort of work that's in my blood. My mind is good at what I do, but my size leaves something to be desired.

I hate guns. More to the point, I'm afraid of them. Ever since I became a teenager, I've hated physical combat. I was always the class shrimp. I never won a playground fight as a child, and I certainly wasn't going to win any battles now.

That presents a bit of a problem because I've got a real short Irish fuse combined with a big mouth. Blue language just seems to roll off my tongue without a conscious thought from me. Being raised by a cop with no female role model around to temper my vocabulary may have had a lot to do with that.

Now that I'm an adult, my primary lines of defense are two: talking my way out of trouble or running. I can lie like a rug if need be, or I can run like a deer, especially if someone's chasing me with the intention of doing me bodily harm.

I found a little garden apartment way up in the back side of Sausalito and moved from San Francisco the first of the month. It's adequate, I guess. The rent is right. Tell you one thing: sure is one helluva lot different having to move a plastic-topped, el cheapo coffee table so you can pull your bed out of the wall, especially when you're used to sleeping in a luxury king-size bed overlooking the bay.

The only view from my new place is the beat-up wooden garage of the main house and a wooden fence in the other direction. I still haven't figured out why it was advertised as a garden apartment. Perhaps because "Garden Apartment" sounded better than "Outhouse".

I had what was left of three thousand dollars in severance pay and my share of that last week's worth of penthouse parties, another twenty-four hundred. I even opened a new checking account in Sausalito because I don't have the foggiest idea what the balance was in my old account. I hate book work, so I didn't take very good care of that either.

Rent on the hole in the wall that I laughingly call my office is four headliners a month. My ratty apartment costs me five hundred dollars, no pets allowed. I guess there's not enough food for resident pests and tenant pets.

Utilities aren't bad, about two hundred for both places. I don't need to spend money on clothing as I have more designer duds than I'll be able to wear out in ten years. Most of it is freshly cleaned and hung in vacuum-sealed plastic bags, neatly packed into cardboard moving boxes. I'll still be able to use a lot of the expensive clothing... once I have a reason to dress up.

When I was on a spending spree, I bought expensive working outfits, and fairly conservative "civilian" stuff, dresses and suits that will be in style for years. Some of those other outfits are more daring evening wear that probably won't see fresh air for a very long time, if ever again. Maybe when I get married, I'll pull some of the sexy stuff out of mothballs and use them on my husband.

Me? Married? Bite your tongue!

My groceries aren't expensive because I can't boil water. On the way home, I stop at delis, take-out restaurants or fast food places and eat greasy hamburgers or pizza, if I'm in a good mood. If not, I go home and eat cold cereal while watching Fox news.

A few times since the day when I was fired and self-retired, men have called me and invited me to eat at some fantastic places. My cell phone makes it's noise...

"Trace? How 'bout some dinner and dancing? Perhaps a few drinks and a show? Or, heh-heh, maybe we can go back to my place, open up this bottle of really great Remy Martin I bought and just fall into a horizontal position early?"

There's been a couple of guys calling who I'd love to go out with... even including the overnight option.

Okay, okay... I admit they were former clients, as I have no boyfriends. A few of my former regulars are super-good guys and I don't think I would say no, even if there was no commerce involved. I nearly accepted a couple of times, but that line of Snaggletooth's kept running through my mind. "Grow up," she said... to my back.

Talk about culture shock. Let me tell you, sitting in your car gagging down a slippery quarter-pounder when you know some gal has probably already rented your beautiful place, eating out in your favorite restaurants, savoring the best that Ernie's has to offer in the company of a good man. Especially when you know they're going to spend the rest of the night doing rather nice things to and for each other in the same cozy bed you've spent innumerable fun-filled nights in.

But I'm doing it. I'm turning down every damn date Nora, from my former service, the Eden Connection, tries to convince me to take. I'm turning down all the ex-customer's friendly phone calls for dates, no matter how nice they were to me. I know if I slip just one time, I'm back in the game. So I'm holding forth.

It's a bitch, but I think I like myself much more this way.

CHAPTER TWO

Interesting.

My first case, and my client wants me to find his daughter after two years of being among the missing. Maybe some of the interesting part was that I didn't like Bradford.

Now that I was working, I decided I could afford to stop for a quick sandwich, then I drove north on to San Rafael and Lincoln High. Stephanie Bradford would be a senior by now, so I asked for the senior class advisor. Her name was Mrs. Quinn.

Mrs. Henrietta Quinn.

I sat with a strange uneasiness on the other side of the metal desk and waited for her to finish her paperwork. When she did, she smiled and said, "Sorry for my rudeness, Miss Cunningham, but I have to get these reports to the principal in an hour."

"Not a problem," I replied and handed her my card that said "Tracy Cunningham, Research and Investigations."

I hoped that was generic enough that I wouldn't get in trouble by trying to pass myself off as licensed. Besides, I did plunk down a couple a hundred for a General Business License as a "Researcher".

"I've been asked to find Stephanie Bradford. She was a student here two years ago. Here's her photo."

I handed the gray-haired woman the wallet portrait.

"Oh, yes, I remember her. A wild sort. Always in some sort of trouble."

"What kind of trouble?"

"The usual... Mostly boys and liquor."

"Drugs?"

"Now, I can't say drugs for sure. I never caught her taking any, or being stoned, or whatever the kids say these days. Considering her sexual reputation, maybe her other habits didn't leave time for pot or coke."

A chill of recognition ran down my spine. This was hitting awfully close to home. "Stephanie lived in Belvedere. Why was she going to school here?"

"Aren't you aware that this is a private high school?"

"I didn't know that."

"We have this campus and we have one in Marin for sixth to eighth-graders. Lincoln Senior Elementary. We make it a point not to call attention to the fact that we're private, for the student's sake. We take the ones who are too unruly and their regular schools are fed up with them. Most of our kids come from good homes but are quite rebellious. Not hard-core delinquents, but can be, if they don't change.

"Take this girl, for example," she said, handing me back the photo. "Stephanie's mother left home a couple of years before Stephanie did. Her father wasn't what you'd call a doting parent. I never heard from him other than the time when he called to ask if Stephanie was in school. She wasn't, and we've never seen her since.

"The biggest crime of all was that Stephanie was a good girl under all that," she added. "When she cleaned up her act, she was quite attractive. She scored very well in her SATS. If she had applied herself, she would have been an excellent student, on the honor roll. As it was, she barely scraped by with Cs and Ds."

"What went wrong?"

"Typical teen-age story. She didn't do her homework. She didn't care. In my opinion, Stephanie had no place to turn to for love except her boyfriends. She wanted to be a member of the gang."

"Did Stephanie have any good friends here? Are any of the girls or boys still enrolled?"

"Only a few of them. It was a pretty tough bunch.

"Stephanie's best friend was a girl named Stacy Reese. She dropped out last year. I understand that she still lives in the area though.

"Stephanie's boyfriend was a kid named Jerry Morresey. When she was here, they were very close. Since she left, he hasn't been seeing any other girls, at least that I'm aware of. Jerry got his act together. He's a nice young man, when he's away from the wrong influences."

She checked a class schedule and said, "If you want to talk to him, he should be on his lunch hour now."

"Where does he hang out?"

"I can't let you roam around the campus, Miss. I can get him in here."

I waited in the outer office, feeling a renewed sense of Deja Vu. I can't remember how many times I was waiting in a room just like this, for a butt chewin' session with the Dean Of Women at good o' R.F.K. High in Los Angeles.

I looked up when I saw a good looking kid of seventeen or eighteen being told to go into Mrs. Quinn's office. In moments, the secretary hung up her phone and asked me to go in.

"This is Miss Cunningham, Jerry. She's looking for Stephanie Bradford."

"Hey." he said politely, but coldly.

"Jerry, do you know where Stephanie is?"

"No."

It didn't take a much of a detective to see that he was lying. "Jerry, it's vital that I find her."

"Why?"

"Because she may need help. Her father's very worried about her."

"Oh, really?" He glared at me. "That's new. Back when, he didn't give a damn... darn... whether the sun rose or set as far as she was concerned."

"Maybe he's had a change of heart."

"Yeah... Right... Sorry. I can't help."

"Can't or won't?"

"You figure it out."

"Will anyone else know about her?"

"Nope." He stood up and asked Quinn, "Can I go now?"

I gave her an imperceptible nod before she said "Yes."

"Okay. Nice meeting you."

"Same here." I waited in the outer office for a few moments, then left. I may have been discouraged, but I hadn't stopped thinking. I just managed to get to my car and cruise past the student parking lot in time to see Jerry slam the trunk on a twenty-year old Chevy and go back into the campus.

Never changes, does it?

I figured that no self-respecting kid with a car is going to use the lockers in the halls. Lockers are reserved for the kids with big heavy glasses, the ones who wear 'Nerd-Packs' in their breast pocket and had Spiderman backpacks. If all went according to plan, and he did know where Stephanie was, the chances were he would lead me right to her.

Piece a cake!

I waited in my car listening to an F.M. jazz station while Morresey got his little head crammed full of important facts like who was second in command at the Battle of Little Big Horn... Things you really have to know in the real world.

Two hours later, his black Chevy came out of the parking lot. When Jerry's field of vision had to pass over Maggie, I was crouching down in the front seat. As I heard the loud mufflers heading away, I sat up. I began to pull away from the parking place then slammed on the brakes. A puffing, stinking, diesel, yellow bus had stopped right next to me! Double parked!

I was blocked in.

"Damnit! Move it move it move it!"

I yelled and honked Maggie's insignificant horn as loud as I could, wishing that the harder I pushed the button, the louder it would sound. After boarding a few hundred computer nerd-types, the bus pulled away, completely blocking my vision of Jerry's Chevy.

Shit!

I pulled around the lumbering bus as soon as I could, just in time to see the Chevy get on the on-ramp of the freeway. By the time I got on the freeway and was at the "Y" that split north and south, Jerry was gone.

Naturally.

Freeway? Hot Car? The kid firewalled it. What kid wouldn't?

My heart sank as I realized that in being so damn coy about not being seen, I completely forgot to look at his license plate. I didn't know where the kid lived. If he was going to see Stephanie, it was a lead-pipe cinch that she was going to go underground the moment she found out her beloved daddy hired a detective to find her.

So that first day at being Tracy Cunningham, Finder of Lost Persons, was a total wipe-out. I'd screwed up more than I'd helped my own cause.

All I had on the kid was his last name and the make and year of his car. I didn't have connection one with the California DMV, so I decided to head over to the San Francisco Cop-Shop and see the one guy I could call a friend. We actually dated one time. I had to break our budding romance off before I fell in love with him.

CHAPTER THREE

I walked into the police station, a bit nervous. I had been here before as an investigator for various insurance companies, which made me a little like an insider. But in my former moonlighting job, the Police Department was our natural enemy.

In a bored voice, the desk sergeant asked what I wanted.

"I'd like to see Sergeant Phillips, please."

"Greg Phillips?"

"Yes."

"Okay," he sighed, going into a memorized routine. "Let's see some ID, sign in on the first available line in the book, tell me you aren't carrying a weapon, and wear this visitor's badge where anyone can see it."

City requirements mean that I had to show two forms of picture ID, and have my name run through a computer, just to get past the half-door that leads to the bullpens.

I did what he told me to do, swore on a stack of Bibles that I wasn't carrying, and carefully clipped a visitor's badge to my beautiful sweater, just knowing the alligator clamp was going to ruin it.

Then I saw a board behind him with a lot of photographed badges, of different colors. They were fairly new looking.

"What are those?"

"ID Badges for regular visitors, people who come in all the time. Attorneys, P.I.'s, people like that..."

"I'm an investigator of sorts," I said. "How do I get one of those?"

Again, he sighed heavily and handed me a stack of papers. "Have Phillips fill out the top form, you fill out the rest, get fingerprinted, have a serious background check run, and get a mug shot taken, bring it all back and wait a few weeks."

"All that," I pouted, "just for a freaking badge?"

"Kid," he smiled for the first time, "if you're going to deal with any agency of any municipal government, you better get used to a lot of red tape and pure bullshit."

"Thanks. Where can I find Phillips?"

"Third floor, second door on the right. Homicide division. Elevator's right over there."

I trotted up the stairs instead. I hadn't been exercising lately, and any excuse to get my heart working was welcome.

I opened the frosted glass door, and was greeted by a uniformed woman wearing corporal's stripes.

"May I help you, Miss?"

"Sergeant Greg Phillips, please."

"Lemme buzz him. What's your name?"

"Tracy Cunningham."

"Sign in here, please." She handed me a log book while she punched in Phillips' number. "Greg? There's a gal out here to see you. Name's Tracy Cunningham.. Okay."

She hung up and smiled. "Go on back. He's got the northeast cubicle in the far corner, on the bay side."

"Thanks." I followed her directions.

Sergeant Phillips was in his office, if one can call a six by eight, half-enclosed area an office, doing some busy work.

"Hi, Tracy." He stood up and indicated a chair. I should say the chair.

"What's on the mind of the cutest insurance investigator in the city?"

"I need some help." I looked up at him. Way up. Phillips is six foot-six tall and kind of wiry. He's got short, light brown hair, blue eyes, a deeper color than mine, and a neat smile. Uses it a lot around me. Maybe he's in lust.

"But before I let you labor under false impressions, I've gone on my own now."

"As what?"

"I'm sort of a researcher."

"You? A P.I.?"

"I'm not a P.I.. I said Researcher."

"Why don't you get a ticket?"

"Personal reasons."

"Uhuh." He made it a point to look me square in the eye." Well, I'm glad to see that you're working again. I heard about you getting canned. What can I do for you?"

"What was that look for?"

"What look?"

"C'mon Sarge. Out with it."

His ears turned a little red. Just like mine do when I get caught with my hand in the cookie jar.

"I heard a few things recently."

I decided that it might be better to be completely up-front with him. "Like me maybe doing a little moon-lighting?"

He nodded.

"What did you hear?"

"A guy from Vice, with a pair of binoculars, saw you go into an office building here where we know a certain escort service operates. He saw you in the office of that service. He came to me and says, 'One a your girl friends is working at the Eden Connection.'

"I asked him, 'Who?'

"He told me, 'That little blonde pixy I've seen hangin' around when you were in Bunco. It didn't take a Sherlock Holmes to deduce who he was talking about, considering you are the only blonde pixy I know."

"What did you think when you heard that?"

"I was boiling mad at first."

"I don't like being conned... then I was disappointed... I thought you were classier than that. Then I said fuck it. If you want to mess your life up, it's not my problem."

"And when was this?"

"Around the beginning of the month."

"Greg, by the first of this month," I said, "I was already out of the game. I was in that office collecting the rest of what I was owed. I quit the Eden a couple a weeks after I got fired from my daytime job.

"True story.

"I've only got my bank account to live on, and that's not much. An' I may have to live on that for six months until I get a good, legitimate business going.

"If you had the slightest bit of concern about me, you'd know that I'm living in a roach-infested slum... and I've been treating myself to greasy burgers, once a day, for sustenance. I'm down to ninety-nine pounds."

Sometimes one must exaggerate...

"Really?" He actually seemed to brighten. "For real?"

"For real."

"So how did you do it? Get out, I mean."

"The Eden didn't have pimps. Nora, who is still a good friend, personally did my booking. When I told her I was quitting, she told me good luck and if I ever wanted to come back in I'd always be welcome."

"Would you ever consider going back in?"

"I ought to slug you for even asking that!"

"You do that and it's assault on a cop." He said, "it's that I don't want to waste my time with you if you're going to turn around one day and decide that being a hooker is an easier way to make a buck."

"Believe me it's not. And I won't."

"Promise?"

"Why should I?"

"Dammit, Girl, I'm trying to make up my mind about you. I want your word!"

I sighed, "Greg, I made myself a solemn vow last month never to prostitute myself again. I promise you the same thing.

He smiled and stood up. "Let's go."

"Where?"

"I'm buying you the best dinner in town, or better yet, I'll offer you a home-cooked meal at my place. The greasy burgers getting to you."

"Huh?"

"You're much too skinny and you've got a zit on your cheek."

"Oh, shit." I blushed and covered my face with my hands.

"Relax." He grinned. "It's a only little tiny one. Will you have dinner with me?"

"Ask me that again," I said, "and you'll be talking in an empty office."

Because I didn't want to see a waiter or a commercial restaurant for a long time, and he did have a rep for being a gourmet cook, I opted for his place and followed him home.

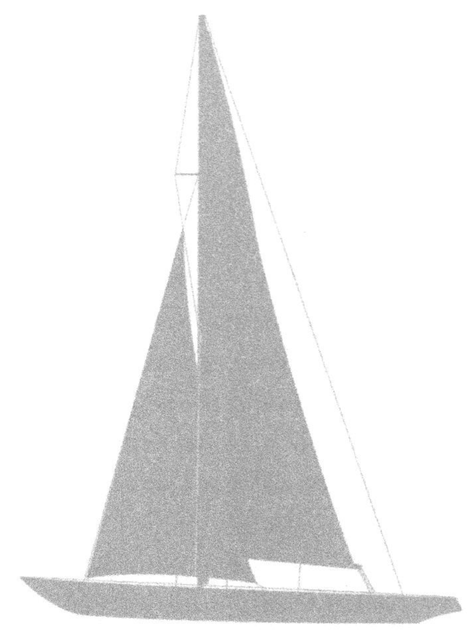

CHAPTER FOUR

Detective Sergeant Greg Phillips lived in a large, clean, condominium in the Sunset hills, on the fifth floor of a fairly new building. He had a view west from his front window of part of the distant ocean, but not enough to make the place overly expensive. His comfortable furnishings were big, almost as though they had been scaled to his size.

The chairs and couches in the living room were gold-yellow crushed velvet. The wood end tables and coffee table were burlwood. The carpet was thick, brown and luxurious.

Soon as I took off my coat I got nosy and explored the condo… just for detective practice, of course. He had a living room… and a kitchen… and a dining area… and a separate bedroom! With a real bed!

A really big bed. Obviously, I was getting too used to living in a one-room shack.

Even though it was a bit cool, I sat out on his breezy balcony watching the sun sizzle into the Pacific. I was unwinding, enjoying my favorite libation, a dry martini on the rocks. We toasted and I took a sip of wonderfully cool Boodles's Gin, very lightly laced with Martini and Rossi Extra Dry Vermouth. My mood warmed quickly.

"We never got around to why you came to my office in the first place." Greg said when we had run the course of small talk.

"I'm looking for a girl and I needed the address of a high school kid. His name is Jerry Morresey. He drives a black twenty-year old Chevy."

"What's his license number?"

"I really screwed up," I blushed, "I didn't get it."

"Some kind of detective, hah?" The way he said it I couldn't get mad.

"Yeah." I grinned. "Some kind of detective…"

"Well, it'll take a bit more time, but I think I can find out for you."

"God, I'll be forever in your debt!"

"Just add it to the dinner tab."

"Okey-doakey." I followed him inside. It was getting downright cold, and I had grown two small, but noticeable bumps under my sweater. "Can I do anything to help?"

"You can peel a couple of potatoes."

"Okay." I was wearing a wide grin. "How do you peel potatoes?"

"Just how good a cook are you?" He began snickering. "... And that's one on me. You said you were eating burgers. Bet you can't cook very well."

"How 'bout not at all?"

"In that case, you just slide up on that bar stool, sip your drink and look cute while I do it."

"I can so do that. What are we having?"

"I've got some fresh trout. How does Trout Almandine sound?"

I giggled, "I don't know what kinda noise a live trout makes, much less a dead one."

"Groannn." He rolled his eyes to the ceiling and began preparing the dinner. During another martini break, he called his office, asking whoever answered to run down Morresey's car and call him at home.

We could hear distant sirens and a couple of car horns. To fill the quiet moment I asked, "Tell me about Greg Phillips, the man."

"Not much to tell, really. I'm from Detroit. My entire family still lives there."

"So why come out here to be a cop?"

"It's something I had to do. I'm the youngest in an extremely domineering family. I needed to breathe."

"I can dig it. What's your girlfriend going to say when she finds out you entertained another girl in your pad?"

"Tracy." He smiled and looked right at me. "Stop fishing. I don't have a girlfriend, I don't have a wife, and I don't have any prospects for any of the above. How about you?"

"Not very interested in a wife," I snickered, "But otherwise, same reply. Haven't had a boyfriend in years." I finished my cocktail and poured another out of the frosted glass pitcher. I was beginning to feel the gin, and I was beginning to like him. A lot.

"Why doesn't a cute kid like you have all sorts of men knocking on her door?"

I popped an olive in my mouth. "You have to ask?"

"I'm sorry," he said. His face turned bright red.

"I'm not," I grinned. "That means, just for a moment, you forgot."

"I forgot before we left my office, and that's the truth."

"Thanks." I smiled at him while his flush receded and he began frying the fish. Those two trout became the second and third things in the condo that were getting fried. Having cut back on so many things, my former daily ration of gin had also gone by the boards, and I was out of practice.

I've always been a cheap drunk.

That doesn't sound right, does it? Let's put it this way. I can feel my first drink, and things only get warmer and fuzzier after my second.

Lest you think I got too blotto to enjoy Greg's yummy cooking, I didn't. As soon as food hit my stomach, I came back. Normally, I like pelagic fish like tuna or swordfish. I don't particularly like those cowardly little fish that swim and hide in reefs.

I guess I'll have to add trout almandine to my "like" list. I love shellfish and mollusks. If it doesn't come in a shell or have claws, it's not for me.

It was one of the best evenings I've had in a long, long, time. The mood in Greg's place was perfect, the trout was perfect, the spinach salad was perfect, the scalloped potatoes were perfect, the wine...

especially the wine... was perfect, and so was the super yummy dessert, an outrageous chocolate Mousse that Greg had in his freezer. Just thaw and eat.

After dinner, I was in much better shape. I helped do the dishes, another chore I abhor. I guess that I'm not really the domestic type. Afterward, we sat on his couch to listen to his great collection of old Dave Brubeck and Oscar Peterson record albums, whilst sipping coffee and cognac.

Yes, records. He says they sound mellower. I can believe it. I don't know whether it was by design or what. I don't know if he planned it, or I subconsciously willed it.

In any event, within a half hour I was far too buzzed to drive home. Maybe it was the quality booze. Maybe it was the quality pad. Maybe it was the quality kisses, I don't know. But I slept with him.

At first, we were dancing and I wanted to kiss him. With our height differential it was clumsy, damn near impossible. So we sat on his couch and tried again.

Mmmm. Mucho betta. It was ten thirty or so and we were still kissing, nicely getting to know each other, when his office called back with the address of the kid. Greg handed me a piece of paper with the information on it.

The romantic mood was broken. Out of the blue I was overwhelmed with loneliness. Saying I was disappointed would be an understatement. Having no reason to stick around, I made a move to say good night and kind of lurched when I went to the hall closet.

Sergeant Phillips became a cop for a few minutes and dutifully instructed me that I wasn't in any shape to drive. I would spend the night. He had plenty of extra blankets and pillows. I could sleep on the couch.

I... don't... think so!

Of course I had to agree with him. I should stay. I had no choice, did I? He was a cop and three times bigger than me. I could be arrested, beaten up, or I could stay willingly.

I stayed.

He sat on the couch, while I reassumed my position of laying across his lap, and we kissed again. He was playing it safe; he didn't put a move on me. After awhile, I murmured, "If kissing when we're on the couch is so good, what's it like lying down?"

"Where?"

"In there, dopey," I giggled, pointing to the bedroom. "If you won't ask, I will."

I got to my feet and held my hand out to him. "Ask again and you'll be talking to an empty couch."

I'd already checked out the bedroom. He had the biggest bed I'd ever seen. He called it his quarter-acre bed, and I was anxious to measure it off.

Passing on using the cute shorty nightgown I spotted in his closet, (When I play detective, I get real nosy) I found a tee shirt of his that covered me like a full nightie and got in bed, waiting for him to come out of the bathroom. Strangely, I was nervous. I don't know why. Greg came out wearing navy Bikini cut Jockeys.

Gawd, he was beautiful!

He had the proper amount of muscles and body ripples. He slipped in next to me and we discovered kissing lying down was a considerable improvement over kissing sitting up. His hand found my ribs, then my breasts and began doing delicious things to them.

He slipped the tee shirt over my shoulders and head. I laid back and lost myself in his lips nipping me ever so gently, his tongue encircling and tickling all my erogenous zones. I was gettin' hot, and when I get heat on like this, my whole body becomes an erogenous zone!

He made it clear that I didn't have to do a thing in return... nothing I didn't want to do... He was the seducer, I was the seductee. And I liked that. A lot.

We changed roles for a while, while I returned the same tender touches and oral explorations he had so delightfully done to me.

I don't like to be on top the first time. I like to be smothered, crushed beneath a hard man. He seemed to understand that. We rolled as a unit and I clutched him like I was going to fall away into a pit of desperation if I didn't. I was doing my part and mouth breathing, my head thrown back, and it dawned on me that the audible moans and gasps of ultimate pleasure that were filling the room were mine.

They weren't fake.

I don't do that... ever. Even professionally, I was pretty quiet. I might vocalize in my client's ear. I usually convinced them that a loud woman was only puttin' on a show.

That was when I decided that I like big men. From now on, if they aren't six and a half feet tall, as far as I'm concerned, they're not keepers. Toss 'em back in the pond to grow some more.

Sometime later during the early hours of the morning, he was snoring while I was awake staring at the ceiling. Occasionally headlights would shine in from the top of the hill that was about level with his bedroom.

I was reflecting that I had a lot of reasons to be happy. I hadn't been invited to a man's home for a home-cooked meal for almost five years!

Greg Phillips was the first man in I don't know how long, that I had slept with, that I wanted to sleep with. He was the first man I can remember who made love to me. He was the first in a long time that wouldn't let me do what most men expected girls like me to do, which was fine by me. As such, he was a man I felt a genuine affection for.

He was single, handsome, my kinda big, so why shouldn't I like him? Besides, he could cook like there was no tomorrow, and made love the same way.

I was in a good, new, business. Sure, crime investigation, be it private or public, is a man's field, and I would probably always have to have a man's physical help, but I didn't mind. Really!

I'm not a dyed-in-the-wool feminist. As a human, I want my rights to do whatever I wish. I like the Supreme Court-granted rights to be an independent soul, and to still be a soft girl. I like having a man around. I'd much rather sleep with one than any alternative.

I like men... period.

I've been around men, under the influence of men all my life. More often than not, I was one of the guys. When I was sailing, I was usually the only female in a boat load of virile males, and never and I mean never did any of the men ever suggest a bit of boy-girl stuff. They all knew how important racing was to me.

I liked Greg. I liked him doing the banging, I liked me being the bangee. Making love with him was something I would do all night long, if he desired. I already told him that. Besides, he'd done me that favor, getting that address.

With that thought, A deep, dark chill pushed the blood from my head. Something way down inside my gut froze. Wasn't what I just did the same old shit?

It was. I had just used my little boobs and my tight number ten ass to say thanks. A man did me a favor and cooked me dinner. I repaid him by screwing him cross-eyed. Tears came to my eyes as I realized I was still putting out for gain.

I was still a whore.

I spent a long time in that delicious bed, watching the occasional light cross over my head, crying silently. I hadn't really changed.

I was still hardened.

I think I knew damn well I was going to go to bed with him the moment he asked me to follow him to his place for dinner. Did I want to sleep with him, or was it the only way I could think of to say thank you?

I cuss like a whorehouse parrot, something that I am really trying to stop. Outwardly, I looked the soft feminine part. Inwardly, the inner me was still a fucking whore.

Was I ever going grow up and be a real woman? The idea of saying, "No, I'm not going to be that damn easy," never occurred to me.

At three-thirty I eased out of bed, dressed and left. If I was still a whore, at least I could still be a classy one. A man doesn't want to wake up with the self-propelled receptacle he used last night. I had a hard time seeing the road through my tears.

Shit.

CHAPTER FIVE

I woke up in my crappy whatever at ten thirty. After a quick shower, I put on jeans and a sweat-shirt with the arms cut off at my elbows. I didn't feel too feminine today, and I was going to be sitting in my car most of the time anyway. I checked my voice mail and listened to two recordings of dial tones.

By twelve thirty, I was across and down the street from the parking lot of Lincoln High. I'd cruised through it once, locating Morresey's car. I remembered my own high school days: a senior usually had a heavy day, then a light day, and so on, through the week. As this was Tuesday, the odds were that he'd be getting out earlier than yesterday. I opened a paperback, hoping to get involved with some fictional character's problems, but I kept thinking about my own from last night.

I kept thinking that Greg hadn't phoned this morning to ask why I left. Maybe he expected it. Maybe he wanted me to steal silently into the night. We both knew I wasn't worried about any virtuous reputation. He makes a phone call, cooks me a trout, I ball him. Seems reasonable to me.

I don't know if I like this crummy life. I don't know if the daughter of man who busted his butt to provide me with a damn good home is cut out to live in a grubby one room slum. In spite of my rebellious youth, I know Dad did his best.

What the hell am I trying to prove by working in a job that's almost exclusively a man's field?

Discouragement overwhelmed me. I really didn't think this case was going to be a rewarding endeavor. I had to do something about my life, and that took money. My extensive indebtedness was almost paid off. There were only a few bills that I still got reminder calls about. I felt a chill of fright from deep inside. If things didn't happen soon, I was going to be right back in the circumstances that made me turn pro in the first place.

With the three thousand dollars seed money dad gave me deposited in a nation wide bank, I packed two suitcaces and drove Maggie to San Francisco. I had lined up a good job, which paid well... for a single girl.

It only took five months to prove that my biggest downfall truly was my inability to manage money. For example, I signed contracts and papers that required me to spend over half of my income for living expenses. Things like rent ($1500) and the furniture lease ($350.00.). This was out of three thousand bucks a month income. I had utilities, phone, food, gas, insurance, to take care of before I could even think about getting some clothes.

I didn't realize a thing about taxes withheld until my first paycheck! All my uncles (Uncle Sam, Uncle Cal, Uncle St Francis) wanted vigorish! I had to pay out almost six hundred and got nothing back for it. That was half my left-over income!

Grrrr!

No matter how hard I tried, I was always down to my last fifty bucks a week before my next paycheck. We all know (now) how long that's gonna go on. The only way I could afford to get clothes more suitable for the bay area was the friendly stores and their plastic money. I got some good deals when I signed up for a couple of them. At least the payments were low.

Suddenly... I was in deep ca-ca.

My rescuer was a neighbor. Nora Pincolini lived alone, so she and I had something in common. She never seemed to have a job, and I never saw her on the arm of a man. The way she dressed, she definitely was not batting for the other side. Once in a while I would see her with one or two absolute knock-out women about my age. Usually different ones. I kind of figured they were models and she was their agent...

Once in a while we would chat. I must have told her enough that she made reasonable assumptions about my financial status. My life changed on a warm Thursday evening. I was swimming laps when Nora swam up alongside of me.

"Hi, Tracy."

"Hey Nora."

"You busy tomorrow night?"

"Not really. Why?"

"I'm having a small get together in my condo, and I find myself in need of an additional hostess type girl. I'd like to recruit you. You can earn some real spending money."

I don't really need a sledge hammer on the top of my head, it dawned on me that she was an agent all right, but her beautiful girls weren't models, they were call girls.

After a long discussion, I walked away thinking about my life and how I had screwed it up so much. I turned around to Nora, knowing I didn't have any choice about my fate. I sighed. "Okay. You just got your pepper pot pixy. Nights and weekends only."

"Great! Tracy, I run an elite operation. Except for the split percentage for my new girls, what you've asked for are our normal conditions."

She looked at me carefully. "But I think I can live with the split, too."

"Why?"

"I see something special in your eyes. Something that tells me you're going to be one of my best girls."

Hooshit!

I almost missed seeing Morresey leave again. He roared past me, never giving Maggie a second glance, and headed out to the freeway. I took off behind him, back as far as I thought was safe.

Tracy's Rule Number Five* of the things I can't understand on TV is the bad guys following a car while staying right in their trunk.

Doesn't everyone watch his rear view mirror? If the same grille kept sitting in the mirror, wouldn't almost any person get the teeniest bit suspicious? I sure would.

Morresey got on the South-bound ramp, heading for the Golden Gate Bridge. I stuck with him, keeping a truck or a car between us all the time. We drove right past my old apartment tower, heading downtown. The Marina was still scarred, but even now looking much better.

I glanced up at my old apartment and saw red curtains.

Ugh! Bet the place looks like a whorehouse inside.

I chuckled to myself, hit a red light and lost Jerry in the financial district. I cruised for an hour before I got lucky and saw the black Chevy heading south on Market Street. I followed a bit closer this time, and he led me right to his Ocean Park neighborhood. By now traffic had thinned out. Once I was fairly certain that he was going home, I peeled off and went back to my shack in Sausalito.

Whoopie.

A whole half hour today on the job. Another day without accomplishing one damn thing.

I spent five fast minutes changing clothes in that depressing place I called home and headed for the Ginnaker. It was the end of his shift, but Dennis tossed a napkin in front of me and asked, "What's it going to be, Trace?"

"A marty," I said sullenly. "A double, dry and on the stem."

"Mainlining, huh?"

"Something like that."

"Something wrong?"

"I don't know, Denny," I sighed. "I think I'm coming to a big damn crossroads in my life, and I don't know if I'm ready to make the decisions."

"Sounds heavy."

"It is."

"What are your choices?"

I looked at him and decided that a bartender is supposed to be some sort of psychologist, right? "Do you know what I used to do? The moonlighting thing?"

"Yeah." He polished a few imaginary spots off a glass.

"Didn't know for sure until your buddy told me yesterday. He said you were a call-girl. He said you were undoubtedly a good one, too."

"The operative word is 'was'. That's what my problem is now. I don't want to go back."

"But you're not knocking down enough money to make it without doing it, right?"

"Something like that." I sipped my martini. Sipped, hell, I drained it and put the glass in front of me in an obvious but unspoken demand for refill.

He poured me a full glass of pre-chilled gin and whispered the word "Vermouth" over it. That was about the right amount of dryness for my self-destruct mood.

"What about the case you got yesterday?"

"I don't think that's going to help much. I didn't charge him enough. I'm not cut out to be an independent businesswoman. I'm the kind of person who does good work but needs someone else to take the headache of running a fuc... freaking business."

"You're a dichotomy, Trace."

"Why do you say that?"

"Because you're a little doll until you open your mouth. Sometimes you sound like a little girl who wants to be the big man. You're going to be stubborn as hell, go it alone until you're forced to go back to working on your backsides. And... from what I hear when you talk, I think you want to go back."

"That's a lot of horseshit!" I snapped.

"Is it?" He walked away to see how the other customers were doing. Five minutes later, he slipped out from under the bar and waved good night to his replacement, a fat Lothario that I wasn't too hot about.

I sat on my stool, fuming, thinking about what Denny had said. As I began to cool down, I reflected about what I'd said, thought, and done over the past month. It soon became a real possibility that my friend was right.

For the most part I was wearing a hair shirt, saying to anyone who would listen, (mostly me) "Look how I've sacrificed my beautiful jet-set lifestyle to become a girl with high moral values!"

Some values. Where did I spend last night, and what was I doing at the time? I was so damn depressed I polished off three more martinis and almost let some guy pick me up to take me to dinner and whatever.

Almost.

CHAPTER SIX

Instead, I went into the dining room alone. I sat by myself in a quiet corner table, by my own choice. Even though there was a window table open, I'd seen the bay at night before. From the way some of the tourists argued about sitting next to the glass, you'd think they'd never seen a body of water bigger than their bathtub.

I treated myself to an Rock Lobster tail with all the trimmings and a pony of good wine.

Hell with my budget.

After dinner, I had a severe inner gut-twisting depression as I walked along the tourist section of the waterfront, still reflecting about my life. I recognized the longer that I kept that miserable Roach Motel apartment, the closer I was to going back to Nora. The longer I tried to make it on my own, the closer I would be to saying the hell with it.

I don't want to work on my back!

I had to drive the tramp from me. l had to excise my demons. Have to do something, change something, but what?

I was about to drive home, but I realized that I had enough liquor in me to blow the Hatch Cover off a Sherman Tank. That was another thing. If I didn't do something soon, I'd become a 'No shit' alcoholic.

No shit. <u>She's</u> an alky?

Starting with a small stagger that mellowed into a teensy-weensy weave, I began walking the three miles to my place. I passed a local's bar and looked in the window at the same time Denny looked up from his shifter (afterwork drink) and waved at me. Knowing the last thing I needed was another drink, I kept going, but he came out and caught up to me in a dozen steps.

By now all the booze had settled into my system and I was quite thoroughly smashed, so I accepted his offer of a ride home. The thought passed through my mind he might want to try me out.

Mood I was in, I didn't care.

S' okey-doakey with me. I could do my part while bombed. Done it before. Be a lot better than sleeping alone.

But Denny was the last of a dying breed. He wouldn't even accept a thank-you kiss. He just made sure I was safe and sound and inside my glorified whatever before he drove back to his warming drink.

I was bawling by the time I had the door locked and chained. I threw my clothes in a corner in a flash of anger and crawled into my sagging bed, utterly miserable. I cried myself to sleep.

I slept abominably that night. Every hour on the hour I'd wake up and remember some of the most horrifying memories about my past. I would have welcomed Pink Elephants and Multicolored snakes.

But no.

Every damn time I'd gotten blitzed, every party I'd ever gotten out of shape at, came gleefully back to haunt me... especially if blackouts were involved, including the summer when I was eighteen or so and whoopsed all over myself, my date, and his huge living room couch. He tried bravely to ignore the stink and take my panties off. Even though his parents were gone and he knew he'd never have a better chance at "becoming a man", he got sick himself. I couldn't even manage a smile at that scene.

I don't think I've ever spent a more depressing, guilt-filled night in my life. Mercifully, I slept soundly from about four thirty until nine. When I got, up, I called the number on the back of Stephanie Bradford's photograph.

"Mister Bradford," I cleared my throat, "this is Tracy Cunningham."

"Yes?"

"I think I've narrowed the area where Stephanie is down to a few blocks. I can have her located in a couple of days at the outside."

"That's great."

"But the reason I'm calling is that I need to take a day off for personal business. It might even be better this way because I've been following someone who I think is seeing her, and if he sees the same car behind him every day, he'll get hinky."

"Hinky?"

"Nervous. I just wanted to let you know what I was doing."

"I appreciate that, Tracy."

"Thanks. I'll keep you posted."

"Do that."

It was a nice warm spring day. The slow-moving cold front had passed into Nevada and was dumping lots of white money all over the mountain ski slopes. I dressed in a tee shirt, Levi jacket and snug jeans and headed back downtown via ankle express, continuing my self-flagellation.

That was a problem, though, because it's hard to keep whipping yourself when the trees are blossoming and innocent little birds are singing, early season butterflies are trying out their new wings, and all the rest of the sunny things about spring are happening all around you.

The more the immediate memory of my bad night last night was pushed back by the super day, the more I began to feel like a still-worthy human being who had gotten herself into a jam that wasn't unsolvable.

My problem was delayed burnout. I was sure of it. But because I was taking the time to do something about burning out before something bad happened to me, I was feeling better and better. It's also quite possible the state of my mental health was because my hangover was going away.

I entered the edge of the tourist area of town and began exploring on foot. The first thing I wanted to do was find myself a place I could be happy in, hang the cost... within reason.

I looked for houseboats to rent, then for waterfront apartments. I got a real fast education in the price of water views. About ten bucks a month per degree of view, plus standard rent, I calculated.

I recovered Maggie from the Ginnaker parking lot, drove up into the older section of town and looked at full sized apartments in the hills. I still couldn't find anything suitable. Nothing but 'toos'.

Too expensive, too big, too small, too run-down. You get the drift.

I returned to the tourist section, parked and walked aimlessly.

Can you believe it? Two grand a month for a one bedroom apartment in the hills. It did have a nice view, though. Damnit, I want to live in Sausalito. It was perfect for me. Lots of sailboats, restaurants, men... no! I have to forget men.

Sausalito has salt air and old beauty, things I crave. But one has to know where to look for it. I couldn't afford any of those places I looked at unless I wanted to go back into the escort business full time, and that's out out out.

Maybe a boarding house?

That's it, a boarding house! I wouldn't have to cook, something that will lead to my slow painful death, and I really don't need a living room overlooking the bay that badly.

I looked around to see if anyone was watching me, then grabbed a local newspaper out of a sidewalk trashcan. While I strolled down the sidewalk, occasionally bumping into tee-shirted tourists, I scanned the ads for boarding houses.

I treated myself to an ice cream cone, wandered a little, looking in store windows, feeling pangs of something like regret when I realized that only a month ago the cute dress in the window would have been in my closet in less than an hour from the time I'd seen it. So would that jewelry, if I was so inclined. All I had to do was hint to the right man, in the right place and time, and it would be mine. I could always buy it myself. Might cost a night's work, that's all.

Now, all that damn dress represented was a month's combined rent. Boy, things sure change in a hurry, don't they? Finishing my ice cream, I bought a local street map at the drugstore.

Feeling renewed, I drove up the hill to the first place I circled in the 'Rooms to let' ads. A big sign out front bragged that there was 'No Vacancy'.

I drove to the second address. I looked over the large converted mansion. It was painted white with green trim. The paint was peeling a bit, but nothing was really wrong with the appearance.

Old beauty. Bet the place is loaded with mahogany.

I parked Maggie, smiling that my car fit in the location so perfectly, and walked up the inclined footpath. The gardens were lush. I felt a wave of discouragement when I saw a man leave. A portly grandmother type was shaking her, head slowly while standing in the door telling him, "Sorry."

Shit... Shoot. This place must be full, too. Dammitall, it sure looks like my kind of place.

Discouraged, I turned to go back down the sidewalk when I heard the elderly woman call, "Young lady! Can I help you?"

"No, Ma'am," I turned and smiled, stuffing my hands in my rear hip pockets. "I'm looking for a room and I just heard you tell that man you were full up."

She smiled in return. "We are... in the men's wing. I have a delightful room for a woman. Please come in, my dear."

The moment I walked in the foyer I just knew this would be the place. I followed the woman up a steep, narrow staircase. I ran my hand lightly along the polished mahogany banister. We were on the third floor and heading North up the hall to a room on the end.

"When this was a private dwelling," she explained, "it was a summer home for a wealthy Italian family who lived in the Napa Valley. This room belonged to the eldest daughter. I've kept it, and the others, as close to the way it was back then. I have to tell you that I've turned down two girls already. Do you smoke?"

"No, ma'am. I've done a lot of stupid things, but I don't abuse my lungs, and I don't abide anyone sending me his smoke."

"Excellent. Do you drink?"

Something told me that I shouldn't try fibbing. I knew this woman deserved more respect than that. Besides, I already liked her.

"On occasion. I have some problems with booze, but I think I can get it under control now. I've never done drugs, of any kind. Well..." I grinned sheepishly. "To be perfectly candid about it, I did try pot... once. I was raised by a cop, and he made it very clear the one time he caught me with a joint in my pocket that he wouldn't put up with a daughter who was a junkie.

"He told me that to smoke pot, I had to learn to smoke. So he sat me on the couch and made me chain-smoke a whole pack of Camel cigarettes... unfiltered! Even if all that hacking and coughing didn't teach me better, after I was finished and the proper shade of green, I really got the brunt of the lesson from my father's favorite belt."

We both laughed gently. "I appreciate your honesty, Miss...?"

Smiling warmly, she unlocked the solid mahogany door and held it open for me.

"Cunningham." I shook hands with the landlady as I walked in the room. "My name is Tracy Cunningham."

I moved slowly in the room, feeling like I did when I was a little girl in pigtails, visiting my grandmother's house. I tried not to look excited while I scanned the room, taking in all the beautiful furnishings. To the right side as I walked in was a large closet. I slid the door open and stepped inside, looking around in awe.

This sucker's bigger than my whole apartment! It was enough for all my clothes.

Back in the room, I glanced around at the pleasant wallpaper and the hand-brushed, light lavender enamel trim.

I love it!

There was a violet area rug under the bed and true hardwood parquet floors. The exposed wood was stained with just the right hues to show the beauty of the workmanship. The old fashioned windows were trimmed with white lace curtains. A four-poster double bed was covered with a white cotton bedspread that had a border-fringe of little white cloth balls.

Ohhh yeahhh. This is my kind of place. It can't be any more perfect!

I looked around and said, "I don't see a bathroom," I didn't want to gush. I had to be more reserved in my attitude, or she'd see a five-foot-two tuna standing in front of her and ask double rent from me. Knowing my present mood, I'd probably pay it happily.

"No, dear. The bathroom is right down the hall, the second door on the right. It has two of everything. Showers, sinks, toilet stalls, and so on. You have to share it with the other girls."

Absorbing the idea it would be just like living in a sorority house again, I opened the bench hatches under the windows.

Tons of room! More than enough.

If I looked out the window facing the back yard, I could see a jungle-thick garden and a moss-covered concrete patio. If I looked out the window facing the east, I could see almost all of Angel Island, most of Raccoon Straits, and the east end of Belvedere Island.

"Oh, Ma'am, I'll take it! " I erupted with joy. I tried not to, but I did. I wanted the room too badly. I so had to have it!

"It's perfect! That is, if I qualify."

The woman seemed to make her mind up quickly. "I'm not worried about that, child. I like people to be, what do you kids say these days?... Up front with me.

"Rent is seven hundred dollars, which includes one garage stall. I charge a security deposit equal to rent. If you want the whole meal package, that's an extra two hundred and fifty dollars a month. That means you can go to the kitchen and snack whenever you wish, just like when you lived at home.

"I serve breakfast and dinner every night, except Monday. That's my night for Bridge. Usually, the boarders get together and make sandwiches."

It was going to take a large portion of my remaining funds, but I didn't care. I sat on the bed, testing it. It too, was just right. Suddenly I flashed on Goldilocks.

"You mean I can have this room and all the food I want, cooked, for nine hundred and fifty dollars a month? I'll take it I'll take it I'll take it!"

I know, I know. It was more than I could afford. But I wouldn't have to deal with all the things of ownership, like electricity, garbage, taxes, and so on. And I wanted it so badly. I needed to like my home.

I hoped if I started liking my surroundings that I'd like myself more. That's one of the things I came up with while I was doing all that thinking.

I really didn't like Tracy Cunningham very much.

"Before we agree," Mrs. Lockland said, "I have some rules. If they're broken, you're out."

"Okay. What are they?"

She went over the house rules quickly. Simply stated, they boiled down to the idea that I had to behave like a responsible citizen. Nothing more than that. I found that the house was an unofficial half-way house for boomerangers... people just like me. Youngish, single adults who realized that living alone ain't all it's cracked up to be, and the old folks live too far away.

I smiled widely. "We have a deal, Ma'am. Just before I decided to move here, I told myself I had to grow up. Now it's almost like I get to be a kid again."

Her skin crinkled when she returned my smile. "Oh, my dear, there's plenty of time for that growing-up business. You enjoy your youth as long as you can. It's over much too soon, believe me. Tracy, is it?"

"Yes, Ma'am. Tracy Cunningham."

"And I am Mrs. Lockland," I followed the hefty dark-salt and pepper haired woman down the stairs. She was portly, perhaps five-six or so, and she had a good carriage. She walked with class. Her hair was braided and wrapped around the top of her head. She looked very old country, maybe German, Jewish, or Italian. I couldn't tell which. Some detective, hah?

Didn't matter. I liked her.

"When would you like to move in?"

"Right away, Ma'am."

"What do you do, my dear?"

"It sounds funny when I say it, but boiled down, I'm an unlicensed Private Investigator."

"Really? That sounds exciting."

"So far it's not. I'm still working on my first case. I'm looking for a run-away teen."

"Does the job pay well?"

"Not yet. I've got to make my bones real soon."

"Or what?"

"Or I'm going to have to find another job. I won't fib to you, Mrs. Lockland. I'm in a bind. I burned a lot of bridges over the past few years. My last supervisor told me that she was going to make sure finding a local job in my field of insurance investigation would be impossible."

"I'm sure things will change, dear," she smiled.

I drove over to my former apartment. The landlord was away at work, and his wife's car was gone. I threw my clothes in Maggie and made several fast round trips. I had just pulled away on my last trip when I saw the landlord return in my rearview mirror.

I felt a bit guilty. I'd just skated on a week's rent, but I didn't want the hassle of trying to convince him I was moving for reasons of mental health. One of these days, I'll pay him what I owe.

At least my office rent wasn't like that. My rent was legitimately month to month, paid on the first in advance. I would lose some money on that, but I considered it part of the price of learning. The pile of paperbacks could stay for the next guy who rented the place.

I am free!

This time, I knew I was doing it right. This time, this new, new start was exactly what I needed. I would be living in a nice home, with a nice bedroom, living with some nice people, and eating regularly.

I wasn't going to worry about an office. From the way things were going, I wouldn't need a damn office, anyway. Actually, my spending would go down. I didn't need to go to Hamburger Jake's for dinner every night.

Look out world! Here comes a new Tracy Cunningham! Are you ready for her?

CHAPTER SEVEN

I woke up late and lazed around, enjoying the luxury of lying in a cozy warm, snuggly private bed while the clock punchers all scrambled about, getting ready for work. When it got quiet on my floor, I showered, shampooing my hair. After using nearly all the hot water on my floor, I checked myself critically in my bedroom mirror.

Results? My boobs still hadn't grown, my butt was still a ten, I still didn't need to worry about errant hairs when I wore a bikini, and now I needed a trim. I stared at myself until I realized it was as good as it was going to get. I made one more inspection turn, went back to my closet and pawed around in my clothes.

I decided that in this new start, I would try to dress properly, not be such a slob. I picked out a navy-blue knee length, pleated wool skirt, a simple white blouse and a blue matching sports coat. I finished my outfit off by knotting a Union Jack scarf around my neck and slipping on my red, white and blue high heels.

Tres Nautique.

I went downstairs into the kitchen and explored the huge commercial reefer. The breakfast cleaning had been done and Mrs. Lockland was outside, enjoying her immaculate garden. Since I'd missed breakfast, I settled for a large glass of fresh orange juice and glanced at my watch.

I had nothing but time. If Jerry Morresey's schedule went according to plan, he would have a full day in school. If he didn't go to the financial district, there was no reason to follow him. So I decided I'd wait, parked near where I lost him. If he drove by, and I was pretty sure he would, I could probably follow him right to wherever Stephanie Bradford was living... if he was seeing Stephanie. If he wasn't, I'd accomplished not one damn thing since I started.

Ah well. I could always use the time perusing the job ads.

I called my old beauty salon in the Financial District and lucked out with an appointment this morning. I drove to the financial section of San Francisco.

Here, I was on familiar turf. All three of the insurance companies I once worked for were located here. I parked Maggie in a secret place (known only to a few worker bees here) and made it to my hair appointment five minutes early.

When I came out, the air on my newly exposed neck seemed a bit chilly. It was going to take some time to get used to my new haircut. Cost a bundle to get it done, but one look in the windows as I wasted time sauntering in the general direction of a couple of my old haunts told me I'd done the right thing. I was going back to the haircut I originally had when Nora made me over. Over the years, my do seemed to get a tad longer as I got a bit older.

I actually looked at my reflection and thought, "Hey. Am I a cute little fox or what?"

I got such a mental lift from seeing a wholesome being looking back at me, I knew the hundred and sixty-five dollars was money well spent. I even looked a little like Tinker Bell, but not an R-rated one. Perhaps more like a PG, now.

I window shopped for a while, then snuck up to my old employer's offices and chatted with the receptionist, a girl who was still my friend. She said she liked my new image a lot. That helped my glowing mood. After, that, I wandered around killing time again, until it was after one, and the luncheon crowd would be thinning at the B and B.

The Bull and Baron is a classy place that serves good lunches at decent prices. The main reason I waited for the crowd to leave was that I wasn't particularly interested in seeing any of my old martini sandwich crowd.

The magnificent back-bar in the B and B is one of those antique, restored Brunswick bars, the ones with the humongous round dark wood columns, leaded glass cabinet doors and small mirrors. The kind that nouveau riche places like the Ginnaker are wont to copy. I stood on the foot rest of the bar, leaned across the mahogany and gave Freddie an air kiss. Freddie was an older bartender, who frowned on the term 'bartender'.

In his vocabulary, a bartender was a type of lobster fisherman's boat on the East Coast. Freddie was a mixologist, not someone who opens a bottle of beer and pours a shot alongside it.

"What may I get you, Tracy?" He polished the section of bar in front of me and smiled." How about something fruity, that's smooth, tasty, with zero booze?"

"Coming right up."

Like I said, another true pro. The fact that I ordered something non-alcoholic for the first time since he's known me didn't faze him in the slightest. I looked around the room. There weren't too many people left over from lunch. I froze for a second when I thought I was seeing my twin.

I don't have a twin…

A girl, built just like me, my age, size and coloring, was sitting at the bar with some guy who was thoroughly entranced with her. Not too hard to figure out why, though. If she rubbed his leg any higher, she'd be giving the guy a hand job. As it was, I could see that he was getting rather uncomfortable just sitting and smiling.

They left about the same time that the waitress came to me with a smile. "Hiya, Trace. Love your hair. Want to order yet?"

"Sure, Joyce. How about a hot Pastrami on Fugassa?"

"Be here in a minute," she smiled, shaking her head at the intertwined couple that had just passed behind her to leave.

I commented "There's no doubt where they're going, is there?"

"You know her?"

"Never seen her before."

"She works at NorCal Gas and Electric. She's a buyer, 'cept she looks more like she's selling today," she chuckled. "Her name's Susan Kennedy. She's been a regular nearly from the day you left. Weird. Almost like she's taken over your barstool here."

I sipped through the straw in my fruit cocktail then said, "Let her have it. I'm out of that crap forever."

"You don't know how happy I am to hear that, Trace. I always thought you were too bright of a girl for that sort of nonsense."

"Thanks."

I turned back to the bar, and enjoyed the yummy peach concoction that Freddie made. It was smooth, tasty, and if there had been any booze in it I couldn't have tasted it anyway. He and I small-talked while I ate my sammer. Traded a couple of ribald jokes.

As usual, he asked me to marry him, but I, as usual, reminded him his wife might not like him bringing me home and asking if he could keep me. I left him a solid toke, and walked to my car, feeling good about myself. I had been in my old den of iniquity, and had come out unscathed. No sleepy drugged feeling, no heavy breathing man hanging all over me.

I settled into Maggie for at least an hour-long wait. I picked up my Kindle, but decided the heck with that, and just sat back and people-watched. During the next hour I saw a few people I knew, but none that I wanted to talk to...

Especially Eunice Martin, Peerless Insurance Company, Vice President in charge of investigations and fraud. My Effing Bitch ex-boss. Also known as Snaggletooth, Moosejaw, Hatchet-face, or Gator Jaws by those who knew and loved her.

Don't count me in the latter group. Unbidden, it all came rushing back. All the pain, hurt and fright from being fired for the third time in less than six years, except this time getting informed that she'd make sure I never worked in the insurance game San Francisco again.

God, how I hate that vindictive old blister!

I stopped myself. I wasn't going to waste time and energy hating a petty middle-aged Old Maid who probably hadn't heard a man rattle out that heady sigh of satisfaction in her ear in years, maybe never!

Sheese, any guy who was bad off enough to take her on would either have to be blind or he'd have to put a gunny-sack over her head and pull it right down to her Uhuh.

Naughty, naughty, Trace. One should feel compassion for her, not hatred. That's the civilized, adult way. Right. EFF her!

CHAPTER EIGHT

Thinking about how cruelly Snaggletooth had treated me nearly had me crying when Morresey's Black Chevy passed my parking place. I slipped in behind him. Following closer this time, I stayed within a block until he pulled behind an old apartment house off California Street. I couldn't follow him in. That would have been too much of a give-away.

I parked in front, in a loading zone, and checked the names on the mail boxes. Disappointment washed over me. There wasn't a Stephanie Bradford there. And in some twenty or thirty mail boxes, there were only a few male sounding names.

Jerry Morresey must have gone in the back entrance, so there wasn't any way to know which apartment he was visiting. I was really discouraged, now. For my day-long efforts, I had narrowed the chase down to one building, a building with a preponderance of female residents. I drove away and parked Maggie in Golden Gate Park, just to have a pleasant place to do some thinking. This was one of my better habits, one I enjoyed a lot.

Where am I? What was it that Bradford said?

If anyone knew how or where to find her, I did... Within the bonus time.

Big deal. Any P.I. in the game would have had that building narrowed down the first day. It took me three days, and I still don't know if I was looking at Stephanie's place. Jerry easily could have had a new girlfriend.

Wonder if the place is some sort of cat-house?

Bradford said that Stephanie was undoubtedly a hooker. Come to think of it, the odds were damn good she was. What else can a girl with two years of high school do for a living? Domestic work?

At her age?

What was Jerry doing coming here every day? Getting some loving?

Okay, Stephanie is hooking. She can't make outcalls because she's too young. No hotel security is going to ignore a teen-aged kid walking in the room halls at three in the morning. Is that place a cat-house?

Must be.

I started Maggie up and drove back downtown to the Eden Connection. Outside, I saw a plain-clothes car with two men sitting in it. I stopped and talked to the passenger.

I didn't even bother to tell them my name. I was pretty sure they knew it. "Make sure you tell Sergeant Phillips that I went in the place after telling you guys."

"Why?"

"Because one of you creeps tattled on me. I don't like that. And I'm going in on legitimate business. I should be out in less than ten minutes."

"What is your business in there, Miss Cunningham?"

"Oh. You do know my name."

"Yeah," he smiled. "Greg made sure that we knew that you're one of the good guys."

"Did he now? All I'm going to do in there is look for a name. Maybe later I can do you guys a favor."

"Kay. We won't log you going in."

"Thanks. I really appreciate that." I walked in, feeling the stares of the two vice cops centering on my tush. I was coming to the opinion that having a sexy butt isn't always a good thing. I stopped at the receptionist's desk at the service.

"Hiya, T.J.," she smiled. "Coming back?"

"Possibly, Roxy. Is Nora in?"

"Yeah. You wanna talk to her?"

"Wouldn't ask if I didn't."

Roxie wasn't too bright. The story was that a long time ago she was the model for "This is your brain on cocaine." Normally no one would have hired a sixty-year old Helium-head. But Nora wasn't a normal employer, and this was the only thing old Roxy could do, since age forced her to quit as a pro.

She buzzed me in to Nora Pincolini's office. Her eyes lit up when she saw me. "Hi, Trace. Gee, you look fantastic! I love your new do."

"Thanks."

"Hey, girl, I got a call from Ramon Castro. You know the drill. He wants only you, and said he'll pay double if you go to his party tomorrow night. Can I call him for you? I hope?"

"Nope," I sat with a smile. "When I quit, I quit, Nora. I do need some help, though."

"Aww, please? Just one more time? One little teensy all-nighter? I'll get him to spring for triple, and you're a few thousand richer, not counting any bonuses you get?"

I actually gave it some thought. Ramon Castro was one rich dude. So rich he didn't want any permanent... read risky... romantic entanglements. When he wanted a woman to bed or a party hostess to make sure things ran smoothly, I was his first and favorite. He wasn't bad looking, and he was damn good in the saddle too.

A few thousand plus the usual extra five hundred tip for doing things his way, was really somewhat tempting. I woke up and forced the thought out of my mind. "Nora, please do me a favor. Don't encourage me, okay? As much as I could use the money, I really want to stay retired."

"I'm sorry, Honey," she smiled, erasing her discouragement. "I'll be your friend, and not try to suck you back in."

I doubted if Nora would ever give up on me, or any recently retired girls, for as long as I or we looked good enough to sell. I'd never tell Nora, but if Ramon ever thought to call me and ask me out on a simple date, he'd probably wind up getting whatever he ever wanted, and save himself the professional fees. I've always liked him that much.

"I appreciate it, Nor."

"What can I do for you?"

"First of all, thanks for the referral."

"That guy panned out?"

"Yep. My first legitimate client. One of these days, I want to find out why you told him I was underdeveloped."

She gave me a coy smile. "Just to keep him from wanting to try to kill two birds with the same phone call?"

"Or losing your cut?"

"Whatever," she chuckled.

"His daughter is a runaway. I'm looking for her. There's an apartment house off California Street that has a lot of female names on the mail boxes. I'm pretty sure she lives there, but her name isn't on the front. I think she's there under an alias."

"Probably a lot of girls are there under an alias. You think it's a cathouse?"

"I don't know for sure. There's some men's names too."

"C'mon, T.J.. Don't be so dense. There's a lot of male prostitutes in San Francisco."

"I knew that."

"What do you need to know?"

"Who's running it? How can I get, in and find one girl?"

"To the last question, I don't know. To the first, same answer, but I can find out."

"Seems to me this isn't a fly-by-night operation. The building's too nice, and the names are too permanent. Nora, what I'd like you to do is find out who's running the place, and maybe recommend me to them."

"Why?"

"I have to get inside and figure out where my subject fits in."

"Tracy, think. How the hell can I pull it off? What possible reason would there be for me to recommend my best escort to a simple cat-house? Why on earth would a five thousand dollar a night call girl go into an operation like that?"

"Maybe I've been busted? Maybe I need the money and I can't be caught in hotels again?"

"I don't think so. Sounds a bit weak to me. I can come up with something that'll work, but are you sure you wanna do this? What happens if you have to turn a trick?"

"I'll cross that bridge when I come to it. Will you do it?"

"I'll try... if you're sure."

"Come up with another way, and I'll listen. Believe me, I'll listen."

"I'll see what I can do. Where can I reach you?"

I gave her my new cell number. I decided that my new home number would remain effectively unlisted. As much as Nora was my friend, I still didn't want her calling me at home with an offer of a date. And believe you me, if the chance of a big score came up, Nora would be burning the lines up, begging me to say yes, just like she just did.

Until Nora called me with something to begin with, I was off duty, for lack of a better term. I drove over to the Police station, went through security again, then upstairs to Greg's office and was greeted much more warmly by the bullpen greeter.

"Hi, Tracy. Greg tells me you're to be considered a friendly around here. The coffee shack is over there, behind that cork partition. Put a buck a day in the big jar, and no matter how much you drink it'll cover expenses. Next time in, bring a cup, and I'll mark it with tape for you."

"Thanks…"

"Kathy. Kathy Barth."

"Is Greg available?"

"Yep. Go on back. I'll buzz him and tell him you're on the way.

Phillips was waiting for me, wearing a wide grin.

"Hi."

"Hi yourself." I said and sat down. "To what do I owe the honor of this visit?"

"How about dinner?"

"Good plan." He almost licked his chops. "My place?"

"No," I said softly. "Not for a while, Greg. The last time I was there, things got out of hand. It's not your fault. it's mine. I knew exactly what I was doing all the time.

"From now on, I'm not going to fall into bed with you at the sound of trout sizzling."

"I don't understand."

"I made you a promise a couple of days ago, and promptly broke it…"

"What are you talking about?"

"I accepted gain for going to bed with someone. You."

"Now you've really got me confused."

I closed the door. It wouldn't do much good, but it made me feel better. I stood close in front of him. "Look. You did me a favor, right? Got a license number and a home address for a kid I was tracking, right?"

"Right."

"And how did I repay you? Not in kind, like a male P.I. would have. I didn't punch you friendly-like on the shoulder, and say, 'I owe you one', or something equally macho like that. No. I batted my eyelashes and climbed into bed with you. How many P.I.'s you sleep with recently?"

"Trace, I…"

"Quiet," I snapped gently. "The copulation was fantastico, but I wasn't so feeling nice afterward. That morning I felt so small I had to look up to see bottom. That's why I left. I figured that if I was still whorin' I may as well be a class pro and not be around when you wake up.

"So if you want to go to dinner, I'll kiss you good night, maybe we can hug a few times, and I won't be too quick to move your hand if it finds itself in the right… er, wrong places, but I won't go to bed with you.

"Sleeping with you is something I want to do, lots and lots, but not so soon. The next time we go to bed, I dearly want to snuggle with my boyfriend, not a over-tall flatfoot who helps me out. Can you understand that, Greg?"

He smiled with a off-center grin that I've already learned to love. "Perfectly."

My knees were quaking, so I sat down with much relief." Great. Now then, can I ask if you'll buy the dinner? I know I invited you, but I'm pretty broke these days."

"I wouldn't have it any other way. Want to get an early start?"

"Less go," I grinned and stood up.

We left my car off the main highway to the Golden Gate Bridge, and went to a small, intimate, restaurant on the coast. This time it really was different. I was going to be a date, not a P.I... once I had told him the rest of the story. I was sure he wasn't going to like it.

I waited until we had a drink in front of us. "Greg, there's something else I've got to tell you."

"What?"

"I think I'm going undercover. I've narrowed down my search for Stephanie Bradford to a certain apartment building. I don't think I can find her without becoming one of the quote, roomers, unquote."

"So?"

"I think the place is a cat-house," I cringed.

"What!?"

Shit. I should have kept my mouth shut." I said, I think it's a cat-hou..."

"I heard," he snapped. "And does that mean, just in the line of duty, of course, you're going to have to put out, too?"

"No," I lied. "I'm not going to do that."

"And just how do you expect to get into a whore house, and not do it?"

"I don't know," I replied meekly.

"No way," he said stiffly. "You're not gonna do it."

Actually, I expected this typical male reaction.

"You can't stop me," I snapped back. "You don't own me!"

"I don't give a damn," he muttered, "if we're going to be more than Cop-P.I... and we are... I still don't want you to do it. I'm not that liberated."

I felt the hostilities go away. "I know that. But I'm stuck. How else can I get in?"

"Tell me where this place is, and I'll go in."

"Right," I replied dryly. "You're going to go in with some sort of search warrant, looking for a girl who I don't have one speck of proof is even in there, right? Maybe you're going to bust the place, and you'll find out it's a boarding house for chaste women. That's all it might, be, you know."

"You believe in the tooth fairy, too? Sounds to me like some sort of operation is going on there. And what will you do? Close your eyes while some guy screws you and pretend it isn't happening.?"

"No!" I snapped, "I'll close my eyes and pretend it's you."

My big mouth gets me in more damn trouble.

"Don't do me any favors, Cunningham."

"I won't, Phillips." We sat in stony silence for what seemed like an hour. Clanks, tinks and tings, people in subdued conversations, all the environmental noises, the sounds of the restaurant, guitar music wafting in from the dining room, seemed to increase in volume. I truly didn't know what the hell to do. I had to get inside that place, and I didn't want to do anything stupid once I was there.

I probably just blew it with Greg, too, and that didn't make me feel any better.

He broke the moodiness first. "I've got an idea."

"What?" I said excitedly.

"Suppose we forget, for the time being, that you want to find a specific girl. Let's suppose we want to find out if the place really is a cat-house."

"Okay..."

"I can get vice to put a policewoman inside and have her wired. We should be able to get some confirmation from conversations, or, at least, we can make a full bust the moment she's been solicited."

"And?…"

"We take everyone in the building downtown and we toss out the culls until we find Stephanie Bradford."

"That's an expensive operation for one runaway kid."

"I know," he sighed.

"How 'bout you and I do this with a minimum of help? Maybe we place some guys at the doors, all with photos. You wire me, and I'll go in. They're probably waiting for me anyway. I'll play the game, and when you think the time is right, you make a loud-assed bust.

"If you make enough noise, won't all the rats leave a sinking ship? Won't Stephanie be one of the ones to run? We grab her at the door. I save my tarnished virtue, and you don't have to look at me like I was tainted meat."

"Was I doing that?"

"Don't worry. I'm used to it."

"From who?"

"Former customers. Why do you think that all self respecting call-girls leave before the bright light of dawn? Because we're vampires?"

"I'm sorry." He waved his two fingers in a sign to refill the drinks.

Cheated death again. He probably isn't going to heave me into the bay.

We sat in stony silence again. Maybe ten minutes later he said, "I've just returned from some heavy thinking."

"To what conclusions?" I sipped my fresh drink.

"Just this. I like you a lot, Tracy Cunningham. I'd like to think we're gonna be a long-term thing. I don't like the idea of sharing you with anyone. We'll figure something out about California Street."

"Why Sergeant," I fluttered my eyelashes outrageously. "This is all so sudden."

"Yeah," he smiled and squeezed my hand. "Ain't it, though?"

It was a real bear trying to drive home that night. Maggie wanted to make a U-turn at every opportunity. I just made it before lock-out.

Damnit, Maggie! Why couldn't you have stalled, just for a while? Another ten minutes, and I would have had to go back to Greg's place!

CHAPTER NINE

I got up early, forcing myself from my cozy bed, put on some sweats and Nikes, and went for a run. I hadn't been a good girl and I had allowed my morning exercise routine to go to pot. Nora demanded that we girls stay in top physical shape. I used to run five miles every day I could. The past six weeks I hadn't put running shoe to asphalt one time.

As part of my new lifestyle, I promised myself that I'd run at least four times a week. I'd already clocked out a circuit with Maggie. My path was down a hundred and twenty wood steps, to the main drag at the bay level. Then north on the main road, so I could enjoy the marinas and docks as I passed, then turn around a stop sign where a big black tugboat was tied up and return. Five miles, perxactly.

The only problem was when I got back, I had to face those same one hundred and twenty wood steps back up to my block. They were a royal bitch coming home.

I have to confess.

I didn't make it to my turn-around point. I felt my legs begin to complain much earlier. Even though I wasn't halfway to the tug boat, at that first suggestion, I turned back. When I got back to the steps, I had to take a break twice on the stairway.

My legs were quivering like Jell-O and my heart was pounding faster than I ever remembered.

I must be getting old.

When I finally got home, I almost fell through the back door and into the kitchen. I came close to knocking Mrs. Lockland down.

"Whew!" I panted. "Those stairs are going to kill me!"

"Not to worry," she smiled. "There will be a time soon when you'll be able to fly up those stairs."

I stretched out in the screened back-porch, encouraged by the smell of fresh ground coffee waiting for me. When I stopped shaking so violently, I went into the kitchen and sat up on the counter, eagerly sipping the aromatic brew and eating a super-fresh breakfast roll that she thoughtfully had warmed for me.

This is one of the singular great advantages to being a shrimp. I can sit on kitchen counters, lick spoons, get snacks early, talk, and enjoy some delicious Deja Vu from my childhood.

After my mother got sick with lung cancer, she centered on herself and forgot the kitchen. Dad was working day shift most of the time, so I never got to sit on the counters at home and enjoy kitchen conversations with whoever was cooking.

When I was a little older, I tried to cook, but I found out that what I was doing to food was criminal. No matter what I tried, it came out wrong. Still does.

Which simply proves not all women are good cooks.

Mrs. Lockland and I chatted, got to know each other better while the sounds from the water pipes began filtering into the kitchen, signaling that the boarders were arising. I checked my voicemail. There was a call from Nora. I was tempted to call her at home, but a woman in her profession doesn't admit the existence of morning.

After breakfast, I took my shower. As long as I wasn't punching a time clock, I didn't need to be in the way of the three other girls who shared my bathroom. Besides, I'm a terrible hot water hog, and this gave the water-heater on my floor a chance to catch up before I drained it.

I wore snug white slacks, and a smooth red, cap sleeved shirt under a navy blue suit-coat. The Don Johnson look, right? The classic old Miami Vice looked pretty good on me. Better me than him. I completed the outfit with white canvas flats.

I don't think I'm the type of shrimp that has a complex about my stature. There's nothing I can do about being a sawed-off pixie.

I wasn't planning on having to run, but if I had to, running in flat deck shoes was a helluva lot more practical, and besides, Greg liked our size differential. It made him more protective towards me.

It was a nice day, so I put the top down on Maggie. With my new do, I could enjoy the wind blowing through my hair and repair it easily when I got to my destination.

The fog was holding well off shore. The winds on the water surfaces were just enough to create ripples and intensify the blue-green surface, but not enough to generate white caps. Around ten knots...

I drove to the Eden Connection and met Nora. "Well," she said while I sat down, "there is some kind of thing going on in that apartment house."

"What kind?"

"I don't know. I've heard of the big mama, though. A gal known as Black Willa."

"Any last name?"

"Nope. Be careful, Honey. From what I hear, she's no one to fool with."

"Is she interested in me?"

"No."

"Why?"

"She can't afford you."

"Why not?"

"T.J., a woman like me just doesn't give a woman like her the best girl she has. Willa has heard of you. She knows you were one of the best girls in the best stable in San Francisco. If I tried to give you to her, red flags would go up all over the place."

"So you tried to sell me." I was beginning to get mad. That wasn't part of the bargain. This was an aspect of the business I hadn't really given much thought. I sure the hell didn't like the idea of being put on an auction block and being sold like a piece of warm meat. "Just like you owned me."

"Honey, women like her expect to buy their prime livestock."

"How much did you ask?"

"Seventy-five grand."

"What?"

"You're worth it. Actually, you're worth a lot more, but I don't think Willa would have given me the time of day if I asked for a hundred fifty."

"I doubt anyone's worth that much bread. No wonder she kissed you off."

"Honey, I have a confession to make."

"What?"

"Before you blow your stack, remember that you were the one who said you wanted in that dump. When that tack didn't work, I made a show of confessing that I was selling raunchy goods."

"Raunchy how?"

"I told her you had the big A. I hoped she would try to give me a distressed sale value for you. She wouldn't."

The big A. AIDS. Here I was, a professional woman who prided herself in never so much as catching a cold from a client! I flew to my feet.

"Goddammit Nora, you just totaled my reputation! Thanks a freakin' heap!"

"T.J. Hooker is history. I'm sorry Honey. I just didn't think."

I was about to really blow my stack when I realized just how much of a favor Nora's greed had done for me.

Reputation? Hey Mon, I don' need no stinking reputation!

"Nora, are you telling me the word is out that T.J. has AIDS?"

"Word like that spreads like wild-fire. I'm sorry. It's going to hurt my business, too, you know."

"Nora, I could just kiss you!"

"What?"

"You greedy old witch, you just saved my life!

Now I can't possibly ever come back! I'm truly and forever Oh You Tee!... Out!"

"This is true, all right," she sighed. "But my dumb-assed goof cost me a helluva lot, too. I've been getting nothing but calls from the other girls telling me they're leaving. No one wants to be associated with a stable who's number one girl contracted AIDS."

"Nor, maybe it is time for you to pull the plug. If you look outside, and down the block, you'll see two VCs sitting in an old Ford. I doubt if the car can move. It's been growing roots to that spot for a month."

"Are you kidding?" She jumped up and looked down at the street. When she came back to her chair, she was ashen and shaking.

I was surprised that she hadn't seen them before. "Girlfriend, I'd venture a guess that you're about twenty four hours from getting busted. It's time to fold the old tent and steal quietly into the night. Shit, girl, you can retire and spend a thou a day, and not even dent your principal."

"This too, is true." After making up her mind, she announced, "I think the Eden has gone out of business... permanently. I'm ready. I think I have been since you retired, T.J. Truth be known, I was a little jealous about you being free."

"You taught me a lot about life, Nora. I'll never forget you."

I drove straight to Greg's office, and poured coffee into an old mug I brought from the boarding house. I flounced giddily into his opulent shoe-box office. "Your girlfriend is off the hook, to coin a phrase."

"Why?"

"Guess what? T.J. has AIDS." His face went white.

"No, no," I laughed. "Not me... T.J.!"

"Who? "

"My street name was T.J.. It's my first two initials. My name is Tracy Jo... and the day my best girlfriend found out what I was doing on the side, she dubbed me T. J.... Hooker," I said. "That was about the same time the nostalgia channel began reruns of the TV program with the same name."

He shook his head in smiling confusion. "Let's start over. Good morning, Love."

"Good Morning to you, too. Greg, Nora got greedy, and tried to sell me... my contract to the madam at the apartment house. By the way, it is an establishment, but we don't know what the specialty is. Any who, when El Madamo wouldn't pay the purchase price, Nora confessed that she was selling spoiled meat. Thought she'd be able to get something for me."

"How much did she want?"

"Doesn't matter. You can't afford it, and besides, I don't think you'd believe it. I know I can't."

"Maybe you're right."

"Trust me. Anyway, the upshot is that I have a shattered reputation. No one would pay five dollars to screw me, not even wearing a firestone tire! Oh Boo Hoo!"

I screwed my face into a phony cry, then laughed and clapped with glee.

His face evolved into a great grin of comprehension. "Aww, gee, that's too bad, isn't it?"

"Yeah. Your little doxy can't bring home any more bacon."

"Never wanted her to in the first place. So. Where does that leave us?"

"Back to Plan B. We have to run some kind of scam on the place. Ol' Black Willa will probably be watching for a short blonde gal now."

"Black Willa? She went underground two years ago."

"Well chum, she just came up for air. She's the head honcho at Stephanie's place."

Greg reached to his phone and punched in a number. "Terry Frankfurter, please... Ter? Greg. Got time for coffee?... Good. I'll meet you downstairs. Buy three cups. Black for us."

He hung up and we headed out of his office. "What's going on?" I asked while we rode the elevator down to the basement.

"Terry Frankfurter is my counterpart in Vice. She's brand-new in the job. What we're talking about is in her operational area. Before I can do anything, I've got to check with her."

We walked into the cafeteria and aimed for a table in the corner, with a tall, nicely-built brunette woman just sitting down with three cups. She wasn't too shabby in the facial beauty department, either.

Greg introduced us. At least he started to.

"I know who she is," Terry said. "T.J. Hooker. One of Pincolini's bimbos."

"No," Greg said in the same tone, "you don't know who she is.

"You know who she was. As I was about to say, this is Tracy Cunningham, Girl Detective."

I injected myself into the conversation. "I quit the EC over a month ago."

"How the hell did you get past a background check for a P.I.'s license?"

"I'm not licensed. I don't carry a weapon, don't intend to, so I don't need a ticket."

You didn't have to be any sort of detective to know that Terry Frankfurter and I weren't ever going to be friends, and that Greg and she had once been very good friends. Three guesses who that cheap-assed pinafore in Greg's closet belonged to.

I'm glad that visual daggers don't hurt. 'Cause when Greg reached across the table for his coffee, his head would have been speared by several thousand, coming hard from both sides.

"Sergeant Frankfurter," I said coldly, "I'm only going to go over this one time, so take notes if you like. My other persona is permanently retired. As a favor to me, my connection dropped the word that TJ Hooker contracted AIDS. I doubt if anyone would touch her with a ten foot pole, even if it was yours."

She ignored my last comment, and me, when she turned to Sergeant Phillips and said, "What is this meeting all about, Greg?"

"How badly do you want Black Willa?"

"You know the answer to that."

"Tracy knows where she is."

"Wait a sec, Greg," I interrupted. "This is going far afield of my original job…"

I took the photo of Stephanie Bradford out of my purse and handed it to Sergeant Frankfurter. "Have you ever seen this girl?"

She looked at the picture carefully. "I don't know. Has she been busted?"

"I don't have a clue. Her name is Stephanie Bradford. She's seventeen. Been on the streets for a couple a years. I was hired to find her by her father. Now, I think she's involved with Black Willa."

"What we need to do," Greg came back in, "is bust Willa's new house, and see if we can bring this Bradford girl out."

"What's all this have to do with Homicide, Greg?" Frankfurter glared at him.

"Tracy's new in these parts. I promised to give her a hand."

"So clap for her, cook her your favorite trout dinner, and do whatever later in that decadent bed… considering her past experiences, of which she's had so many, I'm sure she can be real exciting… But you stay the hell out of my territory!"

"We need your help."

"Take it up with the chief," she snapped and stood up.

"Aren't you interested in Willa?" I asked.

"You bet your tiny tits we are," she glared, "And you can bet we want all you know about her. You can tell Sergeant Phillips all about it, or you can come into my office and you and I will go round and round. When we're finished, I guaren-fuck'n'-tee that I'll know everything you know, slut!"

"Don't hold your breath, Hot Dog," I said with steam venting from my ears. Mostly to her backsides, which was the view in seconds.

I began calming down quickly. I can do that when I don't know the person responsible for my mad that well. "Wow," I said, somewhat in awe, "She's some kind of pissed off, isn't she?"

"Seems like it."

"Wonder why?" I looked aside at, him and casually sipped my coffee.

Ugh.

"Maybe she doesn't like me messing around with a vice problem."

"Maybe she doesn't like me messing around with her property. Is that black lacy piece of shit thing in your closet hers?"

He looked guilty at first, then visibly angered. "That was over a long time ago."

"I suggest you tell her that, Sergeant Phillips."

I stood up and brushed my slacks off. The person who had been sitting there before had left crumbs in the plastic chair.

"Give her that cheap rag back and say that she was right about me. I am exciting."

I calmed down some more. A little. "What now?"

"I don't know. I can't do anything officially, or my head will be mounted to a plaque and placed behind the chief's desk. He isn't enamored of poaching."

"Poaching?"

"Working someone else's area of expertise, or in the case of uniformed patrols, working someone else's beat without permission."

"So we're back to square one."

"Seems like it," he pushed the door-hold button while I fought my way through several big apes to get out of the elevator. Next time, we're using the stairs.

"Okay, where is Black Willa's operation?"

"I just forgot," I said. "That tall toad downstairs is going to have to ask me nicely if she wants my co-operation."

"Game doesn't work like that, kid."

I got mad all over again. "It does for this kid! Read my lips, Hardbody! I never got busted, never had a vice cop look at me cross-eyed! I'm surprised that bitch even knows my street name. As far as she's concerned, I'm an up-standing citizen, and I'm entitled to normal respect! I'll keep you posted, Phillips." I got out of there before he could say or do anything to stop me.

CHAPTER TEN

I'd learned a couple of lessons this morning. Cops are people, too. They have all the normal emotions, one of which was jealousy. I wasn't worried about being the new woman in Greg's life, leaving Frankfurter on the outside looking in. But if I had to tell Sergeant Hot Dog where to find Willa, she'd go busting in like a wrecker's ball and never give me a chance to find Stephanie Bradford.

I couldn't tell Greg, because as a sworn cop, he'd have to tell Hot Dog, which would lead to the same thing. I couldn't ask a Homicide Detective to help me with an old, very cold runaway child case. The territorial imperative again.

So I was on my own.

That's where I should have been a long time ago. If I ever want to be respected as a detective, a self-proclaimed researcher, I'd better learn to do it myself.

I drove to the apartment house off California and sat across the street, watching the place. I didn't have a plan. I just stared and thought. A few people came in and out, almost always in singles. Men only. It was obvious what the place was.

If Black Willa had gone under two years ago, and re-surfaced here, why didn't the vice cops know it? Sure, Nora was in the game, and had an inside track, but for crying out loud, it's not supposed to take this long for the authorities to track down a madam, especially if all she did was move her operation.

However, back to the task at hand. How the heck do I find out if Stephanie is inside? The only way I could see getting in was as a working girl. There's always the frontal approach. 'Ey Mon, don ' got no front...

Shit. How freaking dumb can I get?

All this time I had been wrangling with myself, trying to come up with a sneaky way to get inside the apartment house. I'd totally spaced on the obvious.

Pounding on the front door and lying like a rug.

I wiped all my make-up off with spit and a tissue. For a few moments I was sorry I chopped off my hair. Pigtails would have really turned the trick.

Sorry 'bout that.

The top I was wearing under my coat was a knit cap-sleeved shirt, so I left my coat in the car, along with my bra. When I slammed the car door harder than necessary, taking out my self-disgust on poor Maggie, I didn't look old enough to buy cigarettes. I marched right to the front door, and pushed the button marked 'Manager'.

In a few moments a tall, wide black woman came to the door. At the same time, she looked kindly and hard.

Maybe she looked hard because I knew she really was. "I'm looking for a room to rent, Ma'am." She looked me over carefully.

"How olds are you, kid?"

I hesitated just long enough before I said, "Twenty one."

"Yeah." Her belly shook when she laughed derisively. "An' I'm yo Aunt Jemimah."

"I'm eighteen," I said defensively.

"Doubts that, too, but I let's it lay," Willa scanned me carefully.

My scrubbed, delightful, all-American face, trim, almost boyish, figure and saucy smile won her over. Hey. Don't get on my case about that self-serving description. That's how Nora marketed me.

"Yo looks fo yoself?"

"Who the hell else would I be looking for?"

She ignored my feigned attitude. "Yo gots a boyfriend? An ol' man?"

"No. Why?"

"C'mon in, chil," she smiled, "This be an apartment house only fo gals, Thas why I asks."

"That's what I'm looking for." I decided not to ask about the male names on the post boxes right in the entrance. I stepped over an old earthquake-caused crack in the front concrete slab.

Step on a crack, break your mother's back... maybe I ought to go back.

Black Willa led me to the fourth floor, second from the top in the old place. The paint in the halls was in reasonable condition. Maybe two years old. The red and brown carpeting was showing thin in places. The air smelled of a heavy combination of old must and flowery fragrances.

She unlocked a room door and stepped back to let me walk in. The rooms were just that. A room. Singular. This one was a studio, with a kitchenette set-up in the corner. Each room had a bathroom, of course, but it was small with a tub shower right next to the commode. "Where's the bed?"

"Ra 'cheer." Willa opened a large pair of sliding doors, and a double Murphy bed swung down easily. In all my life, I'd never seen a Murphy bed. Now, in the past month, I'd rented two of the dangerous things.

Dangerous?

Absolutely. I'm so light, I live in fear of being slammed upside down inside a wall if I sneeze while sleeping... I need a man's weight to keep the bed down... Yeah. That's it.

As it was, the room layout was a lot better than that crummy place I lived in before. At least here you didn't have to move the couch and table out of the way to sleep.

Even with the bed down there was room to move around. The six foot long couch, upholstered in worn, dark green, velveteen was tolerable. The wood-grained central table and end tables were all plastic laminate. The view from the windows was of the back parking lot, and a neat garden belonging to the neighbors.

"How much?"

"Six hun an we pays utilities."

"Wow. That's a bit steep for my budget."

"Don' worry none 'bout that chil." She smiled at me, checking out the merchandise. "Theys ways 'roun that."

I'll bet.

"Are men allowed?"

"Sure, chil'," she smiled. "We a modern place. If yo wants to brin' yo boyfrien up, come ahea. Ah don' care. Jes no fightin' and loud noise-makin after el-ven."

"Gee, I really like this place... Can I let you know?"

"Bette takes it quick. Ah gots 'nother gal lookin' real hard."

Suuurrre you does... do.

"I'll call you in an hour. Gotta think about if I can afford it."

"Yo does what yo nee ta, girlfrien," she smiled and locked the door behind her. She led me downstairs and into the large living room. There were several girls of dubious, even tender, age reading, watching TV and playing cards.

Here, I don't use the term girl, like I describe myself. These were girls. "This be the livin' roo," Willa said. "As ya can see, they's lotta ki here. Some even gwine to schoo. A good place ta live."

As she spoke, a couple of kids looked up. One in particular caught my eye. I'd been carrying her photograph around these past days.

Bingo! Good afternoon, Stephanie.

Willa led me through a door and downstairs to a huge kitchen area in the basement. She had a complete cafeteria set-up down here! A black man was cooking something that smelled pretty good. There were several picnic tables with cheap vinyl cloths covering them.

Yep. The whole magillah, including a cash register. "This be whe most the tenan eats. I give's credi, so's the kids can eat regular. So's ya can see, they's all you nee, chil. It's a happy boardin' house."

You betcha.

I ignored Stephanie when we walked to the front door. While I was standing at the open door, trying to catch more of the atmosphere, a man came in. He smiled at Willa, asked if a girl named Joanie was home, and getting a smile and a nod, went right into the living room. Her girth blocked my vision so I turned to leave.

"Well, I kind of like it, but I can't hack six headliners a month."

"I tol' you, we gots ways 'roun tha."

I turned around and gave her my eager-to-please look. "You mean I may not havta pay that much? What do I havta do?"

"Ya agin' men?"

"No." I giggled. "What a dopey question. I like men. Why?"

"Willin's to go on blind dates?"

"Sometimes. Why?"

"Willin's to earn some extra bread?"

"Isn't everyone?"

"Ya a virg'n?"

"Not since I was ten and my old man came home drunk."

One thing about Willa. She doesn't mince words. "Ya focks?"

Focks? "Sometimes. Depends on the man. Why?"

"Supposin' ah finds the man."

"I don't know."

"Fo every man yo dates that ah finds, yo get fifty bucks offa yo rent, and a twenny buck allowance."

"Let me understand this," I said, looking at the big woman and added a tinge of fear in my eyes. "You want me to let any man you say into my room and let him bang me?"

"Thas ri."

"That's prostitution, isn't it?"

"Not if yo don'ts get paid by the mans, it ain't."

"But you drop the rent?"

"Yes'm."

"So I suppose all I gotta is diddle some clown a dozen times a month and I can live here free? And you give me a twenty dollar allowance per each?"

"Yea. Ya can puts it agin yo ren, or agin yo foo. Any lef over I gives ya cash at the ends of the mon fo what ya nee."

"Lemme think on it. I'll call you in an hour."

If I had been just a bit quicker when I stepped out on the front porch, I would have seen the rear end of Jerry's black Chevy when he drove into the back lot. I walked down the street, ignoring my car until I was sure that Willa wasn't watching me through the curtains, then doubled back and drove away. I didn't want her knowing what kind of a car I owned.

When Dad bought Maggie for me, she was already a classic, but the street value of her was less than half what it is now. Dad got her at a drug seizure sale for pennies on the dollar. Had an inside track, he said.

Any girl who's interested in 'focking' at least twelve times a month, and accepting the pricey sum of seventy bucks per value for it, isn't going to drive around in something like Maggie.

There was no doubt in my mind. Willa's place was an out and out bubble-gumming, teeny-bopper cat-house. I know one of the kids I saw couldn't be a day over thirteen. Scrub off the makeup, and I'll bet she wasn't an even dozen years old. That's the sort of thing that makes me mad.

Seemed like a good deal for Willa. First, the rooms are overpriced all to hell. The tenants don't look old enough to know what was a fair amount to pay for rent.

Second, she doesn't question under-aged kids who happen to knock on her door. That's worth a lot to run-aways.

Third, she allows the sappy girls to drop their rent, at fifty bucks a whack. Gives them twenty more in 'Allowance,' then probably takes all that back for the beans and ham hocks that cook was making up.

Betcha the girls never see cash. Wonder what the fat bitch is charging the Johns?

For prime older teens like Steph, at least a couple of hundred dollars per half hour, maybe twenty minutes. Had to be. I don't have the foggiest idea what Kiddy-Diddlin' brings. Gotta be more, though.

Shit. The fat bitch should be whipped until her skin falls off.

Wonder how many of the girls bought that line of crap that they weren't prostitutes, because the John didn't pay them? If they bought it, the combined IQ in that place must be lower than the IRS's generosity.

Times ten.

My blood pressure had to be in the two hundreds when I drove home. I packed a box of old sailing clothes, nothing of the quality of the slacks and shirt I wore in the afternoon.

If anyone asked, I'd just tell them that I wore my best to make a good impression this afternoon. I told Mrs. Lockland that I wouldn't be staying home tonight, and if Greg called, I would probably be calling him later... and a woman better not answer.

I tapped an ATM for a couple of hundred dollars and drove back over to the city. I left Maggie in a high security covered parking garage downtown and took a cab to a block away from the house. When I rang the doorbell, Willa greeted me with a broad smile. "Thoughts yo were gwine to call."

"I decided not to waste time. Still got the room?"

"Come right in." Said the spider to the fly. Except this fly is a hornet in disguise.

I told Willa my name was Kelly McAllister. There really was a Kelly once. I use her name as way to keep her alive in my mind. We two were the pee-wees of our grammar school, and bosom buddies all summer long.

We both had cop fathers and Irish ancestors. We both inherited the classic short fuses. The only difference between us was our hair color. At that age, I was a toe-head blonde.

Kelly had neat dark reddish brown hair and a swarm of freckles on her perky nose and upper cheeks. We always managed to get into giggling girl mischief together. We even had a special nick-name that we were sure was original.

Here comes Salt and Pepper. Let's get them to do it! I remember once, in the third grade, we got in a school-yard brawl with the class bullies, two on two. We lost the fight, but we proudly sported our matching shiners and missing right front teeth like badges of honor. Even the school principal was amazed that we had identical war wounds. To this day, I can't remember which one of our salty little mouths got us into that glorious fight.

The summer we were going into Junior High School, Kelly was killed by Leukemia.

I was moved into Willa's in less than a half hour. I paid two hundred dollars in rent, telling Willa that I was broke and planned on working off the rest., but not tonight. I was tired and in my heaviest days. She understood. Somewhat. "I gots men who likes girls when theys flowin'."

"Oh Yecchhh! " I shuddered, "That is so sick! I'm not available for wet play, an I never will be! Never! Wait a couple a days, okay? I'll let you know."

"Of course, chil'. "After I got a receipt for my rent, I walked into the living room. Along with Stephanie, most of the kids I saw this afternoon were gone, but there were plenty of different girls around, and a couple of effeminate boys playing cards. Most of the room occupants were older teens. Guess the cretins who liked children didn't want to be seen by more normal men who were filtering in for a cocktail-hour quickie.

At first glance, it looked like a college dorm for coed freshmen, but there wasn't any colleges in the area. The difference between a dorm and this was the atmosphere. I could sense depression in the air. You could cut it with a knife.

Conversations were subdued. When I walked in, they got even quieter, until I sat, down and stared at the news broadcast. In a few minutes, a pretty blonde girl sat next to me. "New here?"

"Just moved in."

"What do you do?"

"Work for an insurance company a few blocks away. I'm an entry level file clerk. How 'bout you?"

"I'm between jobs," she said.

"My name is Kelly McAllister."

"Hi. I'm Colleen Brannigan. Live in 315."

"Hi. Another Irish" I smiled.

"Not really, but it's a neat-sounding name."

"Musta got my name in the same cereal box. I live in 420. Glad to meet you," I shook her hand. I looked around and saw that we were pretty much in private. "What's the story around here?"

"What do you mean?"

"Are all the girls and boys puttin' out for rent?"

"Yeah," she sighed heavily. "Kelly, you are aware that this is a cathouse, aren't you?"

"I wasn't at first, but Willa let me know fast."

"So why did you move in'.?"

"I told you a lie. I'm not working. I don't have any other way to support myself. Won't be the first time I made money by spreading my legs."

"Don't feel bad. Most of us are in the same boat."

"Even those with jobs?"

"Yeah. If we don't put out, something always happens to make us lose the daytime jobs, so we're forced to pay off."

"You don't like it here?"

"Not particularly. When I moved in, I didn't know what kind of place this was. I didn't get approached for a couple a weeks. A week after I came here, I got shit-canned from my job, and not one place I went gave me a second interview. I still don't know why. I was getting scared about digging tip money for rent when Willa came to me with her phony accent and an offer of how I could stay."

She looked at me with suspicion. "All of a sudden, I'm answering a lot of questions. How do I know you're not one of the fat broad's snitches?"

"She's got snitches here?"

"Think maybe I'll shut up."

We heard a voice clearing its throat behind us and looked around. A man was talking to Willa, and she beckoned Colleen with her finger. I didn't need to be told that Colleen wasn't happy to see the creep. The look of disgust on her face said it all. She pasted on a weak smile and went to them.

Shit! Talk about timing!

Discouraged, because I was getting someplace with her, I stood up and casually walked over to where the boys were playing cards. I kibitzed for a while, then yawned and went upstairs. Passing on the canned beef stew that was the dinner fare, I stayed in my room, sipping instant coffee made from hot tap-water, yuck, and watching the activity in the back parking lot until well after one a.m..

When I thought it would be clear, I crept down to 315, listened at the door to make sure there wasn't any masculine company in the room, then quietly knocked on the door. I heard rustling of bed covers then the soft padding of Colleen's feet as she walked to the door. She opened it enough to see that it wasn't a late night John, then said sullenly, "What do you want?"

"I'm not a snitch and I need to talk with you. It's important."

"At this hour, it better be. Come in."

"Thanks."

She got back in bed and I sat on the end. She looked at me and said, "Prove you're not a snitch." I'd thought about this while I was waiting to come down here. This was definitely a time to mix truth and fibs. "To tell the truth, I am a snitch... of sorts. I'm a detective from Sausalito."

"A cop? I don't believe you. Show me a badge."

"Use your head, kid. Would I bring police ID in here?"

"I guess not. You look too young. How do I know you're not lying?"

"You don't. You'll have to trust me. And I'm twenty two, just graduated from the Academy. Police often use kid-looking rookies like me for vice scams. No one knows us."

"Why are you here?"

"I'm looking for this girl." I handed her the photo. She turned on her table lamp, looked at snapshot and handed it back to me.

"Why?"

Now for the whopper. "We have reliable information that someone wants her dead. We know there's a couple of pistoleros tracking her. I'm just a few steps ahead of them."

"Why do they want to kill her?"

"She saw something back in Cincinnati that she shouldn't have. At some sort of penthouse party."

She was wilting. That detail about Cincinnati struck home. "You don't want to arrest her?"

"No. We want to put her in protective custody."

"Going to give her a new ID and place to live?"

"Possibly."

"Can you do that for me?"

"Possibly. Will you help me find her?"

Colleen bought it, hook, line and Murphy bed. She broke into a triumphant and warm smile. "I just knew you were a phony. You were too eager to put out for money. None of us were that willin', not like you. Shit, you were just as phony as Willa's accent. Now I can believe you. What do you want to know?"

"Willa's black accent is phony?"

"Shit, Kelly," Colleen laughed. "Ol' Willa is one sharp-assed old broad. I'll bet she's a college grad. The only reason I know is I overheard her telling some other madam off on the phone a few days ago. She spoke very clearly, no Ebonics, no accent of any kind, and was very hateful to the person on the other end."

That had to be Nora. Better be careful. "Tell me about Stephanie."

"Who's Stephanie?"

"This girl in the photo."

"Oh, that's Dannie."

"Dannie?"

"She uses the name Daniele Dumas. She lives on the second floor."

"What's her room number?"

"...But she left about two or three. I'm pretty sure she's trying to split. Maybe those guys you're talking about have found her."

"God, I hope not. How did she leave?"

"Her boyfriend, a kid who comes every day to help her pass a G.E.D. test, came in this afternoon, as usual. Willa allows us to study and have kids our age in to help us out. We're even allowed to take our real boyfriends up to our room if we want, just to keep the images up. No charge. It makes the girls look more like coeds. Obviously, most the creeps who come here are into teen sex."

"Or worse."

"Tell me something I don't know," she sighed. "Dannie and her boyfriend had a quick conversation. They went to the front windows and looked outside at something. Later I looked.

All I saw was a really neat little sports car parked down the block. One of those old classics? Anyway, her boyfriend left. She went upstairs. I saw her toss out some clothing to him, and the next thing I know, she's in his black Chevy, and they're haulin ass.

"Her timing was perfect. Willa was down in the Cafeteria.

"Damn good thing it was still in the afternoon, and the goon squad wasn't here yet. I hope she gets away. She's a good kid, trying to make it on her own."

"Is she the only girl to get away?"

"I don't know."

"Colleen, people have to get out somehow. This place would be wall-to-wall kids if they didn't."

"Some girls move out, when they're over twenty-one. By then they've been balled and blackmailed so much they'll never tell on Willa."

"That's the only way out?"

"I don't think so. Sometimes girls disappear at night. One day they're here, the next day their room is empty. We never hear from them again."

"What does Willa say happened to them?"

"She says, 'Don ask, if we knows what's good fo us.' "

"Why was Daniele putting out to reduce her rent?"

"Same reason. Willa was blackmailing her."

"With what?"

"I don't know. Something about a warrant for her arrest in Cincy."

"Why don't you just move out?"

"I can't."

"Why not?"

"Cause I got busted once. Willa bailed me out.

When I said I was quitting and moving, the old bitch showed me a copy of my booking slip, and told me that this could very easily get into the wrong hands. And she said I owed her five hundred dollars bail money. She had the receipt. I got the hint. I can get my ass kicked royally if I even think about moving out, and she'll call my parents."

"Blackmail, hum?"

"Yeah."

"How did you get busted?"

"I was only walking down the street. A man who had been up in my room a few times stopped me. We weren't doing anything! He was just asking me a few innocent questions, just talking like friends and Zap!, a plainclothes car pulls next to us, and a vice cop arrests both of us! He got off with a lecture, but I was charged with soliciting!"

"What was vice's probable cause?"

"You mean why did they even arrest me? I don't know."

"Didn't they tell you?"

"No. All they said was that I made a offer to screw this guy for some bucks, and I didn't! I'm stuck here for the rest of my life, I guess. Hey, can you help me with that jail thing?"

"Yes."

"Promise?" This time I wasn't lying. "Colleen, I promise that all this is going to get investigated, real thoroughly. But it might be wise to keep quiet for a while. Don't tell anyone, and for Christ's sake, don't let Willa think anything is up."

"Don't worry. Fat Bitch has too many girls tattling on each other."

"Can you run away?"

"No."

"Why not?"

"Couple of reasons. Two of the biggest hoods I've ever seen, park out in the back lot, at night. Supposedly they're guarding the establishment, but they'll beat the shit out of any girl who tries to sneak out. Mess her up good! I've seen it happen."

"Tell me about that."

"A while ago, a girl got her ass kicked so bad she died a day later. I don't know what happened to her body. There never was anything in the paper about finding her, or any anything else about girls our age.

"Willa said that if we even dreamed about what happened, her two men would fuck us a few dozen times, maybe with broken cola bottles, beat the shit out of us, then kill us… slowly and painfully. None of us who were here then are ever supposed to mention it again."

"What was the girl's name?"

"Sandy, I think. That's it. Sandy Reed. I don't think it was her real name though. None of us use 'em."

"What did she look like?"

"My height, five-six. Nice figure. Coppery hair, and a face and neck loaded with freckles. Maybe seventeen, eighteen."

"What color eyes?"

"Gray or hazel, I think."

"You said there was a couple of reasons that you stayed. What was the other?"

"Willa does an in-depth check on us as soon as she can. She knew where to send the copy of my arrest sheet before I got busted, I think."

My blood ran cold. The fat broad ran background checks! I had to get out of there, like yesterday! Stupidly, I'd used Kelly's and my real home town when I filled out the rental papers. If she didn't know already, by the morning, noon at the latest, Willa would find out that Kelly McAllister died when she was a kid.

If Willa wasn't any dummy, she'd put two and three together, and just maybe realize that I wasn't a snot nosed teen and had to be something else, like a cop. Or the infected girl Nora was trying to palm off on her.

Which could lead to mucho kinds of trouble. Not the least of which was getting the crap beat out of me for spreading germs. Maybe removed permanently by the two creeps out back. Dead women can't pass germs.

I told Colleen I was leaving, and had to convince her that I couldn't take her with me. I tiptoed downstairs and looked for light coming from under Willa's room door.

Nothing. She's asleep.

I was about to go back up to my room and retrieve the box of grubbies I brought with me. My plans changed when Willa, who clearly wasn't asleep, puffed her way up the stairs. I didn't know if she was headed for my room, but I wasn't going to wait around to find out.

I slipped out the back door as quietly as I could, and walked around the lot, ostensibly stretching my legs. All the cars in the lot were empty. Apparently, the palace guards were gone.

Piece a cake!

I was feeling pretty good. I'd gone under, found out what I had to, and gotten away, and no one was wiser except me.

A booming male voice scared the pee right out of me. "Gwine somewhere?"

I didn't turn to the voice, didn't freeze in my tracks, just bolted across the lot and over the fence to the neighbor's back yard. I heard a car start up and spin rubber as it peeled out of the parking lot. I made it across the block and was running down the alley in the next block when a car came screeching around the corner. Headlights lit my path.

The car was in the alley!

I panicked and ran faster. I was conscious of wind in my ears, conscious of trying to make my legs churn just a little faster with each step.

Conscious about how far out of shape I was. I was in such deep crap if they caught me!

I ran, arms pumping, breathing deep and hard, trying to keep to the right side of the narrow corridor because garbage cans were on the other side.

A wino was stumbling towards me, oblivious of the action in front of him. My first inclination was to dodge around him, and let him stop the car. My second realization told me if I didn't shove the drunk to one side he'd wake up in the morgue.

I hit him from the side, using all my hundred pounds to block him away from the car's path. We crashed into a metal doorway about the same time the car tried to remove my best asset. It was that close.

The car had passed, and now I was behind it. I doubled back over the same path I had taken; the car couldn't turn around in the alley. I had scant seconds in the deserted street to make up my mind. I could hear the car coming around the block.

I ran through the neighbor's yard again and hopped the fence back into the parking lot of the cathouse. I hid in a shadow-covered corner, behind a trash dumpster, concentrating on quickly catching my breath. I prayed that the turkeys chasing me wouldn't figure I was back where it all started. After a few minutes of heavy breathing, I climbed into the metal dumpster. It was a good thing I did, because the car came back into the lot, driving in a way that the headlights played over the entire property. I could see two men in the car from a small crack in the hatch door to the container. They parked right next to where I was hiding. I was trapped.

"Wonder who that little punch was?" The man with the deep voice asked.

Punch? Oooo.' I've never been called that before.

"I dunno. Never saw that one afore. Willa will tell us in the mornin'. Probably one a the bimbos deciding to try it on her own."

"I wouldn't want to be her when Willa gets hold o her ass."

"Maybe we get a crack at this'n? It be our turn, ain't it?"

"Possible. Ifin' we don't get our asses kicked for letting her get away."

My legs were getting cramped in place. I wasn't comfortable, even though there was plenty of room inside. I couldn't move an inch because the passenger had his car window halfway down. His ear wasn't four feet from me.

C'mon, turn up the freaking stereo! Do something, make some noise so I can stretch out!

I was nearly in tears of pain when something jumped in the trash box with me. I don't know who was more surprised, the cat or me.

Purely from startled reaction, I jerked and made an angry 'Pfffttt!" sound.

New Cat yowled loudly and scrambled up the side of the container, screeching and hissing at the bigger Old Cat already in the box. I used the noise he made as a mask to quickly get comfortable.

New Cat flew out through the top door of the container a yowlin' and a clawin' all the way. One of the voices yelled, "Shit!"

The other laughed with his deep voice, "Hey Clyde, wassa matta? Scared of a little pussy cat?"

"You sombitch!, that sucker was right next to my ear, and I was dozing. If it was you, you'd be shooting the little pissant."

"Well, it ain't me. Here."

The silence and a slight gurgling noise let me know that You Sombitch had handed Hey Clyde a bottle of something. The loud belch and satisfied "Ahhh" suggested it was booze. I was so close I could smell it.

Cheap bourbon.

Hey! I'm cold. Pass somma that stuff in here, would'cha?

We waited out the dawn. Sometime after sunup, the car started up and pulled out. I was out of the smelly trash bin and out of the parking lot in nanoseconds, using back alleys to get a good five blocks away before I found a phone. I didn't have my cell because a girl as hard up for money as I was supposed to be wouldn't be carrying the latest in cellular technology, would she? I jammed my hand in my pocket, hunting for a quarter to make a call.

Nothing.

Doubleshit!

I wandered for a while, and finally spotted the same bum who's life I'd saved. I walked to the sleeping form cautiously, and gently kicked the bottom of his shoe.

"Hah. Wassa?"

"Hey Bro, I need a quarter."

"Beat it." He rolled over to the other side and began sawing logs.

"Hey!" I snapped. "I'm the one who saved your miserable life last night! The least you can do is loan me a quarter."

"Don' 'member. Hey, do I look like a goddamned bank?" He passed out again. Mentally holding my nose I reached in his pockets and found a quarter and a dime. It was the only money he had. I snickered to myself as I walked back to the phone.

Five weeks between being the numero uno Escort *in the circuit to rolling drunks for quarters.*

I dialed Greg's home number.

If Hot Dog answers, I'm going to kill him ever so slowly.

Greg cheated death again. His voice mumbled, "Hello."

"Greg?"

"Who is this?"

"Who do you think it is?"

"Gail? Ann..."

"Before you say one more word, Sergeant Phillips," I growled, only partially kidding, "you better guess the right name or I'm going to make the rest of your effing life hell on flat tires."

"Tracy! Sorry, honey. I didn't recognize the voice, but the vocabulary sure is familiar."

"Very funny. I need help."

"Call the Boy Scouts."

"Gregory Phillips, you *listen* to me! Two big black goons are looking for me. The top three numbers on their hit parade are beating, raping and killing.

"I'm the target du jour! I spent the whole night in Willa's kitchen garbage. I had to roll a drunk just to get the money to call you. Now c'mon, joke's over. Please come and pick me up at California and Fifth."

"Okay," he sighed.

"And bring a trash bag for me to sit on. I stink to high heavens." I stayed in the nearest alley, telling myself I was hiding from the two hoods that might still be looking for me.

But if the truth be known, I didn't want to see anyone who might recognize me. I looked frightful. I had wound up only a couple of blocks from the building where I worked at Peerless.

Greg pulled to the side of the curb. I sprinted to his car, and hopped in. "Phew!" he opened his window. "You weren't lying. You do stink!"

"So would you, if you spent the night in a freaking white elephant with two guys who want a piece of your ass sitting four feet away."

"Want to tell me about that?"

"We were so right. It's a cathouse. Stephanie Bradford was there, but I don't think she'll be returning. She took a hike about the same time I was home getting some grubbies packed.

"Willa gets the young ones in, makes them what they think is a good financial offer to put out, then blackmails them when the girls decide enough is enough. If that doesn't do the job, she's got two big thugs outside waiting to beat the snot out of any girl who tries to leave."

"Sounds pretty small time for a gal with her reputation."

"I thought so, too." I turned on my seat to face him.

"Hang onto your delicious buns, Lover, 'cause I'm going to give you probable cause to be involved in this. There was a murder there six or seven months ago."

I'm glad I had my seat belt on. He slammed on the brakes so hard he almost lost control of his brand-new, obscenely huge, politically incorrect gas-guzzling Ford Explorer.

"A what?! In that place? Who?"

"A girl named Sandy Reed. Five-six, one-twenty maybe, coppery hair, facial freckles, hazel eyes, seventeen to eighteen years old. She tried to go it alone and was beaten to death. And the girl who told me all this said she never saw any kind of Jane Does that fit her in the obits."

He began driving again. "If that's true, her body was probably weighted down and dumped in the bay, or offshore. We'll never find her."

"Maybe you already have, but you only have her as Jane Doe."

"Possibly, but I don't remember any carrot-topped Jane Does who were beaten to death in the past few months."

He pulled into his driveway and we went inside. "Can I use your shower?"

"You're not going to sit on anything in my house until you do. Right through there."

"I remember."

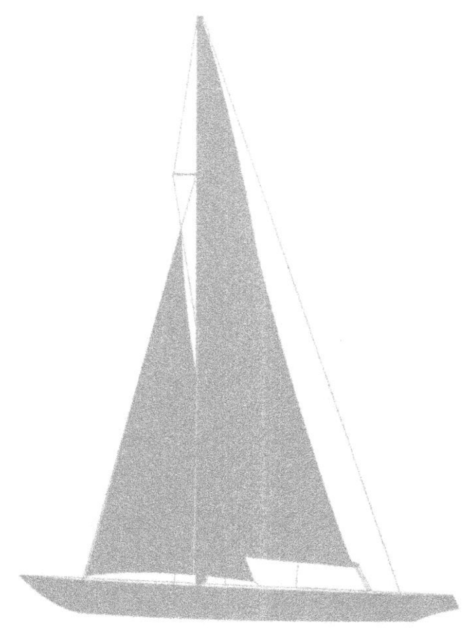

CHAPTER ELEVEN

I closed the bathroom door and peeled out of my clothes, tossing them in a heap in the tile floor. I was shivering from cold more than fright when I stepped in. The shower felt super.

My only problem was reaching the shower head. I've been in many showers in my life, but never one with the head so high. Greg must have had it specially put up to his height. I had to stand on my tip-toes to adjust it. Once I did, I liked it immediately.

When I grow up and get my own home, I'm going to put the shower heads way up, just like this. It was like a hot rain on my head. While I stood under the warming water, feeling the cold parts of my body come back to normal, I thought some about what I'd learned.

Stephanie was there. She was hooking for the house. She didn't like it. Somehow Morresey learned that I was close, maybe already inside. He hauls her out. How could he know about me?

Doublestuff!

I am so stupid! A damn dope! It's so obvious. He must have spotted Maggie sometime, and when he passed by her on the street, knew how close I was. Cars like mine aren't exactly common.

Great. Now how do I find Steph? I need another car.

Questions. Always questions.

Why does Pop Bradford want me to find darlin' daughter after all this time? Why now? She's seventeen, right? What's a...Whoa!

She turns eighteen sometime in the next year! Many things happen when a girl turns eighteen. She becomes a legal adult in a lot of ways. Is that the reason?

"Hey!" Greg's voice boomed in the bathroom, scaring the wits out of me.

"What?"

"There's a robe hanging on the inside of the door. I'll take these ripe clothes and toss 'em in the washing machine."

"Thanks."

Bet it's hotdog's robe. If it is, I'd rather go naked than wear it. Come to think about it, I'd just rather go naked anyway.

I am so bad...

I shampooed my hair and towel-dried it when I got out. Then I finger-brushed my teeth and put on the robe. It wasn't whatsherface's. It was a short one of Greg's. A smoking jacket, like. I looked at myself in the mirror and busted out laughing.

All I needed was the ears and I could pass for Dopey. I looked like a kid playing in her daddy's clothes. The sleeves came clear over my hands, and even though on Greg the bottom hem was above the knee, on me it came close to dragging on the floor. All I needed was a hood to make it look like my dress designer was the same one the Seven Dwarfs used.

I went out to the living room and was greeted by a great smell of bacon and eggs. I climbed up on the barstool and sipped a cup of black coffee while he finished cooking.

"I called in." He said. "And took the day off."

"Why?"

"Because it's the only way I can get involved with you and stay out of trouble."

"Who said anything about being involved?"

"In your case, kid."

I stopped him. "Please don't call me that, Greg. It sounds patronizing."

"Sorry." He grinned and placed two plates of breakfast on the bar. I dove in like I hadn't eaten in days.

I'm a one-way type of person. When I sail, my favorite outdoor recreation, I don't think about eating, say.

When someone like Greg makes love to me, which is my favorite indoor recreation, I don't think about sailing.

When I eat, I don't think about making love... or sailing. And so on. I didn't say a word to my host until my eggs, hash browns and bacon were history, and I was slathering butter on my third piece of toast.

"You eat like a lumberjack." He chuckled.

"I do that. I love food, and you're a terrific cook. Will you marry me?"

"That's my line, isn't it?"

"Yeah, I suppose it is. If you're thinking it, just don't say it for a while. I've got a whole lot of catching up to do before I become Nee Tracy Cunningham."

"Tell me about that."

"What?" I turned to him. "You want my life story?"

"Up to the pro part. Call it pay for the vittles."

"To make it short, I'm the only child of Beverly and John G. Cunningham. I was a normal bratty tom-boy until I was thirteen or so. My mother contracted lung cancer when I was five, but she began to really go downhill around the time I began puberty. It took her a long time to die, almost ten years, and the whole damn time, she kept smoking her friggin' cigarettes.

"In the last few months, she was bedridden. A skeleton with skin. She could barely lift her arms. The last few days the nurse, Dad, or I had to hold cigarettes for her while she puffed her life away.

"That's why I'm so death on smoking. That's why I moved from Southern California when I graduated from college. Unlike most Angelenos, I don't want to see the air I breathe."

"Why aren't you a cop?"

"I'm afraid of guns. I hate the military BS, and at the time, I was too small. Five foot two female cops don't gain a lot of respect."

"So you became an Insurance Investigator."

It dawned on me that he had a great interrogation technique, and I was actually being cross-examined. But I didn't mind. It felt good to get some of these things out in the open.

"And I was damn good at it, too. My problem was and is that I'm an airhead when it comes to finances. I always have been. I got into deep ca-ca with my charge accounts. When I was recruited I think I was completely ready to work."

"And now you're retired. What about Chief Cunningham?"

"What about him?"

"Does he know about the Eden?"

"God, I hope not! He thinks I'm just easy. He doesn't know the truth."

"Are you ever going to tell him?"

"Greg, my father is over six foot tall, and weighs someplace over two hundred pounds, all solid muscle. He's bald and has my temper. I got some bad spankings when he caught me doing things he believed his daughter shouldn't have been doing. The last time, he beat the crap out of me with a Sam Browne. I couldn't dress for gym for a month."

"Why not?"

"If I showed my bruises to a teacher, they would have called in the gendarmes, and my father would have been in it, real deep. Any normal citizen in the world would have been convicted of felony child beating. I would have been put in that school for wayward girls. Dad would have certainly lost his job."

"At least." I could see from Greg's dark expression he didn't like hearing about anyone, even my father, beating the snot out of me.

"How do you think he would react if he found out his only living heir was an escort? We have enough problems without him finding that out."

"What problems?"

"We don't see eye to eye. The last time I visited him, I got blotto and he had to carry me into my room. I woke up at four o'clock, still dressed.

"I didn't pass go, didn't collect two hundred dollars. I left the house before five A.M., still gassed to the eyeballs, and flew straight to San Francisco. I haven't been back since. I haven't even talked to him on the phone in over a year."

"Wow. Kind of heavy between you two."

"You could say that. In spite of it all, I still love him, and I think he loves me."

CHAPTER TWELVE

I'd been completely up front with Greg. By the time we finished breakfast coffee, he knew more about me than any other person alive. More than I wanted to admit, and more than I wanted to know about myself. I was tempted to make him stop asking questions in a way that. would have pleased us both, but that's not why I called him.

Why did I call him?

Because I was right back where I started and I didn't know what to do. Maybe I was once a top-notch Insurance Investigator, but I wasn't so hot at tracking a missing girl.

I'd found her, but instead of going right back into that living room, and dragging her out bodily, I let her get away. I had to get cute. I wasn't as smart as I thought. My walking away from Maggie had only given Jerry enough time to point me out when I got back. Now both Stephanie and he knew what I looked like, and what kind of a car I drove. On the good side, Stephanie was alive and well, and I'd seen her in person.

I yawned and realized that I was totaled. I hadn't had a moment's rest, so I mumbled something, sleepily walked to the bedroom, and crawled into that one acre of decadent bed. Even though I was completely undressed, I was so zonked that if Greg had gotten in with me, I'd have to phone in my part.

I closed my eyes and visualized the image of my quarry looking at me. Stephanie was still quite pretty. Hooking hadn't lessened that. She had a good figure, not slender, not over-blown. Her hair was a medium blonde-brown, and I wasn't close enough to see the color of her eyes, but I assumed blue because the black and white photo showed medium gray eyes. When she looked at me she had smiled. It was still a pretty smile, although, looking back now, it was also kind of timid.

I disappeared and slept until after one thirty. When I woke up, I felt a pang of disappointment that Greg hadn't slid into the bed with me. He had been in the room and obviously had the chance. My clothes were neatly folded on the dresser.

Damn.

A rip-roaring matinee would have been a great way to end my nap. I dressed and emerged from the bedroom, bright-eyed and bushy tailed and climbed back up on my favorite barstool, asking, "If you were me, what would you be doing to find Stephanie?"

"Let's reverse that. If you were me, say, or a cop, what would you be doing?"

"I'd have a BOLO or A.P.B. out for Jerry Morresey. He's still the link between the real world and Stephanie's."

"Agreed. But you can't put out a call. No reason able cause to even hold him for questioning."

"But he is a person of interest, right?"

"Right. You know he's going to be real careful about letting anyone follow him. "Dammitalltohell! I could have sworn that I did a good tailing job."

"From what you tell me, I wouldn't say you did one thing wrong. Unless, of course, your somewhat unique car was the culprit."

"She had to be. I guess... seeing Maggie three times in three days would be a rarity."

Greg nodded and sipped his coffee. "This Jerry Morresey youngster seems like a true blue friend. He's going to see Stephanie every day, teaching her what he learns that day in school. Apparently, he's not overly concerned about her sexual activities."

"Unless he doesn't know," I said. "How could he not know?"

"Beats me. Maybe he's so smitten with her, he just ignores the possibility."

"True. What do you think we should do?" I felt a comic light bulb over my head when it dawned on me that Greg was instructing me. One doesn't get to be a sergeant in the San Francisco Police Department by asking airheads like me what to do next.

"I think that we should capture Jerry, and have a real heart-to-heart with him."

"We?"

"Me, then. But I need muscle."

"And you've got it. Just for the day. Let's go."

He drove his unmarked police car. We figured that if we found young Morresey, his being detained by the police would make him a lot more co-operative. Having a policeman at my side also made the Senior Counselor much more amenable to my requests. All it took was a glimpse at Greg's gold badge.

Quinn sent a student worker to Morresey's class with a pink slip, and Jerry came into the office five minutes later.

"Jerry, you remember Miss Cunningham," Mrs. Quinn said, "And this is Sergeant Phillips of the San Francisco police department."

The boy mumbled his acknowledgment.

"Thank you, Mrs. Quinn," Greg said. "Would you excuse us for a few minutes?"

Mrs. Quinn wasn't pleased that she had been summarily dismissed, but she left.

Nosy 'ol broad.

"Jerry," Greg began calmly. "Can you guess why we want to talk to you?"

"Yeah," he glared at me. "She wants to find Steph again."

"That's right, kid." Greg said, "The difference is now I want to find her."

"Join the club."

"I already did. Where is she?"

"I don't know."

"Jerry," I interrupted, "Stephanie is not in trouble. Nothing's going to happen when we find her, except maybe she can live more comfortably at home, with her father, and not be always looking over her shoulder, wondering if anyone's tracking her."

"Bullshit! Things were just fine, until you stuck your nose in our business!"

"Were they?"

"Yeah. She had a good night-time job, and was catching up with the senior class well. She's going to be ready for her G.E.D. and get it the same time the rest of us graduate."

"What kind of job?"

"She was a fast-food worker. Wouldn't tell me where. She didn't want me coming around and bugging her."

"Bugging her?"

"Soon as she turns eighteen, I'm going to marry her, lady." He stared at me evenly. "Bugging means taking her to a dark corner and making out."

Greg's face turned dark. "Kid…"

"Wait a sec," I jumped in before Greg could say anything to hurt him. "Jerry, Stephanie is in trouble, but I don't know what kind."

"Huh?"

"Her father hired me, right?"

"That's what you said."

"Ask yourself, 'Why? Why does he want her back after two years of 'I don't give a damn what she does?'"

"I don't know."

"Can you find out?"

"Gimme a break, lady. Just who's side do you think I'm on?"

Something clicked in the dark spaces of my mind. "Just hold on." I said. "You should ask me that."

"Why?"

"Right now I'm not sure who's side I'm on."

"True story?"

"True story. Will you ask Stephanie why her dad wants her… now?"

"I suppose."

"Can you call her?"

"Possibly."

"If we go outside and leave you in here alone, will you call her and ask if she knows any reason for her father to want her back now?"

"I might."

"Jerry," Greg said. "We'll trust you, if you'll trust us. You can always tell her to split, that the heat's after her, can't you?"

Realization of what Greg was offering him sank in. "Yeah."

"So don't. Just ask her what we want to know."

"Okay."

Greg and I walked outside and closed the door. The line light on the outer phone went on and stayed on for a good five minutes before it blinked off. We went back in.

"She wouldn't tell me."

"But there is something, right?"

"I think so. Once I mentioned it, I could tell it's scaring the shit out of her."

"Where is she, Jerry?"

"Get me a pass, and I'll take you there. We better hurry."

We were heading for the San Francisco zoo area in five minutes, the red magnetic light atop the car, silently allowing Greg to break all kinds of traffic laws. We pulled up to a run-down apartment house.

"You go with Jerry," Greg shouted while running around to the side entrance, "I'll cover the back."

"Apartment G," Jerry said. I rang all the apartment buzzers, except G. We were buzzed in quickly, and we both ran up to the third floor. I let Jerry knock on the door. "Steph! It's me. Lemme in!"

She came to the door and opened it, puzzled. "Jer? What are you doing here?"

I pushed in beside her. "Miss Bradford, I presume?"

I know, I know. It was a moronic line, but this was my first case and I hadn't thought of anything better.

"You're the one who's looking for me." She looked back at Jerry. Her eyes asked, "Why did you betray me?"

Greg came into the apartment and showed her his badge. Stephanie sat on the tattered couch and began crying. I sat next to her. "I shoudda run the moment Jerry said there was someone looking for me. Shoudda got the hell out of town."

"Coudda, Shoudda, Woudda," I said dryly. "What happens when you turn eighteen?"

"I don't know what you're talking about.."

"Oh, cut the bullshit, Stephanie! Your old man wasn't interested in you until just recently. He knew you were back in California. You're going to turn eighteen soon. A girl becomes a legal adult then."

"That is my business."

"Steph," I said softly. "I told Jerry I wasn't sure who's side I was on. I'm only going to get a grand for finding you. I've already spent three hundred. I can get that back, plus a thousand dollar bonus if I hand you over to your father before the end of the week.

"That's thirteen hundred dollars that I need very much. As much as I could use the bread, I'm not going to turn you over to anyone if there's the slightest hint that it may be dangerous for you. Right now consider me your big sister."

She looked at me with soft light-brown eyes. "Do you mean that?"

"Word of honor." I nodded and told Greg and Jerry that I wanted to talk girl-to-girl in private for a few minutes. They went out to the car.

"Steph, I know what you were doing in Willa's place."

"What?"

"You're a hooker. I rented a place there the afternoon you saw me. I don't know how long it took Willa to have you come around, but she asked me the first time she knew I was interested in renting a pad there."

"A week for me."

"And somehow, you've been able to keep the prostitution a secret from Jerry, right?"

"He's so much in love with me, he'll believe anything I tell him.

"He thinks I work nights. No thanks to you, you blew all that."

"Honey, I didn't let on. He still doesn't know. I won't tell him. But I think you better."

"Why?"

"He says he wants to marry you. Do you want to marry him?"

"Yes. But if he finds out, he'll hate me."

"Better you find that out now than after you're married and some creep sees you in a restaurant and asks you if you want to make a fast buck for old time's sake. If Jerry is truly in love with you, and that seems pretty obvious to me, he'll find a way to deal with your past. It's not like you did street work, you know."

"Not here. I did some streetwalking in Cincinnati."

"Figures."

"I moved back six months ago. I wanted to pull myself out of the gutter. I was doing fine… for a while.

"Oh, God, Tracy, I'm never going to get out!"

"Oh yes you will!" I held her shoulders while she cried. "If I can do it, you can."

"You?"

"Yeah," I smiled. "I've been there too, Steph. Now, what the hell does your father want with you?"

"I don't think he wants me per se'. I'm going to inherit something when I'm eighteen. I was my grandpa's favorite. He and I had a pretty special relationship. Obviously, my father wants whatever it is. I don't know. Something in a safe deposit box?"

"And you don't know what it is?"

"No."

"What did your grandfather do?"

"I don't know. He never told me. I guess little girls aren't supposed to be told things like that. Gramps died when I was still a kid.

"All I remember about him is that he had an old gray soup-strainer mustache that tickled when he kissed me. I know I adored him. I know that he was nice to me, took me places like the zoo, and fishing, and skeet shooting. I was his buddy. He was pretty rich, I guess. He had a chauffeur and a butler with him all the time."

"A chauffeur *and* a butler?"

"Yeah. All the time."

"What does your father do?"

"Runs the family business.

"Which is?"

"I told you, I don't know for sure. He and Mom never talked about it in front of me. He went to the office every morning and came home every night. We had money."

"Why did you run away?"

"Why not? I had no reason to stick around. Mom was gone. Grandpa was dead. I hated my old man."

"Why?"

"Son of a bitch got drunk and beat Mom up all the time."

"But she left you."

"I know. I don't know where she is."

"Who's father was your Grandfather?"

"Mom's."

"And the family business… was that grandpa's too?"

"Yes."

"Well, girlfriend, we're getting the hell out of here."

"You going to make me go back?"

"No way. You need help and it's not the kind that your father can give you."

"Why are you switching sides?"

"I don't know. I want some questions answered before I do anything else."

"Why can't I stay here?"

"Because this is a freaking flea trap! Steph, today is the first day of the rest of your life."

She rolled her eyes and snickered. "Gawd, Lady, gimme a break! That line is so trite!"

Now that I'd finally seen it, she had a really great smile. "Sure, it's a dumb line, but it's also truth. Most trite lines are. Today is the day we pull you out of the gutter."

She didn't have enough clothing to fill a large cardboard box, which she had and was still packed. When we left, I didn't have any idea what I was going to do with her, but turning her over to her father was on the bottom of the list of options.

I know, I know. I'm not supposed to interfere with my client's personal problems. I was hired to find the girl. I found her. I'm supposed to call my client, get my final bonus and expenses and give Stephanie to him.

Cut and dried. Nothing to this game.

What stopped me was that I liked the kid from first sight.

Before I was going to turn her over to anyone, I wanted to get some answers to some very pointed questions.

CHAPTER THIRTEEN

After we drove Jerry back to the school, the remaining three of us went back to Greg's condominium. Once inside, both Stephanie and I complained long and loudly about our stomachs growling. Greg acquiesced to our demands for food and sent out for a jumbo pizza. I don't think any Gourmet dinner in the world could have tasted better.

That was probably because of my mood. I had successfully done what I was hired to do. Find a teen-aged runaway. I knew where to go to find Morresey, over a period of four days, trailed him to Willa's cathouse, saw Stephanie in the flesh, and once that was done, coerced Jerry to take us to her new hiding place. So I'm allowing myself to feel good.

"What's the next step, Sherlock?" Greg said.

"Well, we've got to find a good place to hide Stephanie. Then I want to find out what's going on."

"How about here?"

"Right, Greg." I said dryly. "I'm really going to leave a seventeen year old fox in this den of iniquity."

"Don't be so nasty, Trace." he said with a touch of hurt in his voice. "I meant the both of you sleep here. Stephanie can sleep on the couch."

I didn't ask where I was going to steep. I knew, and that was fine with me. "I'm sorry, Greg," I smiled and looked at Stephanie. "Okay with you?"

"Sure," she said, looking, around Greg's digs. "This is a lot better place than I've been in since I blasted."

"Okay, onto the next phase," I turned to Stephanie, and said, "Let's start with your grandfather's name."

"Angelo J. Martucchi. People called him 'A.J.'"

"A.J. Martucchi?" Greg interrupted.

"Yes."

"Say no more. I can put a lot of this together for you."

I said, "How?"

"A.J. Martucchi was the mob, Trace. I don't mean in the mob, he was the mob. Numero uno. The big Cheese. Ichi-ban numba one.

"That's a lot of bullshit!" Stephanie snapped. "My grandpa was a nice man!"

"Was he a heavy man with thinning gray hair? A thick gray mustache? Parted his hair in the middle? Had a stogy stuck in his mouth all the time? Had his left ring finger amputated because of something called Dupertwan's Tendonitis? Always wore a vest when he wore a suit?"

Greg apparently nailed him cold.

"A lot of men are like that." she replied sullenly.

"He may have been the best Grandpa a girl could know, but he was still a Mafioso Don."

"I can't believe it."

"Steph, those two men always with you? The chauffeur and butler? They had to be body-guards."

"Shit. I think I suspected something like that," she sighed. "Ever since I saw The Godfather, I've often wondered about it.

"I've wondered about the Belvedere Island home we lived in. It was a big compound, like, with a high brick wall around it."

"You're a mafia princess, Steph." I said quietly.

She laughed hard, with a derisive sneer. "Boy, if I am, they sure cut me loose easily enough, didn't they? You'd think they would want me in the fold, where they could keep an eye on me."

"Several thoughts come from that," I said. "One is that they were keeping an eye on you. At least, they did until you moved back to San Francisco. Did you ever get into trouble while you were gone?"

"Not really."

"Never got beat up by a pimp?"

"Oh, no. Never had a pimp. I was always able to make it without one."

"Uhuh." I said dryly. "And I'll just bet you scored pretty high a few times, too."

"I did all right." She said. "I didn't have as many Johns as the other girls, but, I made a lot more than they did."

"How much more?"

"Plenty enough to pay my share of an apartment with another girl and eat well. I got bonuses for being a wild and crazy kid."

"You were getting an allowance from the family, kid. You got protection from the family, too. No girl is going to hit the bricks at the age of fifteen or sixteen in a big city like Cincinnati, and keep out of the stable of some big greasy dude who's going to use the hell out of her bod for his own gain. When you moved, you must have moved so suddenly the family lost you."

"I did. It was no more than a whim. I'd just gotten a postcard from an old friend. I decided on the spot that I wanted to see her and Jerry again. So I piled on a bus heading for the west coast."

"Who was the girl?" I asked."My best friend. A girl named Stacy Reece."

"Did she live at Willa's place?"

"She said she did, but I never saw her. Never found her. Willa said she moved out a few weeks before."

Stacy Reese? Sandy Reed? It had to be. The names were too close for anything else.

I was just about to tell her that, Stacy Reese, AKA Sandy Reed, was dead when Greg interrupted, "Wonder why they didn't do what you did, Trace? Just follow Jerry to Stephanie?"

"I think they tried," Stephanie said. "Once I was back in town, I got a lot more careful. I waited a long time before I called Jerry to let him know where I was. I told him to drive on different streets every day, and if he ever saw anyone following him, he was to ditch them, or not come near me."

"So they used me to find you. Maybe they figured a small woman wouldn't alert Jerry."

"I don't agree," Greg said. "The first thing you did was go to the high school and find Jerry. Maybe they've been following you."

"Do you think they're outside?"

"I can find out easily enough," he dialed his office and asked for a uniformed car to sweep his neighborhood. "If anyone's out there, we'll find 'em."

"Things are all messed up." I stood and began pacing slowly. "We think that something in a safe deposit box is the real reason Bradford wants Steph back. She was probably under some sort of loose protection while she was back east. They lose her because she moves west.

"Five and a half months after Bradford said he heard a rumor that Stephanie was back in San Francisco, he hires a dirt-poor, dumb broad ex-hooker to find her, when he could have probably found her himself, just as easily."

I directed my questions to Greg. "Why hire me to begin with? What has all this got to do with me? If you know so much about Stephanie's grandfather, why don't you know anything about Bradford?

"Steph says he's running the family business. That means he's the mob boss now. I'm supposed to be smart, but I sure the heck don't understand any of this."

"I do know something about Bradford," Greg said, "It's a simple matter of not connecting your Bradford with Mob Bradford. Do you think maybe he just wanted you to do the routine work? Maybe he doesn't have any men who have investigative talents."

"C'mon, Greg," I said. "I don't believe everyone in the mob has a crooked nose and speaks with a thick Detroit-Italian accent."

"I don't either."

Something in the back of my mind started clicking. "Hmmm. I wonder..."

"What?" They both said.

"What if there's a reason they can't be seen or caught tracking you?"

"What kind of reason?"

"Say... and this is just an airhead's speculation... say there's someone else who wants Steph. Suppose... just suppose... this other group is following the mob guys'."

"Like who?" Stephanie asked.

"I don't know. A competing organization? Possibly the Feds?"

"Why would the Feds want me?"

"I don't know. For the time being, let's just pretend that they do."

"That could work." Greg smiled. "Let's see if it fits."

I was onto something and I was getting excited. I said, "Stephanie is going to inherit something. The mob wants it. The Federales want it.

"The Feds can't find Stephanie. The mob doesn't dare look, because they've discovered that the feds are around. They need someone to be a bird-dog. They find me, via the Eden Connection. They don't care who I am, they just would like to have someone who knows enough about the biz to find her quickly.

"It gets better here. The family lucks out and gets the name of an ex-call-girl who's just become an investigator. A gal who never applied for a license and who's never had a case.

"I'm a no-body!

"I don't have a single thing in any official files that says I'm an investigator of any kind! Insurance Investigators are licensed by the state, they're hired by the insurance companies from the graduate lists of universities. No fed can possibly know I exist! Even if they run a check on me, my path comes to a screeching halt at Peerless Insurance.

"I made it a point to burn bridges when I left there. The best part is that I'm so dumb and broke that I'm supposed to find Steph, turn her over without a second thought, and pick up my bonus."

"Seems to me." Greg said, "that our Federales could find one girl, if they wanted."

"How?" I said. "She ran away when she was fifteen. Check any database you can think of and you'll never get this Stephanie Bradford. Right?"

"Right," she smiled. "I've never been busted, booked or ever been inside a police station."

"Colleen Brannigan said Willa was blackmailing you with an arrest warrant from Cincy."

"That's a laugh," Steph sneered. "I went along with that bullshit because I needed a safe place to hide. I knew she was bluffing. I never did a thing that would warrant a warrant."

For just a few seconds, she allowed herself to be a teen and giggled. "Now, what the hell am I supposed to be inheriting?"

"I don't know."

She got to her feet. "Wouldn't somebody know? A lawyer maybe? Obviously, my father knows what's in the safe deposit box."

"Your grandfather loved you, right?"

"Yes."

"Do you think he'd leave you something that would get you into trouble with the police?"

"Ain't no way."

"What did A.J. think of your dad?"

"Not much. He was the only male in the family. Mother was an only child."

"So A.J. was stuck with his son-in-law, your dad," I said.

"Yes."

"A.J. would never put you in jeopardy. That's a given. The mob wants whatever he left you. That's a given. Let's say my conjecture is correct. The Feds want whatever you're going to inherit: assume that's a given. Application: What is the single thing that makes all three of these givens work?"

"I don't know." she said.

"Nor do I," Greg added. "That makes three of us. How about your mother? Would she know?"

"Possibly."

"What's her name?"

"Angel Martucchi Bradford."

"Where do we start"

"Ma'am?" Stephanie asked.

"Call me Tracy. Where do we start to find your mother?"

"I don't *want* to find her. She left me holding the damn bag. One day she's home, and the next morning dad tells me she's taken a hike. I was just thirteen.

"I never... repeat never... got one crummy phone call from her to let me she loved me, was all right, nothing! Least I had enough class to have my father called once a year to let him know I was still alive."

"Maybe she didn't have any choice, Honey," I said softly.

"Why?"

"I don't know. Play along with me on this. If I find her, you don't have to speak to her if you don't want to. All we have to know is what's in the safe deposit box."

"Why not wait until my birthday?"

"When is it?"

"Six months."

"A lot can happen in six months. Have you seen your grandfather's will?"

"No."

"You and your father don't get along, right?"

"You might say that. I hate his guts."

"Suppose there's no love lost the other way. Seems to me if you're gone, your dad automatically inherits your stuff."

"Ohmygod!" She replied in shock. "I never thought of that!"

I looked at Greg. "There's the reason we don't turn her over. We could be turning her over to be killed."

He shook his head in disgust. "It works. Damnit, it all fits! Maybe I'd better see if there's a safe house available."

I stopped him before his hand reached the phone. "Wait a sec, Phillips. How do you know the police can be trusted?"

"Cunningham, you're getting paranoid."

"Just hold on, dammit. Think about this. Didn't I mention who I was looking for in front of Sergeant Hot Dog?"

"I don't remember."

"Well, I do. And I did." I asked Stephanie, "You don't look very much like your father. Does that mean you look like your mother's side of the family?"

"Most people think so, Why?"

I didn't answer her, just kept pressing Greg. "We show a photo of a girl who looks something like her grandfather, and mention the name 'Bradford' not once, but twice, in front of that overstuffed associate of yours and she never asks 'Bradford? The mob Bradford? Is this girl A.J. Martucchi's granddaughter?' or anything like that, does she?"

"No. I guess not."

"Hardbody, it seems to me, you better realize that there's at least a possibility that a cop's gone sour."

CHAPTER FOURTEEN

If Greg thought there was anything to my thinking, he didn't let on. I can't blame him, though. A bad cop is the worst person a good cop can imagine. Even if one was sleeping with the other.

After we got the expected phone call that there wasn't any obvious surveillance on Greg's place, we all breathed a little easier. We knew there wasn't any way we could all stay there. We had been lucky so far.

Today was Friday. I was supposed to check in with Bradford.

If he knew anything about me from Nora he'd know my word was good as gold, and be expecting the call. As soon as I called, unless I was very careful, he'd know something was up. If I had been followed anytime since I began this case, they knew where I was coming for advice and solace. The odds were too good that Bradford probably had put a man or two on Greg's condo, hidden well enough that the uniforms couldn't find them.

We decided to wait until morning before I alerted Bradford.

We watched TV for a while, then I peeled off to go to bed. I was tired again. Greg wasn't long in climbing in with me. We snuggled against each other and I whispered, "Greg, you know we can put a real name on the girl Willa had killed, don't you?"

"I think so. All we need is a conformation of Brannigan's description of the dead girl. I just didn't want you blurting something out we can't prove, honey. All it would do is hurt the hell out of Stephanie."

"I know," I said, kissing him warmly. "Thanks for stopping me. I'm so glad I chose such a nice man to be my boyfriend."

"You chose...? "

"Got that right, Hardbody." I giggled in his ear. "Now, why don't you show me what a super selection I made?"

So he did. Oh man, how he showed me. All I had to do for a long time was make myself comfortable. He did alllll the work.

I almost drew blood when I bit down on his shoulder to keep from crying out in ecstasy. That was all Stephanie's fault. If she wasn't sleeping out in front, I wouldn't have to keep quiet, so I wouldn't have bit him.

I stayed awake for a while. I had just been brought near to the brink of something I never actually experienced before. A climax is one thing. A earth-shattering, ground swelling, tsunami wave culmination caused by someone you love is quite another. I wanted to savor the feeling, the memory of it, all. Even though I wasn't quite pushed over, it was wonderful!

Maybe someday.

I'm sure I drifted off with a most satisfied glow on my face.

After a fun-filled wake-me-up romp early Saturday morning, I dialed the number on the back of Stephanie's photo. I had worked things out in my mind so I wouldn't have to lie. For some reason, I didn't want to work my first case with lies.

"Mister Bradford, this is Tracy Cunningham."

"How are you doing?"

"Not so good. Stephanie rabbitted on me." True.

"What do you mean?"

"She found out I was getting close and took a hike. I don't know where she is."

True. I hadn't looked in the living room this morning. She could have been in the kitchen, I don't know.

"How close did you come?"

"Close enough to see her for a moment." True. A lot of moments, but who's counting?

"Goddammitt, Cunningham, I told you to find her and call me! Now you've fucked everything up."

"That's not fair! I'm doing the best I know how." True.

"Not good enough, lady. You don't find her by Monday, you're fired."

I boiled over. "Bradford, you can go pound sand up your ass! I quit!"

Very true. I slammed down the phone, shaking with anger.

"Did he go for it?"

"I think so. I wasn't acting on my end. I think he believes I'm telling the truth, but we'd still better get outta town."

Over breakfast, we deliberated our options. I wanted to take her to Los Angeles, but Greg reminded me that my father and I didn't get along so well. There were too many chances the Chief would find out I was in L.A., and come to see me. He suggested a hotel right in San Francisco, but I pointed out that was way too close to home. Stephanie suggested Cincinnati, but that was too far away.

Besides, who the hell wants to go to Cincinnati?

We hassled it out, until Greg came up with a positively brilliant idea. A boat! Greg knew someone who knew someone, who lived out in the middle of Richardson's Bay on an anchored live-aboard tugboat.

That person was involved in a line of work that may have interested the Federal Government, Treasury Department thereof. It may have had something to do with the friend of a friend's proclivities for importing various objects 'de art without paying the proper vigorish to the government.

As the items brought in weren't high priority, not narcotics in any form, just bric-a-brac, the Federales weren't looking too hard for the man. However, if they were given the man's name and address, they'd certainly want to have a ten year chat with him.

We were all so paranoid, Greg walked down the street to a phone booth. Once he got hold of the party of the second part, and explained all this, and he explained it to his friend, the party of the third part decided that, yes, he really did want to take some time off. Boston was so beautiful this time of year.

Stephanie and I stopped by my boarding house and packed some clothes. Not knowing how long we were going to be isolated out on the bay, and not knowing what we would do if and when we came ashore, I over-packed.

I always do anyway. Unless it was a trick bag, packing is not one of my things. I brought some business type suits, some sports-wear, some grubbies, and some flimsy things to wear under my clothes and in bed. Especially in bed.

I had to stop myself. Although I was getting more loving from one man than I had in my life, I was also getting positively horny just thinking about sleeping in a boat's bed with Greg. That's one mix I've never had. I can do all my favorite things at one time. Great sex on a boat, followed closely by a chocolate cupcake.

Yum!

I shook the sexy thoughts out of my head and dragged my two heavy suitcases downstairs. Steph could fit into my looser clothes. We only had to wait twenty minutes for Greg to finish his errands and pick us up. Departing from Belvedere, we borrowed a runabout to get out to the tug.

The boat was anchored among other boats, houseboat, rafts and floating... for the most part... barges, all serving as some form of home for live-aboards. Traffic in the water wasn't like summer days on the bigger San Francisco bay when there was a good ten to twenty thousand yachts out recreating.

Not that the small bay we were in was deserted. It wasn't: there were always several boats of varying sizes, from ten footers to monstrous one-hundred footers moving about. If someone was onto us, or even thought that we might be hiding Stephanie aboard a floating safe-house, there was no way they could find the right boat right off the bat.

Greg and his police partner figured this 'safe house' would be good for at least seven days, at which time we'd have to move to new quarters. If we took reasonable care while we were out there, there would be no way to figure out which direction we were coming and going from. In the San Francisco Bay there are hundreds of places we could debark from.

The old tugboat was perfect. There was a big master's quarters, with a queen-sized bed. Greg would have to sleep from corner-to-corner, or hang his feet over the foot of the bed. That was okay. I just nestle myself on top. Otherwise, what was left over was plenty for me. The owner was a bit kinky, I guess. There were mirrors on the ceiling... the overhead. The other bunk room was in the bow and a good fit for Stephanie.

Out on the deck and up in the pilot house, we could see in all directions for at least a half mile. No one would be able to come out and do us bodily harm without us getting on a cell and screaming our little lungs out.

Greg went back to land and the PD to begin hunting down Angel Bradford. It was going to be a very cold trail, because there had never been a Missing Persons report filed.

"This is neat." Stephanie said while she looked over the tug. "Nothing to do except lie around and get an early season tan."

"Not so, my child." I opened a box Greg had picked up while Steph and I were at my boarding house. "You have at least four hours a day of studying to do."

I handed her a U.S. History book and smiled, "Hit the books, kid. You need any help, let me know."

"Hey! It's Saturday!"

"Very astute, Miss Bradford. We'll give you an 'A' in calendar. You've got a lot of catching up to do. They've all been marked out for what you need to do for a while."

"When was all this done?"

"While you and I were at my place, packing, Greg picked up the books at his former high school teacher's house and took them over to Jerry's house for marking."

"That snitch!"

"Calling Jerry names won't help."

"I know...," she smirked, "But he is so going to pay for this.... And just what are you going to do?"

"Work on that tan. No sense in both of us wasting the sun, is there?"

"You are so cold..." she pouted.

"No kiddin'," I grinned. In five minutes I was on the foredeck, behind solid railings, lying on a comfortable air mattress, wearing only bikini bottoms, exposing everything else to the sun gods.

It was going well. I didn't feel one ounce of guilt that I was lying out under the sun, while my charge was studying, and while my new boyfriend was doing all the work.

Just for a while, it was this woman's job to guard home and hearth, make sure the children did their studies, and be available whenever for her man's loving. Like I said, a thrown-together nuclear family.

I didn't give much thought to the future. Let it play itself out. Tomorrow doesn't exist. There's only today. There's maybe tonight. There's me and my man in a snuggly bed. That's all I had to think good things about.

A tour-chopper flew over once, slowed, came around and flew over slower. Self-consciously, I glanced down at my chest and chuckled.

Lying on my back, I didn't have any chest. I didn't bother trying to cover up. At that height unless they had binoculars, there wasn't much to see. They left and didn't come back. I was almost insulted that they didn't at least come in lower.

Around five, I went inside the cabin. Stephanie was enraptured with the history book, reading it voraciously. "Have you been in that book all afternoon?"

"Oh, no. I got all this done," She handed me a chapter's worth of homework each in Algebra, History, Chemistry, Bookkeeping and Life-Science. I Looked at it in awe. This kid was deadly serious about keeping up with her schooling.

"I'm just reading this because when you don't have to worry about memorizing some stupid detail, history is fascinating!"

"I'm impressed."

"Not as much as I am about you, Tracy."

"What do you mean?"

She marked her place, folded the book closed, and stood up, stretching wantonly. "I watched Greg's face in his condo when you figured all this out. I don't know him, but I don't think he ever saw someone work out logical conclusions like you did. If he's that impressed, I'm a whole lot more."

"Just lucky."

"Yeah. Sure... Greg told me some about you. I know you were considered one of the top insurance crime investigators in the city. I know you went to UCLA and graduated in the top third of the class. Are you rich?"

"Where did that dopey idea come from?" I laughed.

"You're not going to make any money at this case, are you? Tell me, how does a lady P.I. do these days? Still get two hundred a day plus expenses, like they do on television?"

"Bingo." I smiled. "But I won't make a dime on this case. One of these days, I hope to specialize in cases that involve finder's fees."

"How does that work?"

"Insurance companies pay five to ten percent finder's fees, if they save a bunch of insurance money. Say I find a stolen cruiser. If the boat is worth a million, and a lot of them are these days, I get at least fifty thousand dollars. It sounds pie-in-the-sky, but I think... once I'm established... that will be my primary source of income. I'll make it, don't you worry."

"I'm not worried about you. I can see the determination sometimes. I know something else, too."

"What?"

"If you can do it, so can I."

"I like that."

"Do you think I can re-enroll before my class graduates, take some tests, catch up and graduate with them?"

"Steph," I laughed and put on a tee shirt. "I'd bet you're ahead of the class. The moment we get all this worked out, I'll make sure that Greg asks the school to take you back. Just keep studying."

"I am. I love history. I think I'd like to be a historian someday. Maybe an archaeologist or a paleontologist."

"Either way, I have a feeling you'd make a super one. Enough is enough. It's Saturday afternoon. You can't go out on a date, but you don't have to stay late in school."

"I know. I'm about to quit anyway. What's for dinner?"

"I don't know. I can't cook, so I'm at the mercy of Greg's tastes."

"You and he are a thing, huh?"

"Kinda. We've only been seeing each other a week. I like him, he likes me."

"Are you sleeping with him?"

"What do you think we were doing last, night?... playing Monopoly? Why?"

"Did you sleep with him the first time you went out?"

"Yeah. Why?"

"I want to ask that. Why?"

"I liked him. I was sloshed and horny. And I was repaying a favor."

"That's three bad out of four possible reasons."

"I know. Why?"

"Because I want Jerry to make love to me, but I'm afraid to let him. I don't want him knowing what I was doing."

"Better tell him, Honey. Tell him soon, and before you go to bed with him."

"Why?"

"Don't give him your heart until you know he wants it. If he loves you, he won't be bothered by the fact that he's not the first one."

"He'll be the first man that I love."

"Don't tell me, tell him."

CHAPTER FIFTEEN

Greg came out to the tug around sundown, with fast-food chicken, and four large bags of groceries. After we all pitched in to put the food away, He and I sat in the afterdeck sipping martinis, while Stephanie drank a Pepsi.

She asked Greg, "What did you find out about my mother?"

"Not much." He said. "I put a request on the line for information on Angel Martucchi, AKA Angel Martucchi Bradford, AKA Angel Bradford. All I could tell anyone who asked, was that she was wanted for questioning. That gives us very low priority. We may not get a response for a week, a month, maybe never."

"Where was her family from?" I asked. "Was there a place where she could run home to Mama?"

"No. Grandma Martucchi died... committed suicide... a long time before I was born. The compound was Mom's home. When she left, there was no place for her to go."

Greg asked, "Why did your grandmother commit suicide?"

"Knowing that Mom and Grandpa called it the 'Baby Blues', I went to a library and looked it up. Nowadays they call it Postpartum Depression. A lot of shrinks are still scratching their heads about why it happens to an otherwise healthy woman. Something went wrong with her mind when Mom was born. Grandmother went into some sort of deep depression, and after Mother was weaned, she took a bottle of sleeping pills."

"About your mother." I said. "Didn't any of the men want to know what happened to her? After all, she was the princess before you were. Wouldn't their allegiances lean more to her than your father?"

"My mother was a sleazy bitch. She was the lady of the manor, could do anything she wanted. She treated people like dirt, especially after Grandpa died. Anyone there was nothing better than her nigger and I'm not making racial slurs when I use that term.

My roomie in Cincinnati was a black chick, so I don't think I'm prejudiced. Looking back, everyone in the compound was probably glad to see her gone."

"How would your mother support herself? Was she skilled in anything?"

"Yeah. Being a witch. Check out Salem, Mass. That's where her kind lives."

"I don't understand, Stephanie," Greg said. "You sound like you hated her, but you also said you were upset when she left."

Stephanie's eyes flashed. "Hey! She was my mother you know! Sure, she was a bitch, but she was still my mother. That woman went through hell so I could be born.

She put me to her breast, gave me her milk, changed my messy diapers, and all the rest. I owe her some respect for that, don't I?"

"I understand, Steph."

This kid sure had her head on straight for someone who was entitled to be real messed up.

"Was there a favorite place she might have gone to?"

"Try a place called Pinecrest." She said after some thought.

"It's a tiny resort town up in the mountains, 'bout thirty miles above Sonora. Grandpa had a mountain cabin up there. If you could say she grew up in two places, Pinecrest would be the other place."

"I'll head up there tomorrow," Greg said.

"Can't we all go? I like being on this boat, but by tomorrow Steph and I will be getting island fever, you know?"

It didn't take much thinking on his part. Not with the look of promise I was giving him behind Steph's back. "Okay. We'll make a day of it." I don't know if my eyes shined as much as Stephanie's, but if they did, we wouldn't need lights tonight.

After dinner, Stephanie browsed through the ship's small library and was soon lost in the adventures of Sir Francis Chichester, the old man who sailed around the globe single handed. Of course Greg and I went to bed.

Of course, we made love. Each time was leaps and bounds better and more passionate than the time before and Greg was getting right to my inner soul. In all the times I'd been in this two-in-a-bed context, never... and I mean... have I been so happy with my partner.

I wasn't just a woman who was banging and getting banged. I was half a couple. I was half of a pair of humans who were expressing love, admiration, and affection in very lovely ways. I was definitely falling in love with the big jerk.

CHAPTER SIXTEEN

The drive up to Pinecrest was pretty scenic. We left early in the morning, maybe nine thirty or so. On the way up we talked mostly about Stephanie, what she did, where she went the two years she was gone.

I'll never condone running away for any kid, but if you have to run away, do it Stephanie's way. Have some secret Guardian Angels with broken noses and thick accents. As we talked, it came more and more clear to us that she had been completely protected all along.

Stephanie thought it was her good luck until all this came to light. We figured that the people who watched her weren't going to try to make her change her mind. She admitted that she could be real headstrong if she wanted. If she wanted to be a teen-hooker, she would be a teen-hooker. If she wanted to be a brain surgeon, she could become a brain surgeon.

She claimed, and I believed her, that she was good at the job. She liked the attention her men gave her, and repaid in kind. Couldn't be any doubt about that. Sometimes when she smiled just right, or subconsciously struck the right pose to display her charms, she would become a truly sexy woman.

Take her Johns, for example. She didn't get as much action as the other girls, but the action she got was exclusively 'Rich, young, playboy' types. Mostly dark-haired Italian and Mediterranean types. Steph simply assumed that was the predominant makeup of the population of Cincinnati.

Sometimes only one or two customers a week would call. Her clients always booked her for the entire night. They were always gentle and kind to her, always left a healthy bonus.

When she told me she was knocking down a cool seven hundred and fifty dollars a week, not counting bonuses, I was convinced of my theory. Independent street-walkers just don't make that kind of easy money.

When she was on the street, she never hooked up with the regular sleaze-bag street-johns. For some reason they avoided her. When she did score on the sidewalk, it was always the same dark-haired yuppie types.

We did a lot of laughing and giggling about our imagined operation of her protectors.

"Can't you just see someone saying, 'Well, it's time to give Stephanie her allowance. It's a dirty job, but someone has to do it. Any volunteers?' Slow men would be trampled to death to get in line."

Any pimps who happened by and talked to her always seemed to take her first "No thanks, I'm doing fine by myself," for a final answer. They'd walk away with a smirk that she would be in their stables in a day, but for some reason, never came back.

She had no other frame of reference as a streetwalker to give her the slightest idea that someone was taking good care of her. She didn't find out the truth of the glamorous life of a girl on her own until she woke up one morning at one a.m., re-read the postcard from her friends and suddenly missed them, impulsively deciding right then to go back to San Francisco. By five a.m., she was headed west on a bus. We figure that's when the guardians lost her. She found her way to Willa's hoping to find Stacy.

Willa told her that Stacy moved out weeks ago.

I interrupted her at that point. "A question, Steph. How did Stacy wind up at Willa's?"

"I don't know. I talked to a couple other kids from my school..."

"Lincoln?"

"Yeah. They just kind of drifted in that direction."

"So Stacy was there, and now you tell me a couple of the other girls went to Lincoln, too? That's a bit of a coincidence, isn't it?"

"Not if you know the kids at Lincoln. Most were real punks, like."

"Was Stacy a punk?"

"No. She had it real hard at home. Her father diddled her a few times, mostly when he got drunk. Her mother caught him doing it once and blamed Stacy for starting it. I guess it was unavoidable that she'd wind up at a place like Willa's. Sure would like to see her... but no one knows anything about her."

"Just out of curiosity," I said, "what did Stacy look like?"

"Last time I saw her, she was a freckle face, and had red hair. About my size and build. Why?"

It was one of the hardest things I'd ever done, but after I got a surreptitious nod from Greg, I broke the news to Steph that Stacy was undoubtedly the dead girl I'd learned about from Colleen.

I'll give her this. She took the news stoically, and didn't break down until a half hour later when we ran out of things to say.

Even then, I wouldn't have known unless I hadn't heard a soft sniffle and turned around to see her staring up at the passing pine trees, silent tears streaming down her cheeks. I almost broke myself when I saw her silently mouth the words, "Goodbye, Stace. We had fun, my friend."

After awhile, we started talking again. In the two weeks after Stephanie moved in to Willa's, she had found a job, lost that job under suspicious circumstances, and was approached by Willa. Willa had a copy of an official-looking document from Cincinnati that Stephanie was wanted for assault and battery, robbery and prostitution, and that a john had been beaten and robbed by Stephanie.

Willa said with that hanging over her head, Steph would never work again, at least not in a normal job. However, if she wanted to stay on at Willa's place, she could hide out, work right there, and earn her rent. Maybe earn some extra money, Stephanie knew it was a fake warrant, but she had enough smarts not to let Willa know she knew.

Then I thought of Colleen Brannigan. I startled Greg out of his wits by my shout. "Hey!"

"What?"

"Hardbody, I want you to check something out."

"What?"

"Call the office and see if a girl named Colleen Brannigan was ever booked for soliciting... sometime in the past six months."

"Who's Colleen Brannigan?"

"One of the girls who lived at Willa's," Stephanie chimed in. "Poor kid wasn't even an easy lay when she moved in. She told me her total sexual experience was comprised of going to bed with her boyfriend... twice... and getting pregnant once. Her parents kicked her out at the ripe old age of fifteen."

Greg had me dial the cop shop. I handed him the phone and after being put on hold for five minutes, he became alert said "Thanks".

He turned and said, "Colleen Brannigan has never been booked."

My blood began boiling when I thought of the dozens of girls Willa had taken advantage of with her blank legal forms and phony booking slips.

"I wondered. Greg, I think that proves someone in the cop shop is dirty. Colleen was arrested for soliciting. She was held in jail, in the women's holding tank. That's a given.

"Willa has a copy of a booking slip, and the receipt for Colleen's bail. That's what she uses to keep Colleen in line. Wonder how many girls have been tossed in the slam on trumped up charges, and Willa has quote, unquote, bailed them out? Seems to me, someone in vice may be involved."

"I'll talk to Internal Affairs or check that out myself." Greg said evenly. "You stay... the hell out of it!"

In seconds, my eyes filled with tears. Of all the responses I could have imagined, that wasn't one of them. We'd been working this case together for a couple of days. We'd been lovers, damn good lovers, for a couple a nights, expressing a lot more than a passing attraction for each other, and now he comes down on me so hard? I didn't understand.

He looked across the seat at me and saw that he'd hurt my feelings. "I'm so sorry, Honey. That didn't come out right. I'm pissed, but not at you. A bad cop is a good cop's business.

"If you get involved with dirty cops, you could easily wind up in a marble slab with friends and relatives standing over you saying, 'Tsk, tsk. She was such a lovely young girl.' I don't want that. Get my message?"

"Yes, sir."

I understood, I agreed, but my feelings were still hurt.

We rode the final fifteen minutes from Long Barn to Pinecrest in strained silence. The snow was melting off fast. It left a messy road that would take a month to dry out.

Greg's new Black Ford-built Sherman Tank was shiny clean when we left San Francisco. Now it was caked with a muddy brown wash. Every time the car in front of us ran through a wet section, we had to use the windshield wipers to re-clear the windshield. Talk about mechanical erosion. I wondered how many tons of dirt are moved from the mountains to the lowlands by cars.

Once, when I was a small child, I had been to Pinecrest with my parents. It was in the warm summer. I think I was about four or five. It was the last of the good times we had before my mother got sick.

I could barely remember the small resort town. A little girl's point of view is a lot different than an adult's. Everything she sees is huge... Gigantic.

I barely remember a great big lodge, with a bunch of high steps that my father had to carry me up on his shoulders. 'Course, that was my favorite place, because it was like riding a horse. I can still remember a red with white fringe cow-girl vest and skirt outfit that I wore all that summer.

I remember the lake looked a little like those calendar photos where you get an overwhelming feeling of nostalgia and expect to see a couple of Native Americans paddling a birch-bark canoe across the mirrored surface.

What was now the community of Pinecrest wasn't the same. The huge old lodge was gone. The neat sporting goods store where Dad bought me my first fishing rod was gone. Even though I never caught a fish with it, I treasured that cheap metal pole and red plastic reel for years.

I hate what they've done to this place!

All that was there now were modern buildings that looked like permanently parked mobile homes, hidden behind a wood facade, filled with ticky-tacky little shops selling ticky-tacky tourist crap. Another place totaled by progress.

Why the hell can't people leave well enough alone?

We stopped in the small settlement to grab a quick sandwich. While munching a pretty decent cheeseburger in the local restaurant, we talked to the waitress. Being off-season, there wasn't much else for her to do, except chat with us. She was one of the less than one hundred people who lived up there full-time.

Strawberry Lake is a half mile across and maybe one and a half miles long. Fed by the South fork of the Stanislaus River, it's formed by an old Pacific Gas and Electric dam, built back at the turn of the 20th century for power storage. In the early summer the water is deep, cold, and fairly clear, the visibility maybe twenty to thirty feet.

Good fishermen can catch Rainbow trout, Black Catfish, and an occasional German Brown. During the summer and fall, the water is released for hydro generators farther downstream.

We finished eating and drove around to the eastern side of the lake. It was spring, the off-season. The ground was soaked. Mud and slush were everywhere. The small lake was just beginning to fill with icy runoff, and wouldn't reach full capacity until late May or early June.

One look at the sticky mud and I knew my shoes were going to be totaled. The closest thing to boots I could come up with was an expensive pair of high-top tennies covered with plastic overshoe rain covers.

Stephanie directed us around to the place where the Explorer, even in four-wheel drive, wouldn't go any farther.

"We'll have to hike in." She was grinning.

"How far?" I asked with some apprehension. Give you three guesses how much proper snow wear a girl who almost never left San Francisco has in her wardrobe.

"Not far. About a half-mile. Grandpa's cabin is remote. He liked it that way."

We set out, me walking last, hounding Greg to take short paces so I could step in his big foot prints.

I began muttering under my breath. "'Not far.' she says. Freaking snow and mud would make ten feet an all-day trip!

It took over an hour to hike 'Not far'. We finally made it to a cabin that sat on a rocky lava slide from eons ago.

Stephanie knew where a hide-a-key was and we entered the icy cold cabin. Not only was it freezing in the place, there were a zillion spider webs all over the interior. It looked like it had been abandoned for centuries.

I wanted be the very next person to abandon it... like in the next second! I looked at my watch and hopefully reminded them that there was only a couple of hours of daylight left.

"If we want to spend the night," Stephanie said, willfully ignoring me, "We'll have to bring up some firewood from under the cabin. I doubt if there's any food, except canned stuff."

"I'll pass," I muttered, shaking uncontrollably from the cold. The temperature couldn't have been twenty degrees inside. "What are we looking for? Whatever it is, let's find it and get outta here."

"My father hated the mountains." Stephanie was perversely and utterly ignoring my complaints. "I doubt if this cabin has been used for almost five years. That's if Mother didn't come here. Can't you two detectives find some evidence that she was here?"

"You'd think so." Greg was smiling at my discomfort. I was getting the definite impression that the SF city girl was out-numbered.

"Trace, you start in the bedrooms with Stephanie. I'll check out the kitchen and grounds."

I hired myself out as a detective, right? I'm the evolutionary result of a skillion generations of romantic couplings that became the Clan Cunningham: the two generations previous to mine produced top-cops, right?

I graduated in the upper third of my class in Criminology and Criminalistics, right?

I'm a well-known insurance investigator, right?

I even answer my cell phone "Tracy Cunningham, Confidential Investigations", right? With all this going for me, finding evidence should be a piece a cake, right?

Wrong.

I didn't have the slightest idea what in the hell to look for. What kind of clues does a woman leave that shows us that she stayed in the cabin as recently as five years ago? If there wasn't a newspaper with a specific date on it, I was sunk.

I pawed cobwebs aside, glad it was off-season for the creepy bugs that left them there, too. Stephanie and I found mouse nests in the bedding. No mice, though. They must have gone to Disneyland for the winter to see Uncle Mickey.

Everywhere I looked, on bedding, bureaus, and elevated surfaces, there were hundreds of little mice turds. Even in the drawers. A cat wouldn't starve in this cabin, that's for certain.

Stephanie looked in dresser drawers, while I checked out the closets. Excepting some chewed up coats, there was nothing of note any place. As far as my uneducated eye could see, there was no evidence that Angel Bradford spent any time here. 'Course, there wasn't any evidence to the contrary, either.

We went back out to the main room. I looked through a stack of old Reader's Digests, finding nothing more recent than five years ago. I gave up. If Angel was there, she didn't leave any clues for me to find.

"Greg?" I called out. "Find anything?"

"I think so. C'mere." We almost ran into the kitchen. Greg had all the canned food out separated into two areas. "Those are cans with no dates. Those are cans with dates on the labels."

"Any in the past five years?"

"No."

"Then what are you looking at?"

"Look in the reefer."

I opened the refrigerator and gagged. There was some food and milk left in it. Thank goodness that it was too cold or the mess was too old to smell. Do you have any idea how bad a container of milk looks when it's been left in a reefer for five years, and the power's been off all the time? Just the sight is enough to gag a maggot.

"Yecchhh!"

"My sentiments exactly, but there's a heavy clue in there, kid."

I let the 'kid' crack side. "What?"

"The 'Use by' date on the milk container,. It's just four and a half years old. We now have proof that someone was here after Angel Bradford left home, and there's another assumption we can make."

"Don't tell me, let me guess," I smiled and closed the door to the hateful sight. "That same someone left in a helluva hurry, or intended to come back. They wouldn't have left the refer like this, not with fresh food in it."

"That's right!" Stephanie said. "The house rules are to take all perishables away, shut off the power and water, and to leave the refrigerator door open when no one is here."

"Then we're getting somewhere," I said with a grin.

Greg began putting the dusty canned food away. "Yep. We're running out of light. I think we'd better go find a place to stay, and come back in the morning."

"Why don't we just stay right here?" Stephanie aimed a gleeful smirk right at me. "There should be firewood under the cabin, and the fireplace is set up for cooking in case the power goes out."

"Great idea, Steph," Greg grinned.

I tried to put my foot down. "I'm not sleeping in a bed that mice have crapped and peed in for five years!"

"There should be some sleeping bags upstairs in metal cabinets. We can sleep on the couches and floor in the living room."

"On the floor? With all kinds of creepy-crawly things wondering what these big animals are doing in their place? Wondering if we're good to eat? No way kid."

"Oh, c'mon, Tracy," she giggled. "Trust me. No one has ever been eaten up here. It hasn't gotten warm enough outside to wake the hibernating kind of critters up. Besides, the mice up here are cute.

Little brown and white guys with big expressive eyes and cute little pink noses that quiver when they sniff you. Mices won't hurt you. You can sleep between Greg and me if little animals scare you. Please?"

I couldn't argue the point. She was right. Staying was a lot more practical than not. But fun? About as much fun as having your teeth drilled... maybe.

I gave in. "All right. But only if there's something we can burn for warmth. I'm not going to freeze my tail off, too."

"Deal," she beamed and lifted up a trap door, under a throw rug. "Down here, Greg. The firewood should be to the left about five feet from the ladder."

Just my luck. There was plenty of firewood! Even some tinder. With an evil smile, it dawned on me that I still had hope. None of us smoked. No matches!

My last chance to spend the night in some sort of rudimentary comfort went out the window when Stephanie came out of the kitchen with a large box of wooden stove matches, two old-fashioned kerosene lamps and a wide grin.

I Immediately resolved that the instant I get back to civilization, I was going to smack her to death! Thanks to the smarmy little brat I was going to spend the night eating canned food, sleeping in bags on a hard floor or a couch, if I didn't mind a little black mice-rice and chewed cotton. The damned sleeping bags were so old-fashioned, that there wasn't any way to zip two together so I could sleep under Greg's...

Protection. What did you think I was going to say?

CHAPTER SEVENTEEN

Another of my many faults is that I'm not a house keeper.

Not even close.

However, I found a broom and once I knocked out all the dead spiders from the bristles, I went through that living room like the old white tornado. I got ninety-five percent of the droppings and spider webs down and outside. The other five percent wound up in my hair.

Another good reason to leave turned up. Even smug little "Kitty Carson" didn't think about water. I was going to keep quiet. Maybe they'd realize it themselves and we'd go back without me begging anymore.

I've got my pride, you know.

Then Greg brought some snow in from a drift on the back side of the house and was soon boiling a kettle full of water for drinking. I decided that he needed some smacking around, too.

The potty! Maybe having no facilities would convince them we had to leave. But when I said that I needed to use the head, they both pointed to the back door.

"There's a comfy tree branch outside," Stephanie giggled.

I looked at them in horror. "You are just kidding!"

"Nope," she said. I could see that she was fighting a laugh.

"It's real easy, Trace. You climb up on the north side porch rail, the one on that side," she pointed left, "stand up, hold onto the tree trunk, turn around and sit on the branch. Hang your buns over. It's not real cold. Be careful you don't fall. It's twelve feet to the ground. Make sure you take some TP out with you. We never got around to putting a roll holder on the tree."

"This is bullshit!"

"Don't forget to kick some snow off the porch to bury it."

I'm going to kill her!

"Sorry, Trace." Greg added to my chagrin with his own smirk. "There's no inside plumbing at all. When I was under the cabin, I saw a lot of split pipes. Even if the water was turned on, it would never reach the faucets up here. All the pipes have frozen and broken."

I gave it one last try. "Don't these old cabins have some sort of outhouses?"

"We have a great one." Stephanie's grin widened. "But there's this teensy little problem. You can see it out the crack between the back window shutters. There's a frozen snow-drift blocking the little house's door. Want to chip away for a couple a hours before you go potty? All you'll ever accomplish when you do get your privacy is doing your thing in a very dark, web-filled, wooden deepfreeze."

"Ohhh! That's just freaking terrific! I bet you both knew all this crap, and didn't bother to mention it to me until it was too late to hike out!" I hate both of you!"

"Aww, Trace." Greg grinned evilly. "Would we do that to you?"

"Assholes." I stomped outside. Shouting as loud as I could, "You're cut off forever Phillips!".

I followed Steph's directions and footprints. She had used the facilities sometime before. The branch wasn't exactly comfortable. It was cold and scratchy. At least, it wasn't hard to climb on. I learned something new in those next few icy seconds.

With my bare buns hanging in the freezing temperature out there, and the oncoming darkness out there, and the silence out there, so quiet that every single noise was a charging beast out there, I learned real quick that you do your business out there and get the heck back in there.

When I got back in to safety, I was giggling. We all began laughing uproariously. It really was pretty funny. If I could do that I could do anything.

Sure felt sorry for the neighbors when the thaw finally got to the drift.

"Not a problem, babe." Greg said. "By warm spring all that stuff out there will have done what all the animal stuff in history has done. Go back to nature."

"Besides." Stephanie added, "There won't be any summer people until mid-June. There's no one within a half mile of this place now."

"Nobody comes here in the winter?"

"Can't get back here in winter."

"We did."

She gave me an adult look. "Little Stephanie Bradford is not a soft summer people. In a lot of ways, I grew up here, too.

Soft winter people have cabins on the other side of the lake. This side are strictly summer cabins. Note the lack of heaters. This side is for hearty people. If we get a snowfall tonight, we may not get out of here for a week."

"We can call someone to dig us out, can't we?"

"How loud can you yell?" Stephanie chuckled.

"No phones?"

"Not even your cell phone can get outta here," she said. "Face it. You're going to have to rough it tonight."

I knew about the cell phone. I tried that a long time ago. "Got anymore effing surprises?" While Stephanie and I unnecessarily held our noses and cleaned out the reefer, Greg cooked some pork and beans, adding some canned veges and tomato sauce. I'll never admit it, but when dinner was ready, it was yummy!

Maybe the cozy atmosphere made the food taste better. The only rough part of roughing it was sleeping next to my guy and not sleeping with him.

You didn't believe I meant that crack about Greg being cut off, do you?

About midnight I swallowed my pride and moved my sleeping bag up to the second small couch. Mice rice and all.

Poor Greg. There wasn't anything long enough for him to sack out on. I rested my head on my hands, swearing up and down that if anything moved under me, no one was going to sleep!

Sometime about three or four, I woke up to the sounds of some night monster upstairs. I froze in my bag, cringing, but not wanting to scream out in terror if it was only a mouse scrabbling around. Even if it was a chainsaw murderer, I had already exposed the wide yellow streak down my back enough. Let someone else scream first.

The noise got louder.

Yellow streak or no, in seconds, I was down in the end of my sleeping bag, pulling my pillow in with me. I even folded the open end under me. I'm glad it was a cotton bag. I might have suffocated, but no freaking Bear or Mountain Lion living in the attic was going to kill and eat me. Not unless he had a pair of scissors to open my bag.

In the morning, we all looked like death warmed over. Even the two mountain goats I was trapped with decided bathing with ice water was too painful a way to go. No one wanted to take the time to warm up enough snow water for three spit-baths. Fine and dandy with me. I just wanted to get the hell out of there, no matter how ripe we all smelled.

Breakfast was some warmed canned spaghetti. Stephanie told me what I'd probably heard was a Pack Rat, AKA a Trade Rat. At the word 'rat' I let out a thirty-second string of French, Anglo-Saxon, and the King's English, letting the two hysterically laughing Hyenas know what I thought about them not telling me there were some big mice in the cabin.

When I began to repeat myself, I calmed down. Steph said that Pack Rats were small little guys who steal shiny objects and sometimes leave an acorn or other rat treasure in return. Very honest animals. They don't eat Tracy Cunninghams.

Really.

We started a new search in the attic, then moved down. Stephanie found and showed me the Pack Rat's nest. Mr. Rat had some old tin-foil gum wrappers and a dime in his treasure trove. He was gone of course, or you would have next seen me running and screaming down the trail.

"Where did he get the wrappers?" I whispered.

"He probably stole them from his girlfriend."

"Thought you said they were honest."

"So I lied. Sue me."

She whispered too. Hopefully we wouldn't disturb Mr. Rat, wherever he was. If she lied about his honesty, what about that part that they don't eat people? I didn't want to be the first human eaten by an eight-ounce, four-footed sneak thief.

I shuddered at the idea that I was calmly looking at a rat's nest even if Stephanie claimed it was interesting. When we got back to the living room, we decided that with the singular exception of the milk carton, there was no, and I mean no, evidence that anyone had lived here.

"Was your mother that fastidious?"

"She was a practical, good house-keeper," Stephanie said. "She followed the rules up here. It's hard to believe that there's no reading material anywhere around. I got my love for reading from Mom. She wouldn't have come up here without a box full of books.

"One of the unwritten rules is that you leave all the books you've read here. There's no TV, and radio reception up here sucks. Reading is just about the only escape there is here."

"I can think of another."

"So can I, but Mother wasn't into boyfriends."

"Looks like we've struck out." Greg said.

"Agreed."

"Well," Stephanie stood up. "We better put the firewood we didn't use downstairs. It's part of the rules. We have to leave the place just like we found it."

Greg climbed down the ladder, and we handed him the four logs we didn't burn. He was climbing up, when he topped, went back down and walked out of our sight. In a couple of minutes, his voice came up softly from the deep shadows.

"Tracy? Steph? Think I've found Angel Bradford."

CHAPTER EIGHTEEN

I held Stephanie while she cried it out. It wasn't the emotional mourning of a daughter for her beloved mother. It was more like she was shocked that any human was buried under what was one of her favorite places. She was shocked that it was the woman who bore her to the world.

From what I knew about the late Angel Martucchi, bringing Steph to the planet was about the only good thing she had ever done. Actually, I think the crying was more for Stacy Reese than her mother.

There wasn't any way we could identify the skeleton, but we all knew who it was. Once Stephanie had settled down, Greg left to find the local police.

Stephanie had fallen asleep, so I took advantage of the freedom and forced myself to down to the hidden grave. What Greg had discovered was a place under the cabin where some animal had dug up some bones. He knew enough to recognize an arm bone from a human.

I imagined that I could smell something, but I realized that what I was sniffing was the normal musty odor of damp dirt that hadn't seen sunlight for decades. The body was so decayed that there wasn't anything creepy, just bones scattered around in a dark corner. I began to wonder where Mr. Rat and his ancestors got their sustenance. I quickly shivered that idea down.

My first case, a simple enough hunt for a run-away kid had evolved to murder. I was supposed to be a detective. Now I better start acting like one. My being a chicken took a back seat to my curiosity.

I stepped carefully, my eyes adjusting to the dim atmosphere. The only light available was from outside, shining through cracks in the shake covering. I made sure that I didn't step near anything that could possibly been a human footprint.

My first deductive conclusion was that she must have been buried nude. There wasn't a scrap of cloth anywhere, yet there were old cloth life jackets hung on nails, which proved that cloth can survive down here for decades.

Head room over the grave site was a bit more than six feet. Not much room for swinging a pickaxe. The killer or killers must have gotten tired of digging a hole in the hard-pack because she wasn't buried very deep, maybe two feet.

All I could see were long bones and a couple of ribs. Most of the skeleton was still buried. After giving the scene a good examination, I shuddered and climbed back up the ladder.

While I sat in the living room, I suddenly had what I'll always consider an inspired idea. I decided to have another look at Mr. Rat's treasure chest. I grabbed a pair of forks and went up to total his castle.

I moved the chewed cotton around, a lot of it from those old World War Two Kapok-filled life jackets under the cabin deck. Whistling loudly and making all kinds of noise designed to keep the missing tenant missing, I kept looking for shiny stuff.

I found some.

A chain necklace with a small crucifix. I was so pleased with my find that I almost missed seeing a dull yellow-colored object. Using a tine of a fork, I picked up a brass case from a bullet. The end still was clear enough to read, "32 Cal. Center-fire Cartridge."

Nice going, Mr. Rat. I take back all those nasty things I thought about you. Thank you for keeping the evidence safe for us.

When I went back downstairs, Stephanie was awake and looking for me. I showed her the necklace. It was Angel's. We now had a positive ID on the victim.

Greg came back with the local California Highway Patrol officer. The Sheriff's deputies were still an hour away, but the CHP guy was right in Pinecrest, drinking coffee at the local saloon-cafe. We three climbed down the ladder.

Even though she said she was all right I wouldn't let Stephanie come down. It was enough that she realized that she had been laughing and having fun right over her mother's grave. She didn't need to see Angel's skeleton in her mind's eye for the rest of her life.

I stayed in the background, kept my mouth shut and my hand firmly gripping a scrap of cloth wrapped around my valuable find. Greg and the CHP went over the shadowy area carefully using two big flashlights. They located a few more bones, but nothing that would point to the identity of the body, the cause of death, or anything else. They didn't think the necklace I found was enough evidence to make a declarative ID.

No matter. I did.

It took an hour for the Sheriff-Coroner and his men to arrive. Once there, they got to work efficiently and quickly. The body was exhumed carefully, in the same way I'd seen when archaeologists search for fossils. Painstakingly brush away the dirt, take a photograph, then carefully lift out a bone.

We were all primarily interested in finding the skull. When the grinning head bones were unearthed, we found the probable cause of death. A clean wound hole in the center of her forehead. No exit wound in the back. She faced her killer or killers.

Inside the hollow death's head was a bullet, not too badly destroyed, according to Greg. He let me look at it after it was bagged in plastic. It was kind of mushroomed, but the last third, I guessed, was still capable of being microscoped.

Now was the time to announce my discovery. "This looks like it's from a thirty two caliber pistol, to me."

My opinion of guns was well known to Greg. He stared at me and said "How in hell do you know that?"

"A little mouse told me?"

Fairly true.

"This is not the time for levity, young lady," the older cop, who was running the show, snapped.

"I'm sorry." I said, unwrapping the cloth in my hand and showing my hand-made bindle. "I found this casing when I found the necklace in the pack-rat's nest I haven't touched it with my fingers, or any form of cloth, so if there's no fingerprints, don't blame me."

I handed it to the boss-cop and asked Greg, "Can a lab find out anything more about the slug?"

"Only if we have something to compare it with." From then on, I kept mouth shut. No wise cracks, no macabre humor was going to emit from this kid. I learned my lesson about that quickly.

I didn't know a thing about on-site murder investigations and I wanted to be able to stick around and use this as a learning experience. I knew lab techniques of course, but the most field experience I had was watching CSI. My pre-conceived notions of police detecting methodology were nothing like the way they really worked. Even if Pinecrest was part of a cow country county, these guys were pros.

Everything was weighed, measured, catalogued and tagged for evidence. Hundreds of photographs were taken. Greg took the time to show me how to draw a sketch, how to make and mark measurements so that the crime was recorded, and even more important recorded in my brain.

Even though all of our cellphones had cameras in them, drawing a sketch was part of my upbringing. It aided in fixing details in my mind.

That was easy for me. My own grandfather was a professional cop before my father was. Grandpa made it as far as Captain, then stopped there for lack of a college education. When I was a wee tyke, Dad was already a Captain. For a while there were two Captain John G. Cunninghams in the LAPD. Grandpa was John, and Dad was Jack.

Still is.

The only reason I didn't get saddled with the name "Johnna" was that my mom and grandmother put their collective feet down, hard.

I'm proud that I got Grandma's name instead. Anyway, as the only child of Grandpa's side of the Cunningham line, I was encouraged to continue the family name in police work. As such, I was given all the police-type education they could cram into a child's head.

Grandpa's favorite game was having me remember what was in my back yard, where all my toys were, all that kind of stuff, and draw him a picture of it.

Since I had already developed slovenly habits, there were a lot of toys to remember. By the time my Grandfather was shot and killed by a cornered liquor store robber, I could play the memory game to a fare-the-well. It wasn't until just now, with Greg instructing me, that it dawned on me why I was taught my grandfather's favorite game.

It also dawned on me, in that cold half-assed basement watching bones being removed with respect for the deceased, that I had probably hurt my father deeply when I so casually disdained police work for the more glamorous insurance companies up in San Francisco.

My grandfather had probably been thrashing around in his grave for the past four years, knowing what the only third generation Cunningham was really doing.

I glanced upward. *Oh Gramps, I'm so sorry. I didn't realize. Take a break up there. You've earned one.*

Just thinking that made me feel better. Maybe he's stopped and was watching me. I was learning true police work, first hand. Maybe there's hope for the kid yet.

After the work under the deck was completed, we three were questioned carefully and allowed to go our own way.

Greg called his office from the Pinecrest Post Office and arrangements were made to keep him on the case, officially. After all, it was a San Francisco citizen, and the case originated in San Francisco, and was discovered by a San Francisco Homicide Detective.

It all came crashing down on me the moment we were in the car. How I'd really hurt the man I loved so much, my Dad. In a second, I was crying. Greg didn't understand why my nose was running and I had to continually wipe tears away from my eyes.

Or why I sat in the back seat and didn't utter one word for an hour on the way back to San Francisco. I look back now, and I think I matured more in those twenty-four hours than I had since I turned sixteen.

We got back to the tugboat before sundown. The sky was gray, a precursor to a healthy storm. It fit my mood, somehow. A rain storm washes away dirt. I was mentally washing away the dirt... Washing my mind down to the clean-cut kid of fifteen who still loved her mother and father, who had big ideas about being the first female police chief in L.A.

That's where I had to start from. Rebuild my life, relive almost ten years, except do it faster, and this time do it right. I realized that I went from a happy teen to a hardened woman in a few short months. I missed all those great growing-up years.

When the good girls were being asked to the prom by the good boys, I spent my first prom night in the back seat of a car in the Gymnasium parking lot drinking and doing things with one of the school hoods that I was suddenly very ashamed of. A lot of guilt came thundering down on me with a vengeance.

Several screaming matches with my patient father, over why I couldn't do something I wanted to do re-visited me. What he was asking me to do wasn't unreasonable.

There wasn't a good reason for a fifteen-year old to go out on a school night. There was no good reason to sneak out through her bedroom window and meet a boy down the block to drink and rut like animals in heat.

I wouldn't let Greg touch me that night. I had a skillion things to work out in my mind. Not the least of which was a face to face meeting with Dad. It was high time I rebuild some charred bridges of my own.

CHAPTER NINETEEN

Greg was still signed out on official vacation. I begged him to stay on for one more day that Monday, even though he had Angel's Homicide to investigate and he wanted to get cracking. All that was happening on Stacy Reese's killing was a search for a Jane Doe of her description throughout the western states.

"Why?" he asked.

"I want you to stay with Stephanie. I have something very important to do in L.A., and I can't take her with me."

"You have to go running off to L.A., now?"

"Yes. I'm sorry, but it's vital. I can't continue like this until I make peace with my father. God, Greg, please understand."

"I do. You were mumbling in your sleep last night and the name 'Daddy' was very clear, several times. But Kitten, are you sure you have to go now? Running off like this is about as unprofessional as it gets."

I put my hand on his forearm. "I'm aware of that and I'll never do something like this again, but you have to realize I'm thinking about the rest of my life, Love. Not just the next week.

"Besides," I said, moving to all even more intimate distance." I promise I'll be a better woman when I get back."

"You're already out of sight Honey." He held me in a comforting hug for a long time. "I'll stick with the kid."

"Thanks."

It was still early in the morning when Greg took me to the waterfront of Sausalito. I walked up to my boarding house, showered and packed some clothes. I was on a commuter to good old Smokey town an hour later.

When we made our final approach to LAX, I looked for my old home. Even though it should have been only a couple of miles away from the flight path, I couldn't see it. The onshore breezes had shut down for a few days, and all of Santa Monica was obscured by thick yellow smog.

After a few minutes wait for a taxi, I told the cabby to take me to Parker Center, the address of LAPD headquarters and sat back, chewing the inside of my cheek and nervously going over in my mind a hundred different apologies for the last ten years. When we pulled in front of the imposing building, I got out, squared my shoulders, took a deep breath, and carrying my suitcase with me, walked straight back to my father's secretary. She was a new woman, a pleasant Hispanic, Sergeant Divas, according to her name tag.

"Yes, Miss?"

"I'd like to see Chief Cunningham, please."

"I'm sorry," she said kindly. "I'm afraid he's very busy."

"Please? I'm Tracy Cunningham."

"Tracy?" Her eyes lit up. "The Chief's Tracy?"

"Yes."

"Of course, you are!" She grinned widely. "I can see the old man all over you. 'Cept it looks a whole lot better on you than it does on him."

She dialed his office number and winked at me. "Chief? There's someone out here to see you."

She winced and held the phone away from her ear, grinning. I could hear him barking over the phone and down the hall at the same time. She rolled her eyes to the ceiling and recited in a bored voice, "Yes, chief," at the same time enthusiastically waving me to go on back. She wasn't going to let him say "No."

I stood, my suitcase in hand, really worrying the inside of my mouth, in his doorway. It took him several moments to sense that I was there. He hung up the phone slowly and smiled. Not a great smile, but at least it was a smile.

"Hi baby," he said. "What are you doing here?"

Dad was still his handsome old self. He's bald as a cue ball, and has deep blue eyes. He was a bit trimmer than the last time I saw him, and he had a more intense tan. One glance told me that my prolonged absence hadn't adversely affected him.

"Hi, Daddy. I want to talk... Change that to need to talk. May I come in?"

"I'm sorry." He smiled and stood up. He let me give him a hug and we sat in his couch. That was a good sign. If he was still mad at me, he would have sat behind his desk.

"How are you, Princess?"

"Fine, Daddy."

Neither of us said anything else for a few moments. I smiled, he smiled, and all my carefully memorized apologies flew out the damn window. Before I could say another word, tears began streaming down my face. The only words I could get out were, "I'm so sorry, so sorry for being such a total shit!"

Not exactly what I had in mind, but the effect was magical.

He put his arms around me and held me for a long time, stroking my back, not saying a word. He didn't know what I was sobbing and heaving about but I don't think he cared. You see, he was bawling, too.

That's right, my pop, the hardest cop in the department, a man with crust so thick he sold excess to the Mother's Frozen Pie Company, was sniffling and blowing his nose while I let it all go.

I'm glad no one came in then, because he'd never live it down. Jack Cunningham doesn't like to admit he's a human being. Somehow being human isn't quite good enough.

After a long time we both quit. I went into his office bathroom and washed my face. When I came out he was at his desk. I sat across from him.

"Honey, what the hell is going on?"

"A whole lot, Dad. For starters, since I've seen you last I've been fired… twice."

"Why?"

"Let's just say I wasn't a very good girl and leave it at that. I haven't been a very good daughter, Daddy. The reason I'm here is to try to patch it up between us. I've come to the realization that I love you very much, and that I owe you so many apologies if I said them all, you'd be listening to them for a year."

"No need for that," he smiled warmly. "I accept them all.

"What brought about this change?"

"The last woman who fired me told me that I had to grow up. I began growing up, or so I thought at that time. But yesterday, it all came thundering down on me."

"What did?"

"All the love you and mom gave me, which I thought was so much bullshit. All the love that Grandpa showed me. I suddenly realized why people were doing things for me. It was out of love, nothing else, and I knew I hadn't returned that love."

I'm turning over so many new leafs, Daddy, it's like I'm looking for a dime in an oak forest in autumn. There's so much I have to do. My very first priority was to come here and see if you'll have me back as your Helium-headed daughter."

"I would be most pleased, Honey." He smiled at me, but I could see a tinge of suspicion.

I deserved it.

I couldn't just come waltzing into his life after a three-year absence and expect him to welcome me with open arms. I'd hurt him too many times too badly."

Dad, I know what this must look like. I don't want a thing from you. I'm not here hat in hand, asking for a handout."

"What, exactly, are you doing now?"

I cringed a bit. Even I knew that Dad's opinion of Private Detectives was legend. "I'm working as a P. I."

"What?"

I sat back to let it sink in. "I better not repeat it. You look like you're ready to strangle me as it is…"

"Girl, what in the hell made you become a goddamned P.I.?"

Here, please note the adjective 'goddamned' and the noun 'P.I.' were expressed as one word. GoddamnedPI!, and don't forget the exclamation point. I fought a giggle.

The expression on his face was as though someone just spooned a load of pigeon droppings on his tongue.

"I couldn't find work."

"Why not?" he snapped."

"Because I was politely informed that I would never find work in San Francisco again."

"Why?"

"If you must know the truth, I was messing around with someone I shouldn't have been."

"Who was he?"

"Does it matter?"

"I guess not." He sighed. "But a P.I.?"

"Daddy, I said I was working as one. I'm not licensed. You know how I feel about guns. I figured that a person doesn't need a ticket just to ask questions. Besides, what's so bad about being a private investigator?"

If there was ever a time not to ask such a stupid question, that was it.

He leaned forward and stared me in the eye. "My dear girl. With very few exceptions, a P.I. is low-life. A garbage-eating mangy mongrel is more venerated than they'll ever be. GoddamnedPI's sneak around back alleys with the rest of the vermin, taking smut photos for divorce cases. They chase ambulances for shoddy shysters. They're knavish bounty hunters. They mess up more of our cases than they'll ever help."

That had to be a memorized speech he gave all the newly licensed Private Investigators.

I stared right back. "Does that mean I can't marry one?"

He chuckled and sat back. "You could say that, Honey. Why don't you move back down here? I'll find you a decent job. You know it's not too late to join this year's class at the Academy."

That was one of his heart-felt dreams. A third generation Cunningham in the LAPD. But as much as I loved my father, I couldn't see me in a uniform.

"Daddy, if I've done one thing right in my adult life, it's that I haven't come running to you every time I get a bloody nose. I'm not about to start that now. Besides, I have a case to finish."

I'll give him credit for not laughing in my face. I know he wanted to, though.

"What sort of case? Divorce? Or is it maybe a heavy fender-bender hit and run?"

"How about," I said, casually looking at my fingernails, "A runaway teen who turns out to be a North Bay Mafia Princess, a seven month old homicide and another one that's almost five years old?"

He started to laugh, then thought better of it. He probably saw my Cunningham-bred Irish arising quickly. "You've been reading too many Mario Puzo novels."

I maintained my cool and said, "So don't believe me. I really don't care. I know I'm not making this up."

"You've got to be kidding..." His manner was softening, like maybe there was a glimmer of truth in my tale."

"If you want to verify my story, check with your own Homicide section. By now there should be a San Francisco request for information about a young red-headed Jane Doe who was beaten to death about seven months ago.

"Or better yet why don't you call the San Francisco P.D. and talk to one of your brother Chiefs and ask what Sergeant Gregory Phillips just discovered in Pinecrest... the one on Highway 108."

"Pinecrest?"

"Yes. Remember when you bought me that toy fishing pole there?"

"I sure do."

"The same place. While you're at it, ask who was with Phillips when the discovery was made. Ask who found most the evidence."

"I don't need to verify your stories." His tone was softer. I was pretty sure that he believed me, but I was also enough of his issue to know at the very first opportunity, he'd get the low-down on Sergeant Phillips, Stephanie Bradford, and everything we'd said and done.

"Before we go one word further," he said, leaning forward and jabbing his finger at me, "If you really intend to become one of those people, I think I should inform you that you must have a license… pistol, rifle, M-1 Tank or no. That is the law, and we obey the law. *Capish?*"

"Yes, sir."

He looked at his watch. "Shall we continue this meeting over lunch?"

"I'd love to."

"Why don't you go straighten out your make-up, and I'll get us a table."

He was on the phone in seconds after I closed the door to his private bathroom. By the time I had re-washed my face and put some eye shadow and mascara, he had told Sergeant Divas out in front to find out all she could and call him.

I waited until I was sure had finished his hushed call. Paternally, he even put his arm around my shoulder as he walked me out and across the street to the Beefeater's Bar and Grille.

I'd only been in there once before, a lifetime ago. It was the place where all the Lord High Mucky Mucks of the LA Government ate lunch. I'll bet more political business was conducted over martinis in one hour than the rest of the city fathers did all day.

I was introduced to the fire chief, and three of his seconds in command. I re-met the mayor. Most mayors had been to the house once or twice when I was a small girl. I even met the Lieutenant Governor.

They were sitting at one table. Since the Lt. Governor and the Mayor aren't of the same political persuasion, and don't care for each other too much, I figured there must have been an important meeting going on. Like I said, one whale of a lot of wheeler-dealing.

The Chief and I sat in a comfortable booth away from the action. Dad wasn't afraid to introduce me to his compatriots, but just in case I pulled my old stunt of drinking my lunch, we were far enough from the action that his friends and associates wouldn't find out he raised an alcoholic.

The first surprise came when we ordered drinks, and I asked for a white wine cooler. Dad knew I never drank wine for cocktails. Not when there was gin available to mainline. I'm sure he purposefully delayed ordering lunch so he could watch me. Cagey he is, subtle he ain't.

Two can play that game.

Drinking a wine cooler was one of the things I consciously planned. I honestly don't like them. If I'd ordered something non-alcoholic, it would have been too radical a change, and he wouldn't believe I was sincere.

I barely had my second glass half done when the waiter came by for the fourth or fifth time asking if we were ready to order yet. Dad ordered club-house sandwiches for both of us. Throughout all this testing of Tracy Cunningham, we talked.

Talked?

It was a third-degree grilling in a two-way mirror lined room.

I told him what he wanted to know about my life in the City. I freely volunteered everything, except my less savory second occupation. He made a few cracks about my easy virtue, and I admitted a lot more. But I never could tell him about my former profession. To do that would serve no purpose except to shatter our fragile reunion and break his heart. One of us living with that Sword of Damocles was enough.

As our luncheon went on, people drifted out, some waving or coming over to say good-bye to Dad. And we got to know each other better. The curtain of suspicion slowly lowered. He let me into his life... a little. He had a steady woman friend, but he wouldn't tell me her name. He was playing a lot of tennis, which accounted for his physical fitness and his tan.

A few times we sat in silence, both waiting for the phone call from his secretary. Then, a tiny telephone ringing said that we were about to confirm my story.

Dad was good. His eyes didn't let on what he was getting an ear full of. He only flicked his eyes to my face a couple of times. After a few moments, I could see a tenseness in his jaw and lips as he began fighting a grin.

It was going to be all right!

He hung up and signaled for the waiter.

"Well?" I asked with a smirk.

"Well, what?"

"'C'mon, Daddy. You're not *really* going to keep pretending that I don't know exactly who that call was from, and what and who it concerned?"

"You knew?"

"Hell, I'm a Cunningham, aren't I? No dummies in the family, right?"

"I have mixed emotions, girl," he said gravely.

"One, I'm pickled tink that you are what you say you are." I giggled at his terminology. "And two... How shall I word this?"

Uh-oh. This isn't going to be good. His face turned beet red in less time than it takes to say it, "I want you out of this! Now!"

In a second, tears flashed to my eyes. I cowered back, wondering what in the hell I'd done that was so wrong.

"Daddy...?"

He saw that he had over-done it and had really hurt me. "Damn. I'm sorry, Baby," he panted. "That wasn't fair. I shouldn't have yelled at you. Pickles, we're just getting back together. Now I find out that you *are* involved with a mob case."

"That scares the pee out of me. Those guys are big timers. They swat twerps like you as easily as they do a pesky gnat."

I didn't hear one word he'd said. I was still reacting to the name 'Pickles'. It used to be his very favorite pet name for me. Grandpa tagged me with it. He said that with my big mouth and tiny fists that I was always in a pickle.

"What did you just call me?"

"Pickles."

"Daddy, you haven't called me that since I was sixteen!" And that started my bawling all over again.

CHAPTER TWENTY

We spent the rest of the day together. Never left the restaurant. Even stayed to eat dinner there. If any crime occurred in Smogville that needed Dad's personal attention, it wasn't going to get it. I went home with him to the old house, the place he and Mother bought after their honeymoon.

The house was a lot smaller than it was when I was a little girl, but it was the same old two bedroom house with a remodeled kitchen and an add-on den and bathroom cum family room. We lived inland enough so that even though our address was in Santa Monica, normally a clean-air city, we got a lot of Los Angeles' Smog.

I slept in my old bed, watching the same old ghosts that crawled on the ceiling when I was four or five. They always came around whenever a car drove through the curve at the end of our street. Took me the longest time to figure out what they really were.

I said good night to the boogeyman who lived in my closet. When I was a preschooler, I was frightened of him until Dad came in one night and ordered him out of my room and off the property, threatening him with a billy club.

Even though I knew the Boogeyman was standing behind Dad holding his hand over his mouth and giggling while Dad was making wild gestures to chase him out, I was never scared of ol' Boogey again. It was our secret that he never left. I had to let my Daddy think he'd done a good job, didn't I?

I blinked back some tears caused by my consummate contentment, said a few words of to Whoever Up There would listen, tucked my old pillow under my arm, like I used to do, and fell asleep, safe and snug, sleeping tight, and no bed-bug better come around to bite.

I got up early, so I could surprise Dad. From the time I stepped from my bedroom, everything went wrong. My poor pop walked into a cloud of smoke billowing from the stove, where my French Toast was gleefully burning, charring the pan, the stove, the ceiling, and my temper.

"Go ahead!" I shrieked, stamping my feet, my voice rising to an unbelievable pitch, "Burn, you flipping sonsabitches, burn! Ruin my surprise breakfast, you no good, miserable, bloody little bastards!"

Dad calmly placed a cover on the offending pan and put his arm around me, stifling a laugh. I pushed away, glaring at him, "Oh, no you don't! I've got a good mad on right now and I want to enjoy it to the fullest!"

I slammed my hand on the counter for emphasis and accidentally knocked my notes on how to make them from Greg to the floor along with the remainder of the gooey egg-stuff in the mixing bowl.

It was that kind of morning.

He began laughing at me. My robe, face and arms were splattered with spots of egg batter, powdered sugar, accented here and there by black smoke smudges. A grin cracked my disgust, then I laughed uproariously with him.

After we settled down, I sat at the table with a smirk. "So much for trying to be a domesticated daughter. Gotta give me props for trying, though. I swear I can't cook warm water!"

He bent down and kissed my forehead. "Ahhh, don't worry, Pickles. It's the thought that counts."

"I wonder why I'm such a lousy cook..." I blinked back some tears and went to the sink to 'wash' up some pots. I still wasn't used to hearing my pet name.

Suddenly, tears began streaming down my face. I went to him, put my arms around him, crying and whispering, "Oh, Daddy, I'm so sorry for being such a shit all this time! It wasn't mom's fault she got cancer. I hated her for still smoking. For ten years all I could think of was that she was intentionally abandoning me. Maybe being easy was my way of getting back at her."

Dad stroked my back gently. "I never told you this. After you quit going to the department shrink, I had a long talk with him. He says you were punishing yourself for feeling the way you did. He said that you wouldn't stop until you came to grips with the whole situation."

Even before she left us, Mother understood and made me promise that I would always be there for you, no matter how bad things got. She loved you very much."

"OhhhhGoddd!" I held him tight and cried for my mother. The emotion got to him. Silent tears dripped down his face while he held me. I broke away and left the room, still bawling. When I returned twenty minutes or so later, I felt a new calmness. Dad told me later that that day even my voice had matured, just the slightest. I sat down and held both his hands on my lap.

"It took a while, but I was able to grieve for Mom. Before I leave town, I want to visit her. Would you like to come along?"

He sniffled and blew his nose with a loud honk. "Not this time, Pickles. I think maybe you and Mother should be alone."

"Perhaps it's better that way. I've got a helluva lot to tell her," I glanced at the kitchen clock. "My Gawd, look at the time! You're going to be late!"

"It's okay," he grinned. "I know the boss."

I walked him to the door and put my hand on his cheek. "Dad, I'm heading back up to San Francisco, so we should say good-bye now. I'll stop at the cemetery on the way to LAX."

Smiling in his eyes lovingly, I said softly, "Daddy, I never said this before. Thank you, Pop. Thanks for raising me with the love you did. Thanks for hanging in there with your airhead daughter. Thanks for being my Dad. I love you so very, very much."

I put my arms around his chest and hugged him hard.

"Bye, baby," He said huskily. "Keep me posted? Call me more than once every six months, just to let the old man know how you're doing?"

"Plan on it, Daddy." I kissed his cheek, smiled and gently closed the door behind him.

CHAPTER TWENTY-ONE

The Tracy Cunningham who flew back to San Francisco really didn't need an airplane. I bet I walked five feet above the ground. The Cunningham family lives! Dad and I had each other back. It felt so good to be loved!

I took a taxi directly to Sausalito, and paid a kid five bucks to take me out to the tugboat in his skiff. When I got there, Stephanie and Greg were involved in a heated game of Seven-Toed Pete, a domino game. I kissed them both hello, beaming from ear to ear.

"May we assume all went well?" Greg said.

"You have no idea, Hardbody," I grinned. "I've got my Dad back. We're both very pleased at the outcome of the big peace conference."

"Did you tell him about T.J.?" Stephanie asked calmly.

"No. I didn't have the guts."

"See where I'm coming from about Jerry?" She stood up and went outside.

"You're going to have to tell him one of these days," Greg said, putting his arms around me.

"I know," I sighed and snuggled into his steely body. "Honey, I don't want to think about that part of my life again. I'm too happy."

I looked up and he got the message. He bent down and kissed me. A lingering, tender kiss. "Greg, I made myself a promise on the plane. I'm never, ever, going to call myself a whore again. Far as I'm concerned, that word doesn't exist in my personal dictionary."

"I like that. What else has changed?"

"I'm going to enjoy life. I'm going to try to find a way to recover the last ten years of my life, live them over, and do it right this time."

"How do you do that?"

"Well, let's see," I pulled away and went to the galley and grabbed a cookie. "For starters, on our very next date, we won't go into a single place where minors aren't allowed. I want to go to a movie and have a hot-fudge sundae afterward."

"Then what?" he leered, cocking an expressive eyebrow. "We go find a romantic place to make out... in the car."

"You're serious, aren't you?"

"Deadly, Hardbody. Better get some practice in undoing a bra with one hand again... on second thought, no damn practice on anyone but me."`

CHAPTER TWENTY-TWO

Greg Phillips went back to work the next morning. He waved with a smile as he moved the shore boat up to a medium plane.

Sure. He could smile and wave. He was having fun and doing something to solve the crime.

I was still stuck with watching Stephanie on the tugboat. I hate baby-sitting. Always have. But I liked staying with Stephanie. She was a great kid. She and I acted a lot like sisters. Got along fine, then a spat over some stupid thing would flare up, then everything would be cool again.

I knew what my problem was. I didn't want to be stuck here doing this. I wanted to be on the front lines, working side by side with Greg, contributing to the investigation. I had to find a way to keep Stephanie under wraps, and get on the mainland.

Humph. Already talking like we were on an island.

All I could do was fret about my inactivity. I had suspicions who killed Angel Bradford. Greg said he thought the same way. But dammit, he was able to do something about it. My first case, and I'm freaking marooned in the freaking middle of freaking Richardson's Bay!

I had long since confiscated Steph's cell phone, and now I was tempted to pull the fuse out of the VHF Radio-Telephone and leave Stephanie alone, but I knew if I did, 'specially with my luck, some bad guys would find her, she'd have no way to call for help, and I'd be responsible for maybe getting her killed.

Doublestuff!

Stephanie had already tried to call Jerry Morresey once.

Fortunately, she didn't know how to use the VHF, and got the Coasties instead of the Marine Operator. I almost slugged her when I caught her, which begat one of our more colorful arguments.

It didn't dawn on her that since Greg, me, and she had vanished, anyone looking for her would keep an eye on Jerry, just like I did. Making her promise not to call him was futile. She was seventeen, it was spring, and she was in love. Hormones were running rampant. Audible sigh... if it was me, I'd sure try to let him know where I was...

Hmmm... if all she wants is her boyfriend, why not? Why not, indeed? Spring break is coming soon, like maybe it's going on right now...

I called Greg after checking on Stephanie. She was on the deck, topless, shivering occasionally as a cool breeze wafted over her. Even though she was protected from crosswinds by the solid railings, and even though it might be cold enough to keep her nipples taut, by damn she was going to get an early start on her tan. If any phones were monitored, it would be Jerry's, not the P.D.'s. I doubt even the mob has the guts to tap the cop-shop phones.

"Homicide, Phillips."

"Hardbody, I just had an idea. Can you get in touch with the boyfriend and maybe have him spirited to our twenty for the duration?"

"Why?"

Let's not get into a long discussion over the cells. Can you do it?"

"I guess so."

"Good. Will you do it, please?"

"I'll try."

"Thanks. I'll explain when you get here." I tried to mellow out about not being ashore after the call. I didn't want to get Stephanie's hopes up, so I didn't tell her what I was doing. I tried lying out on the deck with her, but every time I got a chill, my skin got prickly and I lost sight of my chest. I completely out-classed lying next to a seventeen year old fox.

The only reason I knew which goose-bumps were my boobs was that I remembered where they were the last time I saw them.

It was too cold to enjoy the sun. I got dressed and sat inside, reading an old Yachting Magazine and listening to Rush Limbaugh. My father is on the far right, which is why I grew up with Limbaugh. I'm not as militant as they are. But I can hold my own against most California lefties.

I must have looked at my watch a hundred times. An hour or two later, I heard Greg and Jerry's hail, and a delighted squeal from Stephanie.

She threw on a sweatshirt and ran to the rail. When the Boston Whaler pulled alongside, Jerry Morresey was in the bow, grinning widely when he tossed her the dinghy's painter.

Stephanie gave him a hungry kiss the moment his feet touched the metal decking.

Home was the hunter, home from the land or sea or whatever.

He dropped his duffel bag and kissed her back, cautiously. Poor guy was mindful that both Greg and I were watching, and he didn't know how we were going to react.

I pecked Greg on the lips and the two of us went inside. I just knew all was going to be well.

"Want to tell me what all this is about?" Greg asked, pulling me back to our room.

I sat on the edge of the bed while he stood in front of me. "The only reason Stephanie wanted to be ashore is Jerry," I explained. "He's here. She's here. She's very happy. If you got him away without being followed, there's no reason on earth why Stephanie won't fully cooperate by staying here voluntarily, and I can come ashore and do some detecting."

"You're going to leave them alone?"

"C'mon, Greg." I said with disgust. "Did you forget Steph's an ex-hooker? She's not your daughter. They're almost eighteen, and most kids their age have been humping like Jack Rabbits since they found out why their plumbing is different. If Steph wants to go to bed with Jerry, what the hell do we have to say about it?"

Greg gave up. "Well, we got him away clean."

"If you didn't know what was happening, how come he brought a duffel?"

"A bit of fortunate luck. He and some buddies were going camping. Wormy and I intercepted him when he drove to his friend's house."

He sat down next to me. "Now tell me exactly what it is you want to do ashore."

I gave him my adorable look. "Help you solve the murder?"

"Tracy, I'll preface this by saying I like you very much..."

Uh-oh. I don't like the sound of this.

"Let's change that to love you. We are good together. I hope to be romantically involved with you for quite a long time."

My confusion must have shown by then. I had no idea where this preamble was going. "The feeling is mutual."

"Good." His voice turned cold when he said, "However, you are not going to investigate the death of Angel Bradford. That's the business of Professional Policemen. You are not my partner. Wormy and I have been a team for a long time. Bluntly put, I don't want you or any other P.I.s getting in my way and tearing up my evidence.

"On your request, I brought Morresey out here. I have problems with your reasoning, but I'll learn to live with it. However, bringing her a playmate does not reduce your responsibility to protect her."

He was deadly serious when he said, "Woman, you mess with my homicide, and even though I love you, I'll toss you in the can for interfering with a police officer in the course of his investigation. You will stay aboard. End of speech. There will be no rebuttal."

I was floored.

My surprise gave way to my Irish temper, real quick-like. "Your case? I figured out most of this for you! I was the one who figured out why people wanted Stephanie, maybe wanted her dead, Sergeant! I figured out where the primary evidence of the murder weapon was, and I retrieved it!

"I was the one who put a tentative ID on a pile of bones in a freaking basement in the goddammed mountains! I even gave you a probable Jane Doe homicide you didn't even know happened! And now you're not going to let me participate?

"In your blinking ear!"

I got to my feet and got right in his face. "I do the brain work and you get the bust? Bull-freaking-shit! I'm an independent, I don't answer to you, or anyone! I don't need your permission to do a goddammed thing!"

He held my shoulders. I tried to wrench away, but there was no way. "Trace, don't fight me. It's out of my hands. I didn't make the decision."

"Who did?" I snapped bitterly.

"It came down from the head-shed."

All of a sudden it came down to me, too. In an instant, I knew precisely where the edict had come from. Good ol' Jack Cunningham.

I thought Dad had dropped the matter of me getting involved rather easily. All he had to do was call a Brother Chief, and I'm in the bleachers, or worse yet, standing in line to see the big game. I felt like I'd just gotten to the ticket booth and they closed the window, saying, "Sorry, we're full up."

I blew.

I cried, struggled, stamped my feet, pounded my fists against Greg's chest, taking my frustration out on the poor guy. He held on stoically, taking all I had to dole out. Finally I ran out of steam, and sat down, sobbing, my temper tantrum finally running out of steam.

"Honey, I'm sorry."

"So am I," I sniffled and tried to smile. "At least we found out I can't beat you up. I know what happened. My father told on me."

"He's only trying to protect you."

"That's not fair! I don't tell him not to get involved, do I?"

"That's different."

"Yeah!" I snapped. My Irish was back. "He's a man, and I'm an itsy-bitsy woman! Women don't belong in the real goddammed world! We're supposed to get married, clean the house, cook dinner, and gratefully spread our legs whenever the master of the house wants a good screwing! You've got the 'Four F's?

"We've got the three 'Cs'. Clean, Cook, and Copulate!"

"I think you're being unfair."

One of the things I hated was Greg's calmness. It's hard to fight when one of the combatants is super-rational.

"So what? I didn't start this, you guys did!"

I settled down after that. I had gotten in my shots, not that they did any good. We talked for a few more minutes. I didn't give up, though.

I tried being calmly professional, tried pleading, tried logic, and finally trotted out my cute little pixy-pout, some thing that as a rule works wonders, and got no-freaking-where.

I even sat in his lap, put his hand under my sweater and began lap-dancing him. I slipped my hand under his belt. I breathed hard, panted, licked, kissed and tongued him like the horny woman that I was rapidly becoming.

I tried my damnedest to get him turned on. The creep enjoyed the hell out of all my ministrations, but he wasn't going to budge one inch. When Greg left, he made me promise not to do anything.

A promise I made with fingers firmly crossed behind me.

He said he'd be back about, eight and be ready to go on a date. I even kissed him goodbye with feeling, but my mind was already a thousand yards away.

On shore.

I went to the galley and made myself a PB and J sandwich, plotting on how I was going to get ashore, and what I was going to do once I was there.

I looked around the boat for Stephanie and Jerry. During the argument, they'd disappeared. When I heard some familiar sounding moans drifting, back from the bow cabin, I knew where they were and what they were doing.

God, I hope you told him, Steph. Don't do as I do, do as I say.

CHAPTER TWENTY-THREE

I turned on the radio to an FM jazz station, cranked up the volume loud enough to drown out the audible portion of Stephanie's lovemaking and harkened back to my college days. My roomie was as much into men as I was, so it wasn't uncommon for one or the other of us to have a male in our room after hours.

While one of us would hit the books, the other would be in the bedroom. Not that we had a separated bedroom. All we did was rig a rope clothes-line device that held a bedspread like a tarp across the end of our twin beds. Even though we had agreed that the one recreating would do her best to be quiet, the one studying invariably had to turn up the Ghetto-Blaster to mask the distracting moans, groans and sighs.

Good ol' Deja vu.

I went to a desk and found a steno book. I sat down in the comfortable recliner with a cup of coffee and began marking out a thinking page. When I want to lay something out in my mind, I write everything down as fact. Proven or unproven.

One of my old professors told us one of the most effective ways to deduce was not to worry about proofs, at least not at first. Consider the most reasonable scenario, and work from there.

Use Occam's Razor. "One should not increase, beyond what is necessary, the number of entities required to explain anything."

A serendipity of this is that I can think in my shotgun style, but lay it out on paper in a reasonable order.

What do we know?

We know that Stephanie is going to inherit something that fits in a safe-deposit box when she's eighteen. We surmise that her father wants this thing. Can we surmise that he knows what it is? Who does know what it is?

The mob wants what Steph is going to get. Why? So do the Feds. Why? Her grandfather loved her, so he wouldn't be leaving her something that would land her in jail.

On to the murder. Angel Bradford takes a hike, never to be heard from again. Leaves a daughter behind without a by-your-leave. Grandpa Martucchi dies a year or so later. He doesn't like son-in-law Bradford.

That's obvious, or he would have left that whatever to Bradford. I wonder if our Mafia Princess is going to become the world's youngest god-mother?

What the hell's in that safe? Who would know?

A.J. Martucchi, but he ain't talkin'. How about Martucchi's lawyer? Wouldn't he know?

He would.

Sure. A Mafioso Consigliore going to tell me. How do I find out who the mob mouthpiece is?

I giggled and told myself to leave the dumb dialogue to the old-time Hollywood script-writers. Edward G. Robinson, I ain't.

My immediate problem is that I've got to find a way to find said attorney. How? Ask another lawyer.

Hmmm. Sounds reasonable to me. The family compound was in Belvedere. Is it a reasonable assumption that the Consigliore lives or works there, too?

In the bad ol' days, Peerless constantly went to war with an attorney from Belvedere. If they fought him and lost, he has to be a good guy... Snaggletooth once mentioned that he was a sailor. Anyone who's a sailor is my kind of people.

What was his name? It had something to do with water. River? Rivers... Lake?... no, Brooks! That's it. Ellis Brooks. Like the old Oakland car dealer.

I called the office number of Brooks and Brooks, Attorneys at Law, talked to the secretary and made an appointment to see L.S. tomorrow. The operator and I had a little problem finding his number, because he was listed as "L.S.," not "Ellis."

I was just signing off when Stephanie and Jerry came aft. He had the most ridiculous, delightful expression on his face. Stephanie winked at me with a wry grin. Later, she told me that she had told him everything. I was pleased. I hugged her and told her so.

"Now it's your turn to tell someone, Trace," she said. "Confessing my sins was the hardest thing I've ever done, but Jer understood, especially when I told him that I'd had a Guardian Angel making sure I didn't get into trouble."

"He knows about your family?"

"Yeah. I had to tell him. One thing led to another. He says it doesn't matter to him. We really love each other."

"Great." I said.

"Jerry just turned eighteen. Just as soon as all this shit is finished, he's moving out and we're going to live together. We'll both go to college. He decided that after we graduate, if we're still of a mind, then we'll get married."

"What are you going to live on?"

"I figure if I'm a mafia princess, why can't I get some of the money? I'm going to call someone and ask for a healthy living allowance."

"Who?"

"Not my father, I'll guarantee you that."

"Then who?"

"Grandpa had some friends back east. I know the name of one of his closest friends. Betcha he's a Godfather, too. Maybe he owes my family. Maybe he'll take care of it."

"Think you can talk him into it?"

"It is so in the bag." she said coldly. I got a shiver down my spine when I saw her look of determination. Somehow, the kid we'd rescued from that flea-trap had matured one whale of a lot in the past couple of days.

I almost told her what one of my priorities was on my first trip tomorrow, but I decided I'd better wait until I had something more concrete. It was getting dark. I took a shower and dressed.

I wore a pleated plaid (Cunningham Tartan, of course) wool skirt and one of my favorite Angora sweaters, a hunter green one. At the mere mention that Greg and I would be off the boat for a few hours, Jerry's nostrils flared.

Now that he had been allowed to explore the pleasures of the Garden of Eden, he was going to sample all the fruits on Steph's Yum-yum tree. More power to him. I have a feeling he's going to need it.

Greg and I spent a lot of valuable time instructing the teens what to do if this or that happened, and elicited a solemn promise that they'd stay aboard, not call any friends, do nothing to attract attention.

Once we were ashore, Greg surprised me by escorting me to a Chevy convertible. It was a cream and bronze 1956 Belaire and was in super-clean condition. I laid the back of' my hand on the ultra-smooth fender and felt the care the owner had put into it.

"Where did you find this treasure?"

"I borrowed it from a friend. When I told him that my girlfriend wanted to go back to the future, he handed me the keys and said it was probably before your time, but it was the best he could do."

"It's dynamite!" I laughed and slipped across the seat to sit right next to him. We drove into a drive-in movie and watched Chain Saw Murder or whatever.

Greg must have planned the night out carefully, or else why would he take me to a drive-in where I could scream and squeal and hang all over him? We really did watch the dumb movie... well... some of it.

During some of the duller parts, Greg began warming me up for later. I played the game. Every time his hand got under my sweater, or found my bra, I pushed it away. Wasn't easy, but I did it.

Then we drove across the bay to Walnut Creek, where there was a revival drive-in restaurant. All of a sudden, I was all the way back to the fifties, long before I was born. I learned why the baby-boomers treasure their teenaged years so much. If our date was any example, they had a ball!

After a yummy Hot Fudge Sundae, with extra walnuts and gooey hot fudge chocolate and whipped cream, Greg had one more surprise in store for me. We drove up to Grizzly Peak, overlooking Berkley and the whole damn bay area, the prime parking place for kids to play huggy-body.

The view was magnificent. We could see most of night lights within thirty miles. Course we didn't spend much time looking out the windshield.

During a deep kiss, a big warm hand slipped under my sweater. He fumbled at my back a couple of times, but it wasn't too long before he had my bra undone... with one hand yet.

Even though I had said what I said, it's a good thing that he's too tall, the seat was too small, or we'd be doing something we wouldn't want to get caught doing when the local cops came by with their bright spotlight. As it was, I was straddling him and had maneuvered my body to a real delightful place, and was getting rather vocal with my body heat.

His hand slipped under my skirt and was at the top of my panty-hose when I stopped him and said no. He stopped just like a gentleman should...And kept, trying, just like a boy would.

After an hour or so, he was in physical pain, poor guy.

We drove back to the house where Greg got the great car, and drove his car to the shore boat. It was dark and the FM was still on. Greg moved to turn it off, but I put my hand on his arm to stop him. No doubt, Steph had figured out the benefits of background noise.

My super-terrific date of the past was over when Greg kissed me good night at the cabin door. My fantabulous date of the present began the moment I held his hand and led him onto the bed.

CHAPTER TWENTY-FOUR

It had been a special night. Back to the fifties, then fast-forward into what life would be like with Greg as a permanent fixture in my bed. When I woke up at ten thirty, I was back in the present and Greg was long gone. I got up and dreamily took a shower, and dressed in a colorful outfit, one of my favorites. I was making a statement with my hot pink skirt suit. I was telling everyone I. was happy and sunny, and that I wanted the whole wide world to feel as good as I did about being a woman.

By now I was pleased about my incredible wisdom of bringing lots of clothes. Things sometimes turn out well, don't they? Even if they are mistakes in the beginning.

I was shocked to see that Stephanie and Jerry were cracking the books. He was actually giving her the same mid-terms that he had just taken. Except it, it was a lot harder for her, because she was taking them orally!

Stephanie was positively radiant. I don't know who glowed more, me or her.

I called a boat yard in Sausalito and got a shore boat to come out and take me across Richardson's Bay to Belvedere. The offices of Brooks and Brooks were across the street from the San Francisco Yacht Club.

I walked to the building. The lawyer's office building was a converted mansion. There were several shingles in front, all attorneys of some sort. I breathed deeply to relax myself, and went inside.

The offices of Brooks and Brooks took half of the bottom floor. I opened a frosted glass and dark walnut door and timidly closed it behind me. I looked around the empty office in awe. There was a lot of money spent on the waiting room. The expensively decorated office was pre-Yuppie. Walnut wood walls and spring green splashes of color. On the walls were beautiful nautical oil paintings. I checked out the weather panel mounted over the long chocolate brown, real leather couch.

Every instrument; the anemometer and wind direction, the barometer, a tidal clock that was useless on the west coast, the outside air temperature, even the clock were all matching brass Danforth gauges.

I stood at the front counter and waited a few minutes before the secretary came out from a hallway and greeted me. Just for a flicker of a second, it seemed like she recognized me. She was a pretty woman of indeterminate age. Meticulously groomed, she looked like she just stepped out of the pages of a fashion magazine. She was about five eight, and had a nicely rounded, but trim figure. Dark hair, and brown eyes that looked like they didn't miss a trick.

"May I help you?"

"Yes. I have an appointment with Mr. Brooks. My name is Tracy Cunningham."

"Have a seat, please."

I made myself comfortable in the deep couch, thumbing through Yachting magazine, a wish book for all those who love boats. That's my kind of people. Twenty minutes later, a tall man, in his mid-forties, came out from the hallway. "Miss Cunningham?"

I hope my jaw didn't when I first saw him. He was some kind of awesome hunk. Make that incredible hunk. All I could say was, "Yes."

"I'm Leland Brooks. Call me Lee." He shook my hand warmly. "Come on back."

While he led me down the hallway, I resolved never to wash the hand he just touched and mentally checked off his description. Just for practice, of course.

He was six two or three, and too handsome to be for real. He weighed about a hundred and ninety, broad chest, flat stomach, tight, muscular butt, jet black hair with silver temples, expressively beautiful blue eyes, a super tan, and a crooked smile with perfect porcelain-white teeth.

He was wearing neatly pressed slacks, and a shirt with an embroidered polo pony. Unmarred cream-colored Topsider shoes. The originals. His shirt matched his turquoise blue eyes.

'S no fair!

Why do men always get the good eye colors and long, curled eyelashes?

Sheese. It takes me a half-hour to get my eyelashes that good. If good old LSB's law practice didn't work out, he could always be a male model for the pre-Geritol set. I think I was in heavy lust and already giving thought about how to juggle both this hunk and that tall guy.

I grinned to myself and shook off the prurient thoughts.

Sorry 'bout that, Greg.

By the time I finished my mental exercising, we were in the office at the end of the hall. He walked around his desk and said, "Have a seat, Miss Cunningham."

"Hi." I said nervously. "I'm a research assistant. Sir, I only need enough of your time to find out the name of the attorney who is the mafia man."

"Want to run that by me again?" He could have laughed outright at my stupid, amateurish opening. He didn't though. All I heard was a soft, gentle chuckle. Obviously, he knew that I was green and he was kind enough not to throw me out.

"I'm working on a case. It involves the Bradford clan," His blank look told me he didn't know everything. "Perhaps you know them better by the patriarchal name, Martucchi."

He sat forward and rested his hands on his desk. "Yes. I do know that name. How does this concern a pretty young P.I. like you?"

"I'm not a P.I. I'm not licensed."

"Why not?"

"I don't carry any weapons..."

"Why not?"

Even though I wanted to be his friend, I was getting a little teed-off with his constant questions. I was cool though. I bit my tongue and replied, "I don't like guns, and my client is Stephanie Bradford.

She's about to inherit something from her very late grandfather. Something in a safe deposit box. Everyone in the whole world wants whatever this thing is. I hoped that I could find out what it is."

"Why?"

"Because there's a homicide involved, Mr. Brooks..."

"Lee." he interrupted with a soft voice. He smiled kindly. I melted.

Now I know I was in lust. Not only was he a fox, but he was a nice one.

"Stephanie's mother was murdered about five years ago. We just found her remains last weekend. I suspect that the contents of the safe deposit box have something to do with her murder."

There. I got it all out before he could pick me up by the scruff of my neck and see how far he could throw me.

He sat back in his massive desk chair, studying me, his hands, fingertips to fingertips, doing horizontal pushups against each other.

Outside I could hear the raucous squawking of a Steller's Jay. A gray squirrel was chirping, probably in an argument with the jay over an acorn. The flag halyard on the metal flagpole in front was clanging against the pole rhythmically.

I don't perspire easily, but for some reason, I could feel sweat begin to pop out on my forehead. I don't know why. I know enough about men that I knew he already liked me, but his steady gaze scared the hell out of me, and yet I knew he had to be a kind man.

After what seemed like an hour, he smiled and said, "I'm assuming that you are here to tap into my vast knowledge of law. If I'm to be your attorney, my sage advice and counsel requires me to tell you that I think this is a bit above the level of your expertise, Miss Cunningham. In other words, you mess with those guys, and someone might want to hurt you."

Doublestuff! There's the old "Let's protect the little girl from the big bad guys" again.

"That's not your worry," I snapped.

"I know." He smiled my rising temper down. "I didn't mean it like that."

"How exactly did you mean it, Mister Brooks?"

He let me glare at him for a moment, then said, "Why don't you go up front, get a cup of' coffee, and cool off?"

"Man," he chuckled, "I'm sure glad you're not bigger. You'd be kicking ass and taking names all the time! Let me make a few phone calls. If I can find out what you want, I'll tell you. if I can't, I don't think you ever will."

"How much are you charging me?"

"You should have asked that first."

He was right, of course. "Well?"

"Tell me the truth. Are you on retainer?"

"No." I let out a sigh. "I was, but I changed allegiances, so I'm on my own nickel now."

"In that case, the fee will be a dollar and other consideration."

"Now you just hold on, right there, Mister Brooks. I don't want any favors!"

"I understand where you're coming from, Tracy," he said. "I like your sassiness."

He smiled and held his hand out expectantly. I was puzzled at first, then I realized that he actually wanted a dollar. I put one in his hand.

He folded it gravely and put it in his wallet. "I'm not doing you a favor. The term, 'dollar and other consideration,' is legal mumbo jumbo. It means I'll be your attorney for a buck, nothing more."

"What's the 'other consideration' stuff'?"

"The quote, other consideration, unquote, is a promise from you that you will be available for work."

Huh?

"Say again?"

"There may come a time when I want you to do some investigating for me. If so, are you, and will you be, available?"

I don't believe this is happening.

"I'll have to check with my crowded schedule, sir." I grinned. "Hell yes, I'm available! That is, if you want a wet behind the ears, green girl who doesn't even know what to call her occupation."

"I might. Go up and introduce yourself to Renny. I'll see what I can find out."

I walked to the front office with a dazed look. I couldn't believe all this! Yesterday, I telephoned an old friend who works in Peerless' law department. He told me that L.S. Brooks was one of the few people who made a habit of whipping Peerless in court. He was exclusive, a top-of-the-line insurance law man. Not an ambulance chaser.

He writes insurance law! He spends a lot of time back in Washington, D.C., testifying before all sorts of legal committees. And he wants me to work an occasional case for him?

Think I wasn't swept off my feet? I stood at the walnut counter and smiled at the secretary. "Yes?" she asked."

I'm supposed to introduce myself to you and beg a cup of coffee. Mister Brooks is checking something for me."

"Hi," She stood and smiled. "My name is Renny Babington. Spell Renny with a 'y.'"

"Glad to meet you." I shook her hand. "I'm Tracy Cunningham. I'm an investigator."

"Is that so?" She walked to a back closet and brought out a cup of steaming black coffee. I took a trial sip. It was delicious! It had to be fresh ground, expensive stuff. "I'll bet Mister Brooks asked if you'd be available for an occasional case."

"Yes, but how did you know?"

"Well, first of all, we've been mulling something like this over. He's an unusual man, Tracy. He loves to champion the underdog. He's a man who loves women and women love him… but not in a romantic sense. He's very married. But anytime he likes a woman and he can throw some business her way, he will."

I was excited hearing this, of course. Renny's next comment brought me down to earth. She had been watching me carefully while we talked. "I'm not clairvoyant, Tracy. There's probably another, more personal reason, Mr. Brooks has asked you to do some work for him."

"What?"

"Physically, you look a lot like his first wife. Angie was your size and coloring, had the same athletic build, and was a cute little thing, just like you. She died of breast cancer a long time ago. Lee barely survived. If it wasn't for his second wife, I don't think we'd be here discussing all this."

"I'm sorry Angie died. Are you worried about me ruining things?"

"Should I be?"

"I see no reason to be. I've got a good man and home wrecking isn't my bag."

"I'm glad to hear that. Part of my job is looking out for my boss. He wears his heart on his sleeve. Please don't let me find you doing anything to hurt him."

"Message received. It's not gonna be a problem…"

Lee summoned me from the hallway. "Miss Cunningham?"

"Yes, sir?"

"C'mon back," I followed him again, watching his tush all the way, but it wasn't quite the same, now. The thrill of the chase was gone already. I sat more at ease, sipping my coffee.

"I know the attorney who represents the Bradford family. He's a good man, and a friend. I had to tell him why I was asking, but I kept your name out of it, of course. I was getting nowhere, until I mentioned Stephanie and the discovery of the body. He immediately became quite attentive."

"And?"

"He says he wants to do some thinking."

"God, I hope he can be trusted."

"He can. He tells me he isn't a fan of Bradford's."

"Why work for him then?"

"A.J. Martucchi asked him to, in a manner that commanded attention."

"May I assume that if push came to shove, he'd be more on my client's side?"

"That would be a safe assumption."

"Will you tell me this man's name?"

"No. I told him I'd keep our mutual knowledge of each other confidential."

"You are the go-between."

"Yes."

"Okay, let's try this. My client wants a comfortable living allowance. To be completely up-front, she can't pay me, and I'm flat busted."

I paused, waiting for the standard reaction to my double entendre, and was most pleased to see he didn't try to respond with some sort of trite come-on. That's usually my final test. I continued, "She refuses to deal with her father, for a hundred good reasons. Will you call this man and arrange some sort of stipend for her?"

"I can do that."

"Secondly. This should tell you how much I'm laying my cards on the line, Mister Brooks. We're hiding out in an old tugboat in the middle of Richardson's Bay. Can you arrange a safe house for my client and me? One that will be safe from all those who would like to get Stephanie under their control?"

"Why do you want to come ashore?"

"I hate sitting around and doing nothing. I want an active role in working the murder case."

"What are your credentials?"

It was my turn to give him a little jab. "You should've asked me that a long time ago."

"Touche'," he smiled.

"All I have on my side is a sharp mind, almost five years worth of background in insurance investigations, and degrees in Criminology and Criminalistics."

"From?"

"UCLA."

"Good. That's quite a bit, when you look at it.

Insurance crime investigations, hmmm?"

"Yes. I worked for PacMarine, SQE, and Peerless, but you won't get a good report if you're thinking of checking up on me."

"Why not?"

I wanted to see just how far the man would reach out to help a woman. "For too many reasons to go into now, I moonlighted in an evening job. One that gave me a chance to explore hotels a lot..."

Again, I paused, waiting for an untoward reaction. Again, nothing. "You understand?"

"I believe so. Apparently, you were a call-girl."

No emotion. He said it like he might have said I was a blonde.

"Yes. The operative word is 'was'."

His expression told me that he understood what I was telling him, and that he didn't care, one way or the other. It was none of his business. My past was my past. Period.

"My supervisor wasn't enthralled when she found out that a close relative of hers knew me in my other line of work."

"What was your supervisor's name?"

"Eunice Martin."

In a perfect deadpan he said, "Ol' Snaggletooth?"

I cracked up. "Yeah, that's her. You know her?"

"Somewhat," he grinned. "Okay, Tracy, take off. I'll expect a call from you tomorrow."

"It'll be on cell phone. Cell phones can be eavesdropped on, so we have to be somewhat circumspect during any conversations."

"I understand."

I trotted back to my water taxi and while the kid was taking me back out, I handed him forty bucks. Half that was a tip, I didn't care that it was the last cash I had on me. I felt too good.

I had a feeling that my impulsive phone call for an appointment yesterday had already changed my life. A week ago I was fighting cockroaches for total domination of my office, and today I met a man who could do me one helluva lot of good.

I might make it yet!

CHAPTER TWENTY-FIVE

The next day, I was awake early. The second Greg was gone, I showered, dressed in a slightly less colorful pants suit and paced the aft deck waiting for a civilized time to call Mr. Brooks' office. I even tried some fishing to waste time.

I began giggling at myself. Here I was, dressed as primly and properly as I could be, groomed to the last hair, and I was standing on the stern of a smelly old tugboat, fishing! To top all this off, I hadn't been fishing in eons! I hoped I wouldn't catch anything.

Stephanie and Jerry hadn't come up for air yet. Every once in a while, the moral values of what I was openly condoning bothered me. Just as often, the voice in my head kept telling me to bug off.

It's none of your business. Leave them alone. She knows exactly what she's doing. She 's happy, they're happy in their little romantic hide-away.

But, still, they're kids.

One eighteen, one seventeen... Not really kids anymore. Butt out.

Whatever.

About nine thirty and a half, I called the office. Renny answered with a cheery "Good morning, Brooks and Brooks, Attorneys at law."

"Hi. This is Tracy. Is Mister Brooks in yet?"

"Not yet, kiddo," She said. "He said that you'd be champing at the bit. He also said to call him around eleven."

"Okay," I sighed, hoping my disappointment wouldn't come over the phone. It must have.

"Tracy, he's out working on your case now. Relax."

"Easy for you to say," I muttered. "You've got something to do."

"Tell you what, Sherlock. While you're waiting, why don't you come up with a detailed resume?"

"Why?" Suddenly I was excited.

"I think it would be a good idea to have one available one of these days. A girl never can tell..."

"Yes, Ma'am!" I grinned and rang off.

My Gosh, maybe this isn't all a dream! Maybe he does want me to come and work some of his cases! Maybe he wants me to come to work for him! I already told him about my past and still he wanted to talk to me.

Boy, telling the truth up-front sure pays off sometimes.

I sat in the recliner with my trusty laptop, and wrote out a five-page detailed personal history of Tracy Cunningham, starting back when I was a kid. If he wanted to know the people he was associated with, by God, he'd know me.

My time was occupied until the lovers came out of the forward cabin, both with stupid grins pasted on their faces. I filled Stephanie in on what I was doing, and told her that I thought maybe she wouldn't have to get in direct contact with the man she knew of in Detroit. She was pleased at that.

"And," I said, "You'd better give me a dollar."

"Why?"

"So I won't be telling a lie when I say that you're my client." I learn fast, too.

"A whole dollar?" she smirked.

"I'm sorry I'm so expensive," I replied in kind. "What the hell, you're going to be rich. I think you can afford it."

"In your old job, that's probably enough to pay for one grunt."

"Not even close." Since Jerry had gone back forward to clean up, I turned serious. "Steph, I've made myself a promise. I'm not going to dwell on my past. If I have to tell someone, I will. If I don't, it's none of their business. Maybe you should take the same tack."

"I have." she smiled. "Except with Jerry. We can even make a joke about it. He wants to start putting money in a piggy bank every time we do it. Poor guy's going to be broke for years!

"Trace, I believe that I wasn't really a hooker in Cincinnati. I was only a run-away who had some Godfathers looking out for me. Far as I'm concerned, the men who I slept with were paid boyfriends."

"Want to run that by me again?"

"Just suppose I was uglier than hammered shit. My father or grandfather would probably go out and find me someone and pay him enough money to make him think I was lovely, wouldn't they?"

"Possibly."

"Well, that's the way I want to believe all this happened. You know, I only slept with six guys in Cincy. Six different guys, many different times. Statistically, that's changing boyfriends every three months or so. Not a real promiscuous record, I'd say. Not in this day and age. For all intents and purposes, I didn't become a hooker until I moved into Willa's home for women. Even then I was forced into it."

"How did she keep you there if you knew that warrant was a phony? I can't believe you stuck around just because it was a good place to hide. I also don't believe you wanted to be a prostitute."

"I didn't. The fat bitch stole all my money the week before my rent was due. Then she threatened to call the cops on me for 'Defrauding an Inn-keeper,' or some such shit like that.

"She compelled me to prostitute myself. Since I whored against my free will, I can hold my head higher."

"I'm glad, honey," I went back to dotting the i's on my resume. If she wanted to rationalize her past to something other than being a hooker, that was fine with me. I'm glad she can.

Wish I could.

Can't dwell on what might have been.

Right.

At Eleven o'clock, I was listening to the phone ring in Brooks' office. I was put right through. "Mister Brooks, this is Tracy."

"I know. Are you on the boat?"

"Yes, sir."

"Per your first request: My friend says it will be arranged as soon as he has a place to send it."

"Fantastic! Ask him to get on it and send it to you."

"That shall be done. About the other requests, I think we'd better meet and discuss this in a more private arena."

"Fine, sir. Where?"

"At the place you landed yesterday. I'll send a boat for you."

"It'll take an hour."

"Fine. Noon it is. We'll do lunch. Bring your appetite."

When I walked into the San Francisco Yacht Club, I was properly attired in a colorful yachty-looking suit, (not the same outfit I was fishing in), and met Mister Brooks in the lounge. He was wearing his club blazer and a necktie. First thing I spotted were the three silver Past Commodore stars over the SFYC tangled anchor seal.

Later I'd find out that the only times he wore a tie was when he had important meetings or had to appear in court. I ordered a Virgin Mary because I didn't want to give him any bad vibes about my drinking.

He carried our drinks and we were seated in the dining room, next to the window overlooking the docks. I was nervous at first, but after telling sailing stories to each other, I began to relax and enjoy myself. Once the meal was ordered and we were munching on a delicious icy tray of relishes, He asked, "Did you bring your resume?"

"Yes, sir." I was puzzled that he would ask for it so soon.

All I had thought when Renny told me to make one out was that maybe, some day in the future, he might ask to see it.

"May I see it, please?"

I handed it to him, and suddenly was scared spitless because I had put so much detail down. As he read it over, going back to earlier pages, I fretted, Tracy, you dumb bunny! Why so much? You didn't need to put all of' it down! You've stripped yourself naked and said here it is. Take it or leave it.

He chuckled at a few lines of humor I wrote, and went back to the second page. What did I write there? At last, he handed it back to me with a smile.

"You write well. I'm glad to see that you didn't leave anything out."

I glanced at the page he kept going back to. I breathed a quiet sigh of relief when I saw it was only the page that dealt with my avocation. My legit avocation. Sailing. "How do you know I didn't?"

"I have a confession of my own to make. I had already accomplished most of what you asked for when you called at nine thirty. I was on the other line, talking to Mrs. Martin. Later, I talked to several others who know you. I can tell you that you don't have a lot of fans in the Financial District."

My heart sank. It was all over. Well, it was fun anticipating the chances. After Lee's chat with Snaggletooth, I don't stand an ice-cream cone's chance in hell of ever getting work from him. Too bad. I like him.

"I didn't think I would have."

"However," he intoned gravely, "you might be surprised to know that every person I talked to, even those who don't like you, say that you are one of the sharpest, most adept crime investigators they've ever worked with."

Huh?

"I consider that much better than getting a glowing report from some ex-boss who likes you. I've found out some other not so glowing things, though."

"Like what?"

"In lay terminology, your credit history sucks. I've come to the impression that you're a total space cadet when it comes to handling money."

"That's true," I said noncommittally. "I told you that in there." I pointed to the resume. "Money problems are why I got in trouble."

"Miss Cunningham, maybe I'm moving too fast for you."

"Nosir!" I said. "You just go ahead and move as fast as you want."

"Well, it seems to me that I can use a full time investigator. This isn't a whim. I've been giving this move a lot of thought over the past few months. When you so cheerfully brightened up my office yesterday, you had the great good fortune to be the right person, at the right place, at the right time."

"Sometimes I get lucky."

"Sometimes I do too. Tracy, I have a lot of work that I'm farming out. It's very expensive. Perhaps we can come to some sort of arrangement, whereby you rent some office space from me, and I'll keep you working. In slack times, you can take outside jobs."

"What about the fact that I'm unlicensed?"

"You've been avoiding a background check, haven't you?"

I looked down at my glass. "Like the plague. But my father insists that I get one."

"Suppose I pull a few strings here and there, and I tell the authorities what a stellar, persona you are, toss a few names around to insure that a legitimate background check breezes through? Would you like to be a licensed P.I.?"

I was someplace between a face-splitting grin and tears of happiness when I replied, "You have to ask? Absolutely!"

"Good."

"You want me to go to work for you?"

"No. Not work for me. Do work for me, as a private contractor, not as an employee. I can't make an employee rent space from me. There's some rather silly legalistics involved here."

"I'll do anything you want, Mr. Brooks." It was then I remembered that I negotiated a better deal for myself in the beginning with Nora. I wasn't trying to hold Lee up, but I felt now was the time to get it all on the table.

"I can't afford to rent space from you. Not in that super office building."

"We'll work the rent out. Rent, secretarial help, bookkeeping services, telephones, all these can be put on a ledger against future earnings."

"Mr. Brooks, I have to live, too. All my money will go back to you."

"As most of the finances will be a paper exchange, I think we can make arrangements for you to draw an adequate living allowance. We'll call it an advance against earnings."

There it was. My golden opportunity. I had to give this a lot of thought. I spent maybe ten seconds hesitating before I blurted "Yes!" loud enough to raise the eyebrows of the people sitting at the near-by tables.

My ears turned red, a sure sign that I was either mad or embarrassed. I sure the heck wasn't mad at anyone. No siree bob. "Ooops, sorry. Under those conditions, I'll be happy to do your investigating."

"Good. You'll begin now."

"Now?"

"Now. Welcome to the office building of Brooks and Brooks, Tracy. I'm hoping that we'll have a long, happy, professional relationship."

"I'm depending on it," I smiled and shook his hand. Too bad I couldn't show my thanks in a more physical display of hugging and kissing.

But... hell with decorum. Hell with being reserved. I shouted "Yippee!" loud enough to attract everyone's attention. My ears turned red again.

Hell with them, too.

CHAPTER TWENTY-SIX

"Now that we're a team, Tracy, want to fill me in on your case?"

Mankind, did that word 'team' ever sound good to me.

"Yes, Sir," I answered and relaxed. The total shock of what had just come to pass wouldn't sink in for a while. I mentally squared my shoulders and became as professional as I could. I didn't ever want my new boss to be sorry for the day I walked into his office.

I know, I know.

He wasn't my boss, I wasn't his employee, just an independent contractor who would spend most her time working his cases. The fact remains that I had someone who was like a boss now. I could gear my mind to thinking about what was going on and not sweat surviving the next week. He could make the heavy decisions, decisions I wasn't ready to make in my life.

I was safe again.

"This began as a search for a run-away seventeen year old girl named Stephanie Bradford. Her father hired me, paid me a thousand dollars advance retainer. I found out later he hired me because it takes a thief to catch a thief, except this time we can change the word 'thief' to 'tramp.'"

His expression darkened just enough to tell me he was getting tired of my bringing that subject up. "I think we can let that more colorful part of your past die a quiet death, Miss Cunningham. Let's not dwell on it again. You are what you are now, not what you were sometime in the past. Understand?"

I felt about an inch tall when I said, "Yes, Sir. Anyway, all I had to go on was the fact that she had run away to Cincinnati and had dropped out of sight..."

I went on to give him a half-hour dissertation of what and who had led me to this table. "People like Black Willa," I began my summation, "should be buried in the beach, sand up to their necks and be allowed to watch a very slow, high tide come in and drown them."

If I thought his face turned dark before, he was positively livid, but under control. "How in the hell is she getting away with all this?"

"I think she's got someone looking out for her interests in the P.D."

"What makes you think that?"

"I talked to a girl who was busted and arrested for prostitution in the street. That was the blackmailing item that kept her in line. Willa had a copy of the booking slip and a bail receipt, and was threatening to send a copy to the kid's parents."

"What does all this add up to?"

"Hold it a sec, boss," I smiled. "You answer that. What did your friend tell you was in the safe deposit box?"

"He didn't tell me."

"Get any hints?"

"No."

"Goddammitt, how in hell are we going to figure all this out if we don't know what the big secret is?"

"Slow down, Tracy," he said calmly. "He didn't tell me because he doesn't know what's in the box."

"Who does?"

"No one. All he knows is the box number and bank's name. He can't divulge that. If the IRS knew, they'd have that thing open in a second."

"Hmmm." I finally finished with my lunch and sipped some coffee. "Given: Grandfather Martucchi loved Stephanie more than anyone in his family. Given: He wouldn't leave her anything that would get her in hot water, would he?"

"I wouldn't think so."

"Question: If this was an object of value, or papers, say to the ownership of his estate, wouldn't Stephanie be in a jam with the bagmen?"

"She sure would. So would the trustee attorney. Uncle likes his share up front."

"Conclusion: The thing can't have a high value, can it?"

"Not monetarily."

"Bradford, Senior, wants whatever it is. Maybe he doesn't know what it is, but he thinks he does. And I'm beginning to think I know what's in the box...

"Bradford wants the contents...

"Valueless in bucks, but obviously a high intrinsic value...

"I wonder..."

"What, already?"

I had him on tenterhooks." I wonder if the safe contents have something to do with the untimely demise of the late A.J. Martucchi's daughter, Stephanie Bradford's mother?"

My new boss sat back and smiled. I looked at him, perplexed. He watched my face long enough that I had to say something.

"What is it?"

"I was right about you. In that doll-like head of yours resides one hell of a logical mind. You're a diamond in the rough that needs cutting and polishing. Can you make all this fit?"

"I don't know, sir."

"Stop with the 'sir' bit, Trace. I want you to call me 'Lee'."

"Yes, si... Lee. I need to find out a few things. If I can put Bradford in Pinecrest about the time of the murder, will you go to the lawyer and convince him to open the secret door?"

"Absolutely."

CHAPTER TWENTY-SEVEN

"What about the safe house?" I asked over our second cup of coffee. I'd been watching the time. If he had to go to court, he must have had a late appearance."

I can find one, but I don't think it'll be any better than what you already have. You might be better off just staying out there."

"I can't operate out of a tugboat all the time."

"Why not?"

"My boyfriend is using the shore boat. He doesn't know what I'm doing."

"That would be Sergeant Greg Phillips, San Francisco P.D?"

Yep. He'd done his homework, too. "Yes. He's working the Angel Bradford homicide.

He wants me to stay aboard and baby squat Stephanie."

"Why aren't you?"

"That is reactive. I can't sit around doing nothing. I've got to be proactive, doing something to help. I'll bet I'm already a lot farther ahead than Greg is."

"I won't take that bet. I assume you can operate an outboard?"

"If it's not over a twenty-five horsepower, and I don't have to pull-start it, I can."

"No... that won't work."

"Why?"

"I was going to lend you my dingy. If you don't want your boyfriend finding out you're working the case, you can't leave another shore boat tied up out there. Here's the phone number of the club."

He wrote out a number on the back of his business card. "I'll tell the management that you are to picked up and delivered whenever you want. If you need to, you can use my car."

I found out then why he was wearing a tie. The background noise of the dining room, although somewhat subdued, ceased. That's right, all noise simply stopped. I looked up and watched one of the most beautiful creatures I've ever seen ease her way past the tables.

Some men in the place must have known her, as they smiled and she returned the smile. Others simply let their jaws drop. She was heading in our general direction.

"Apparently," Lee said without turning around, "my wife has just graced the room with her presence."

Talk about timing.

She gave him an air kiss on the cheek and looked me over critically as he introduced us. Her name was Candi, but even this early on, I was thinking she couldn't be sweet.

Candi Brooks was five-five or so, had raven black hair, and the most incredible royal blue eyes I've ever seen. Her eyes were naturally wide-innocent and hinted of bedroom. Her face was flawless, a combination of all that men field in high esteem. Perfect damn nose. Perfect damn lips and mouth. Perfect damn everything. And her perfect skin, perfect cheekbones.

I hate her.

Perfect damn figure... it matched all the rest. Perfect. Not too much, not to little, just what I and every girl wished for every single night we went to sleep as underdeveloped adolescents.

Perfect proportions.

She was wearing a coat over a thin cotton dress that left very little to the imagination when she slipped the coat off and sat down. She didn't need mechanical contrivances of support to display her shape.

Strangely, throughout all this mental cataloging on my part, I kept thinking that I knew her. I was sure I'd met her, but I'd sure remember meeting anyone as beautiful as her. All that came to mind was my best girlfriend from high school who had the same physical and facial description, and was almost as lovely. And Lee's wife wasn't Shelly.

"I'm so glad to meet you, Miss Cunningham."

"I'm likewise pleased, Mrs. Brooks," I smiled.

"Why don't you call me Candi?" She oozed. "After all, I plan on calling you Tracy. Honey."

She turned to Lee, who was just getting comfortable. "Be a darling and get me a drink, please?"

"Sure," he said, getting to his feet. "Be right back." Candi didn't have to add, "Don't hurry." It was written all over her face. Perhaps she was the most lovely animal I'd seen in a long time, but I was already getting a well-defined impression that she could be a bitch, and not have to work at it very hard. The only thing I was mistaken about was the part about having to work at it at all.

She didn't. "Let's clear the air, before there is any air." she said evenly.

I tried to match her manner. "Might be a good idea.."

"Lee told me all about you last night when we were pillow talking in bed."

Now how did I know she was going to stress that? "He won't do anything without consulting with me first, you know," she said. "And to be perfectly blunt about the whole idea of you working for my husband..."

She drew a deep breath, and stared into my eyes. "I don't like the idea of a two-bit whore wandering around in his office."

That set the tone, real quick.

We were going to have this conversation in street language. "Mrs. Brooks," I said as coldly as I could, "Don't confuse me with people you may have known in the past. I was an escort. We both know that the difference between a two-bit whore and me is about the same as the difference between Lassie and you... if there is any difference... come to think of it, there isn't much distinction, is there?"

That stopped her for a moment. "We're not going to be friends, are we?"

I had to be reserved. Even though it had been sitting since lunch began, I took a carrot stick from the relish tray and bit it in half. "Doesn't sound like it. What the hell are you worried about? Believe me, Mrs. Brooks, the office situation is not generally a seething pot of sexual orgies."

"Nevertheless, I am married to a man who is very handsome. I trust him, but I don't trust you. I'll bet you've been wondering what he's like in the sack since you laid eyes on him."

I managed a slender smile. "I'd be lying if I said otherwise. On the other hand, I've seen enough men in my life that I can't imagine there's anything I haven't seen. We used to have a saying: 'Take off their clothes, stand 'em on their heads, and they all look alike'. Mrs. Brooks, believe me. I'm not interested in bedding your man."

Hope my nose doesn't give away that lie.

She almost smiled at my claim. "Looking at you, I'll have to concede that you're not ugly. Don't construe that as meaning I think you're competition, though. You're cute, but simply put, not in my class. The mere idea that you liked getting laid enough to make it an occupation doesn't sit well with me."

I sat forward. "Read my lips, lady. I am not active in that life. Sex isn't that big a deal with me."

I have got to stop this. My nose is going to start growing any second now.

"So you say. So Lee says. So I say, just keep your mind on doing whatever it is that you're getting paid for, and keep your porno-dreams out of my man's pants. Dig?"

"I dig. Look, if you're so dead set against me, why did you agree to me coming on in the first place?"

"I don't tell Lee what to do in the office. I only suggest. If I didn't go along, he'd do whatever he wanted anyway. He's a bit childish about things like that.

"The only difference is, that if he was tempted to see what made you so valuable to men, he might give you a tumble. Now that I've said okay, he won't. It's a matter of honor with him. You do know what that word means, don't you?"

"I'm aware if its existence," I sipped my coffee, hoping she didn't see my hand shaking from fury.

Out of the blue, her manner changed. She softened just a little. "Can I have your word that you won't mess with Lee?"

"I thought you didn't trust me."

"I've got a feeling with you, all's fair and all that shit, but I've also got a funny feeling that your word is good."

"It is."

"Well?"

"You have it," I sighed. "I give you my word that there will never be anything untoward between your husband and me."

"Thank you." For the first time since she sat down, she smiled. Not a great smile, but some, and she was even prettier when she smiled.

Smile or no, I was still incensed about being asked like a kid to promise. "Not that it makes any difference, Lady, but I made myself a promise a long time ago that I was going to change my act. There's plenty of well-equipped singles around. So you don't have to worry about me teaching your man what a terrific joy and a pleasure sticking his pen in a real appreciative woman's inkwell can be."

A look of shock and something akin to fright flashed over her face. In that micro-second blink of an eye I read it all.

Oh my God, I don't believe this!

Score: Lions Zip, Christians!

I had accidentally hit on her Achilles Heel. That flash of fear in her expression said everything. She was scared to death of me! The walking, talking Venus sitting across from me was completely, one hundred percent, insecure!

Considering the conversation, I should have guessed it. It shouldn't have taken a Sherlock Holmes to figure out that if a Prime Fox like Candi was worried about a skinny kid like me, she must not have been all that good when the lights were out. And she knew it.

We were of equal value to men, and she knew I knew it. Her fear of my implied skills more than made up for her physical beauty. We sat stone-faced, staring at each other like two strange alley cats. I was beginning to wonder what happened to Lee. Thank God, he came back soon. He must have been watching the discussion from out in the bar and waited for a calm.

The three of us chit-chatted inanely for a few coolly civilized minutes, then Candi stood up, pecked Lee on the cheek and said she had to scoot. She'd see him about six thirty. Aerobics, and all that.

I calmed down the moment she left. I think Lee knew what the subject of the conversation was, and decided to see if I could hold my own. It didn't completely surprise me when he didn't ask a single question about it.

We walked across the street to the office and Renny asked the moment we walked in, "All set?"

"Yep," Lee grinned. "She's here for the duration."

I didn't know which 'she' Lee was referring to, but I assumed it was me.

"Welcome, Tracy." Renny came out from behind the counter. "Allow me to show you to your office."

While Lee stood at the front counter and leafed through the afternoon mail, Renny led me back and opened the door across from the men's rest-room. I was staggered when I entered. The office made any office I'd ever seen in Peerless look like a cubicle.

The walls were rosewood paneled, and the floor was covered with soft blue carpeting that was so plush the first thing that came to my mind was to take off my shoes and go barefoot.

My eyes were drawn to the two oil paintings on the wall. They were both originals, one a beautiful seascape, the other an old multi-masted clipper ship that was in deep trouble.

"Whoever painted this obviously wasn't a sailor," I said.

"What makes you say that?"

"Come take a look," She walked over and stood next to me.

"With the size of the ship, the angle it's sailing, and the beach so close in the foreground, there isn't a chance in a million that square-rigger isn't going to ram itself ashore, within the next three minutes, with all sails flying."

"I can see it now." she laughed. "Wonder if Lee ever picked that up?"

"If he didn't, he's never going to sail my boat."

I sat behind my new desk. The polished rosewood top was bigger than my car. In the rest of the monstrous office, sitting behind an inlaid parquet coffee table was a full length forest green leather couch. Opposite the table, facing the desk, were two very comfortable dark turquoise leather guest chairs. Renny pointed out a fully equipped wet bar behind a louvered set of doors, then opened the drapes to proudly show me the view of a mossy old garden in back.

I was still in awe when I asked, "Who's office was this?"

"It originally belonged to Mister Brooks's father. He passed away from liver and prostate cancer two years ago. You must be something special. Lee hasn't allowed a soul in here since Brooks Senior died."

On the desk was a photograph of a few smiling Army officers on some Pacific Island, during World War Two. Since there were signatures over all the men except one, the man in the center had to be Lee's father, Shelby. A rather handsome man himself.

"I don't know why I'm given such an awesome privilege," I said. "I could have been comfortable in a converted broom closet."

Then I blurted out defensively, "Please believe me, Renny, I didn't do or promise anything special to deserve this office!"

"I know," she laughed. "May I assume that you've met Lee's wife?"

"I've had the experience." I said coolly. "Who is she? I mean, she looks so familiar."

"Remember a few years back when there was a program on TV about three beautiful stewardesses who were always getting into silly adventures?"

"The Flying Foxes?"

"Yeah. Remember the dark-haired one? That was Candi. Lee and Candi have been married for five years and the honeymoon is still going strong. Whenever the two of them are together, it's kissy-face, huggy-body, pawing each other, and whispering nasty little love words to each other.

I suppressed that sickening image and said, "I don't think it's going to be a big secret that we didn't hit it off too well."

"Why not?"

"I don't know. I was still saying I was glad to meet her when she came down on me like a ton of bricks. She was spring-loaded to the pissed off position from the moment we were within talking distance."

"Damn!" she said. "I'm sorry, Tracy. That may be my fault."

"Why?"

"She called me this morning and asked all about you. What you looked like, personality, that sort of thing."

"What did you tell her?"

"The truth. That you were a cute petite blonde."

"Like Angie?"

"Yes. Like Angie. I'm sorry, Tracy."

"Don't worry about it. She would have known the moment she saw me anyway." I appreciatively ran my palm over the smooth wood on the desk. "Bet I can guess why I'm in this office."

"Why?"

"Has Mister Brooks ever had a female associate? Even one as remotely connected to these offices as me?"

"No. Only me."

"I thought not. In Lee's mind, I'm no threat to replace Mister Brooks, Senior. He probably hates the idea of this office not being used. It's not rational to keep it empty. It's obvious no man will ever be allowed to use it. No law says a woman can't though. You can't, because your job requires that you stay in front and defend the inner sanctum. I'm truly honored."

"You should be. Sorry to say, there's another reason you got this place." Her eyes were twinkling.

"What?"

"It's the only other office in the suite."

I felt my ears burning. "You could have told me that instead of letting me ramble on, you know."

"Oh relax, kid." She chuckled and changed the subject. "Once you get used to this place, you'll find out that Mister Brooks travels first class, in everything he does."

I looked around the office. "I can tell."

It was delivered with as much warmth as possible, but I fully understood what Renny said next was a thinly veiled warning. "First class also describes the people who are allied with him in any way. That means you, Miss Cunningham. Please don't let him down."

I matched her stare. This was unquestionably the day for warnings from Lee's women. I'm now number three. If a fourth woman ever came in, wonder if I'd react in the same defensive way? I hoped not.

"I don't intend to."

"Then I don't have to worry about you, do I?" She broke into a great smile.

"We're going to have good times together, Tracy. You're the first female in here, excepting clients, since I was hired ten years ago. If you look in the deep drawer, you'll find paper and pencils. All the pencils are sharpened. If you require anything, my number is one zero."

"Thanks, Renny. I use a laptop for most of my notes. If I want to see Lee, should I call you first?"

"I would appreciate it." She left the office. The hell with it. I toed my heels off and luxuriated in the delicious feel of the rug.

Excuse me, Shelby. Ahhh.

CHAPTER TWENTY-EIGHT

I spent a half hour getting the feel of my new digs. Half an hour luxuriating in the deep rug, trying out all the couches and chairs, snooping into closets and the bar, looking over the office stock of booze, (All top quality stuff, of course, even my favorite brand of gin, Boodles), even trying out the couch as a napping spot. I quickly dismissed any other good reason to lie down on a couch.

Even though Candi Brooks and I had an immediate dislike for each other, I gave her my word. I wouldn't mess around with her man. The problem was, as much as I would love to be as intimate with my new boss as he wanted, any time, any where, doing anything, I fully intended to keep my word. There's even honor among us bitches.

I got the wiring for my laptop out of the case, and wired up the desk for it. Turning it on, I discovered a few wifi nets. A couple came in full strength.

I sat behind my desk, getting back to the problem at hand.

How am I going to place Bradford at the cabin in Pinecrest? It was four and a half long years ago. About the same time that an airhead girl was telling Nora Pincolini her conditions for becoming a party girl, Angel Bradford was being shot in the forehead by someone she knew.

I tried to visualize Angel's terror, the wet, smacking slam of the bullet snapping her head backwards, her mental death, profound blackness, bones and muscles turning to soft rubber in a second, being undressed, her arms and legs flopping to the floor as the clothes were pulled off her body.

Then being dragged to the trap door, being dropped through it, lying in a heap in the cold dirt under the cabin, timelessly waiting for someone to scratch out a two-foot deep grave, being dumped in the cold hole, and the smell and feel of shovel-loads of damp musty-smelling dirt landing on her face and bare skin.

I shuddered and hoped she was fully dead when all this happened. In my vivid imagination, I pictured Charles Bradford doing all the work. Maybe he didn't have to strip her. Maybe he went up there, convinced her to make love with him for old time's sake, made love to her and shot her in the head.

The final climax.

The ultimate end. Dying while experiencing the penultimate ecstasy. I wanted to be convinced that's the way it happened. I really hoped Bradford was sexually good to her that last time, and that Angel Bradford died mid-orgasm.

It's the way I want to go. Die in a body-washing orgasm. At the same peak that Greg had me at last night.

Oooo yeahhh! 'Cept I don't want it to happen until I'm a hundred and ten or so.

Back to work. How do I find out if anyone, especially Charles Bradford, drove up there? Gasoline credit cards? It was when? Spring? Fall? Winter?

I had already ruled out Summer. Stephanie said the cabins were all occupied during the warm season. A gunshot would echo around the lake at night, and I couldn't see all this happening in daytime.

There wasn't any rational reason it couldn't have been a summer day, but I just didn't see it happening that way. I kind of ruled out winter-time, too. I couldn't get a good mental image of city-boy Bradford slogging through the mud and snow to go copulate with his bitch wife then shoot her.

Besides, he'd have to be more careful than that. All the cabins in the area were summer places. There isn't any recreational-type attractions on that side of the lake basin in the winter. Nothing but snow, trees and rocks. Things Steph and Greg liked. I can handle it, once I'm inside a cozy warm cabin with a good man, a fireplace, a big ol couch, and a steaming mug of hot chocolate with a shot of Peppermint Schnapps, but not before.

Bradford couldn't take a chance that someone patrolling the area wouldn't investigate his tracks in the snow and eventually find the body.

Spring-time would be wrong, too. The body would have a long time to decompose with the resulting odors attracting attention before the first freeze. So that kind of narrows the time of death down to sometime after Labor Day, and before the first heavy snowfall. Four years ago.

Of course I could have just asked Greg what the date was on the milk container, but I felt better about thinking this out myself. Tonight, I would confirm the date.

So how do I prove Bradford went up there then? I could always ask him.

I could always get my head blown off, too.

I didn't even have a photo of the man to show to a hundred gas station attendants, and that might be a washout. How long does a gas jockey stay at the same station? How many guys will remember putting gasoline in a specific car four years ago? Besides, there's always the possibility that Bradford's car was full and he didn't buy gas.

The Ranger station? There's one up there... would Ranger Raccoon get curious about a single woman living in a summer cabin, off-season? Hmmm. Let's say that Angel was there. it's off-season... cold... dark...

Electricity!

Bing-freakin'-go! She wouldn't have lived there without electricals! Even if it was already on when she was there and she never had to call Reddy Kilowatt to have it turned on... Someone had to have the power turned off!

I grabbed the phone book and dialed the general offices of Pacific Gas and Electric in San Francisco.

When a woman answered, I asked hopefully, "Can you connect me with someone who can tell me about electricity being turned off four years ago?"

"I think so. Residential or commercial?"

"Residential."

"Where, Ma'am?"

"Pinecrest? A small summer town 'bout thirty miles above Sonora? On 108?"

"A moment, please. I'll connect you."

Already, I felt better. The woman never wavered, as though my request was impossible. When the next voice answered, the connection sounded like long distance.

"PG&E."

"Can you tell me about someone's service being shut off four some-odd years ago? In Pinecrest?"

"Hold please. I'll connect you."

While I waited, I remembered some conversations with a cousin on my mother's side. Stewart was about ten years older than me, and was one of the few people who treated me like a real person, not a pip-squeak kid.

During our rare family reunions, I was the only child of my generation. All the rest of the children were Stewart's age, but he was the only one who treated me nice, not like I was a pest.

If you can call a ten year separation in age being in the same generation. Stew worked for Edison, and when he'd come over to visit me and Dad, sometimes tell us about his work. Some of the terminology he used came back to me.

"Customer service."

"I'd like to find out who ordered a service disconnect about four years ago."

"Yes, Ma'am. Residential or Commercial?"

"Residential."

"What's the address?"

"I don't know. It is the Pinecrest summer home of August J. Martucchi. Permanent residence in Belvedere, California."

"I'll check. Hold please."

Piece a cake. All you have to do is think things out, and presto, you're a detective.

Or get bullshit lucky, and think you're a detective.

"Ma'am?"

"Yes?"

"The service was disconnected at the request of a Charles Bradford on October Twelfth, four years ago. Do you wish to have it re-connected?"

Bingfreakinggo!

"No thanks, Ma'am. Is there any possibility I could get a copy of that record?"

"I think so. May I ask why?"

"I'm a detective from Sausalito. I want it for verification of time. It has nothing to do with your company."

"I'll be happy to send you this, but I don't think it's going to do you much good."

"Why not?"

"It was a telephone request. We have no way of verifying the name of the caller."

"Oh. Well, could you e-mail me what you have anyway?"

"Address?"

"TJH at gardenconnection dot net" I have to get that changed. You can guess what gardenconnection dot net was assigned to. I asked Renny if she could set me up with a new email address. It was getting on about four o'clock and I had to be back at the tugboat before Greg.

I said good night to Lee and Renny and never touched the ground while I walked across the street.

CHAPTER TWENTY-NINE

That night, after dinner, in our cozy bed, I got one verification of the homicide date from Greg. The milk container was dated the fifteenth of October. That matched the date of the service disconnect, the twelfth of October.

Angel Bradford was killed on or about the dozenth of October, probably by Charles Bradford. Most important, I discovered that I knew a helluva lot more than the so-called professional cops did!

How do I know? If you're the least bit surprised what a girl can find out in bed, doing her man in a very intimate way, don't ever sleep with a spy. Don't get me wrong. I wasn't doing those lovely things to him because I wanted his information. No way, Jack.

It was my turn to do him, and I'll bet he doesn't forget last night for a long, long time. I know I won't.

Audible sigh.

All Greg knew was that the skeleton was Angel Bradford. Dental records confirmed that. And that she'd been shot once with a thirty two caliber automatic pistol, probably a Ruger.

Except for the name part, I told you that.

The cabin had been re-searched by the sheriff's department, and there was a possibility that the Crime Scene Unit found evidence of blood on one of the couches.

I shuddered, wondering which one of us, Stephanie or I, was the one who was sleeping where Angel was killed. Clothing belonging to the dead woman was never found.

Not a problem. Bradford probably hauled it all away.

The area around the building and the trail to the parking area was checked for tell-tale clothing. Same results. Nodda.

You're never going to find blood-soaked clothes, Hardbody. She was starkers before she was shot.

No evidence what-so-ever to the identity of the killer.

Ask the power company who shut off the juice, H.B. Better yet, why don't you ask the dumb broad you've been banging for a week?

I fell asleep with the same silly smirk I woke up with.

Wonder if 'ol Mona Lisa was a horny P. I.?

The four of us had breakfast together. I didn't sweat the teens blabbing to Greg that I was gone during the day. I had told them if they ratted on me, and I got stuck on this barge baby-sitting, I'd make sure that they wouldn't get within shouting distance of each other.

There was no way we could keep this up much longer. Jerry had to return home pretty soon, as the guys he had quote, gone camping with, unquote, were due to come home tomorrow afternoon. If I wanted to get back to a normal life, I had to bring this case to a close in thirty hours.

I had fantasies about bringing in the head hood, handcuffed, and serve him on a silver platter to the Chief who had instructed Greg to get me off the case. Better yet, go to the source of the problem, give Bradford to my dad and say, "In yo face, Pops."

Greg was just getting the shore boat onto a speedy plane, ever so smug in his belief that I was being a good girl and following his orders, when I was on the cell, calling for my water taxi.

I changed out of my Levis and UCLA sweatshirt and into a conservative navy blue sweater and gray pants. I bounced into my office bright-eyed and eager, grinning a good morning to Renny and Lee, and going behind the desk and into the coffee shack.

There was a package with my name on it. I opened it and found a big coffee mug. It was one of those tip-proof cups, shaped like a Captain's bottle, with outline drawings of sailing boats on it. Lee and Renny were going out of their way to welcome me to the office family, that's for sure.

Wonder if Lee felt a bit guilty about Candi coming down on me so hard?

Let's face it. She must have bragged how she put the little tramp in her place. She'd never be able to keep her mouth shut. And I know she'd never repeat the final portion of the conversation. She'd never be that honest.

I came out with an effusive "Thank you," and followed Lee back to his office, at his request. Once I settled onto a comfortable chair, he said, "You took off so fast yesterday you didn't tell me what you had accomplished."

"I'm sorry, boss," I smiled. "From now on, I'll write out a thumbnail report, okay?"

"That'll be fine."

"Well, I did some thinking, and I imagineered myself a way to find out if Bradford was at Pinecrest when the murder occurred."

"And?"

"He was. Angel Bradford was killed while making love with her estranged husband, by her estranged husband, on or about Columbus Day, four years past."

"What makes you think that?"

"I called the power company and found out who had the electricity shut off... and when."

"Ohhh, that's great! It's so simple, it's pure genius!" he almost shouted. "Was it Charles Bradford?"

"Exactemente."

"That doesn't prove he killed her."

"No sir, it doesn't. But can you tell me how he knew when to have the disconnect done? There are no phones up there. No cellular towers. Angel certainly didn't call him and say, 'I've just been killed. You may as well shut off the power'.

"Unfortunately, I can't prove he was the one who called. All the power company can say is that someone, purporting to be Bradford, called and asked for a service disconnect."

"You're convinced?"

"Yes, sir," I smiled. "Aren't you?"

"I am."

"Can you take that to the bank?"

"I can sure the hell try," he grinned back and punched in a number on his desk phone. I went to my office to give him some privacy, even though he didn't ask for it.

I even wrote up a crime report explaining my thought processes for the files. I was up front, waiting for Renny to download my flash drive when Lee came up, and shanghaied my arm.

"Grab your purse, Sherlock."

"Where are we going?"

"We're going to meet someone at a bank."

During the drive, I asked if I was going to meet the Mafia Consigliore. Lee looked me straight in the eye and lied. "No."

That was good enough for me. I didn't want to know any old mob mouthpiece anyway.

We met a man whom I was introduced to by first names only. 'Harry' led us back to a private room, one of those rooms in safe deposit areas where you could open your treasure box in privacy. We waited while he left and returned with a box, holding it so we couldn't see the numbers.

I wasn't about to ask why he was in possession of the key. If whatever was in the box was so valuable to the family and the feds, he must have had one helluva good hiding place for the key. He unlocked the box and opened it slowly, bring out as much drama as one could in the five by five enclosure.

"Well, I'll be dammed!" he said. "What is it?"

"A pistol in a plastic bag." I jumped to my feet excitedly. "Don't show it to me, don't tell me, let me guess! It's a 32 Ruger Automatic!"

"How did you know?"

I laughed lustily. "Gawd, it's delicious!"

"Want to fill me in?" Harry asked. I was just about to, when I stopped myself. "No. Harry, I don't know you, and I don't think I'd better say anything more. I want to discuss this with my attorney, and he can inform the proper parties."

He understood. It was part of the game. I hadn't met the Family attorney, and since my information only concerned him and his clients, I wouldn't discuss the matter with an unofficial stand-in.

Back in Lee's gas-hogging Continental Convertible, he said in a mock Chicago accent, "Okay, Babe. Spill it."

"Do I have to?"

"Huh?"

"I want to get all the interested parties in one place and tell everyone at once. I've got some things to set up, too. Can we wait? Please?"

"Okay," he smiled. "The grand finale?"

"Something like that, boss. Thanks."

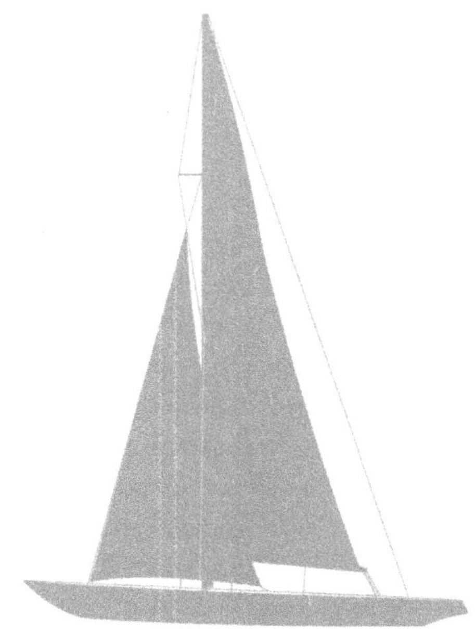

CHAPTER THIRTY

I really felt self-conscious and nervous. It was like this was something out of the movies. The only difference was that instead of the eccentric old male P.I., the Saucy Sleuth reveals all her surmises and conclusions before the clients, suspects and the police. All I needed was a thunderstorm and a huge fireplace. Failing that, we all met in Lee's office.

You could cut the atmosphere with a chain saw and sell it to a psychology class. Stephanie Bradford sat across the room from her father. Greg Phillips and his partner, Sergeant Wormy Dunnegan, sat between the two Bradfords. Lee sat behind his desk, while I got to pace the floor. Renny was in her secretary's chair, flexing her fingers over her court-reporter's stenotype machine. Everyone was ready except me.

I was scared to death. Greg wasn't too yippee-skippee to discover that I had gone behind his back. Yesterday, I had convinced his partner to help set all this up and not tell Greg. If he found out too early, he could and would have quite literally, screwed me out of the information.

My possibly new ex-boyfriend wasn't very pleased when he found out that I had allied professionally with a prestigious attorney. Or that I had an extravagant office, done all this while he was under the impression that I was being a good... make that obedient... girl.

A half hour ago, I took Greg to one side. Actually, I dragged him into my office, closed the door, and, using a combination of kisses, pouts, cute looks and a complete preview of the meeting, had gotten myself out of hot water with him.

I hope.

"It's time to get this going, Trace," Lee whispered.

"I know," I whispered back. I turned to my audience and nervously cleared my throat.

"I'm going to describe what I think happened. To do this, we have to go back to when Angel Martucchi was born."

"This goes back that far?" Wormy asked.

"I think so. A lot of this is conjecture, as you all know. Let me lay it out and you can draw your own conclusions. When we discovered what was in A.J.'s safe deposit box, everything began falling into place."

Now that I was talking, I was a little less nervous. "When Angel was born, her mother, A.J.'s beloved wife, went into postpartum depression. It's not uncommon, but since it's a fairly recent diagnosis, the Martucchis had no idea what was happening to her. Six months later, Mrs. Martucchi took an overdose of sleeping pills and died.

"Angel Martucchi grew up, best described as an unqualified bitch. She probably was this way because she sensed that A.J., consciously or sub-consciously, hated her for being born, for being the reason his cherished wife was dead.

"Before she was twenty, Angel married a man who has big ideas of becoming the Godfather after A.J. dies. Charles Bradford is a venal, willful man. A.J. knows it's only a matter of time before Angel and Bradford come to blows, and he's right. Angel takes off four and a half years ago.

"Now the time is right. A.J. goes to Bradford, and tells him that he too, despises Angel. And if Bradford has any ideas of taking over, he, A.J., wants him, Bradford, to go up to the cabin and shoot Angel to death."

Stephanie shot to her feet. "That's a lot of horseshit! Grandpa wouldn't do that to Mom!"

"I'm so sorry, honey," I said softly. "Nothing else logically fits."

"I'm not going to sit here and be vilified," Bradford stood up.

"You're already vile." I shot back.

"Sit it down, Bradford." Greg said calmly. He never took his eyes off me. "I'm enraptured by Miss Cunningham's recital, and I don't want you disturbing a moment of my enjoyment."

"Shove it."

Bradford took one step towards the door. In that second, Wormy, a man who I thought couldn't get out of his own way, was out of his seat and standing in the doorway, his coat unbuttoned to expose his revolver. Bradford meekly decided that sitting was better than the alternatives.

"Where was I?" My knees were clattering together like castanets."

A.J. put out the contract," Lee said.

"Right. Bradford goes up to Pinecrest and shoots Angel. I've got a sneaky suspicion what they were doing at the moment of death, but I'll keep that to myself."

Bradford turned beet red. "When Bradford returns from Pinecrest, he tells A.J. the deed is done. To keep Angel's body hidden, A.J. declares the cabin off limits and somehow acquires the murder weapon.

"Obtaining the murder weapon is one... probably the prime reason A.J. instructed Bradford to do the job himself. A.J. puts the pistol in a safe deposit box, waiting for the only person he loves in the whole family to turn of age. Shortly thereafter, A.J. dies, or possibly takes himself out.

"Stephanie, being crushed by the death of her beloved grandpa, and hating her father, soon runs away. Bradford lets her go, doesn't give a damn what happens to the ungrateful kid.

"I believe that A.J. had Stephanie watched and cared for from the moment he died. Stephanie says she knew of a Godfather in the East. I'm sure as a favor, that family looked after Stephanie.

"Sometime after Stephanie leaves, Bradford discovers his Ruger thirty-two automatic is missing, remembers Stephanie's strange inheritance and puts two and two together. Now all of a sudden he wants her back, dead or alive, preferably dead.

"That was when I came into the case and you all know the rest."

"Most interesting, Miss Cunningham," Bradford said, trying to joke his way out of my glare. "I suppose you know you've blown your bonus?"

"I figured. No big loss."

"It's a good story, but you don't have one shred of evidence," he said.

"We can directly link you to the murder weapon, can't we, Sergeant Phillips?"

"Yep," he said calmly. "Your fingerprints are all over the pistol, Bradford."

"That's not enough to convict."

"Maybe yes, maybe no. Want to drop the other shoe, Trace?" Greg was smiling only with his eyes.

"I'd be delighted, Sergeant. Mr. Bradford, the way I see it, there may be enough to get you jailed for a while, maybe not. However, if you give the police a complete confession, it may be better for you."

"Why?"

Stephanie stood up, right on cue. "Because I called that Godfather back east. You know the man I'm talking about. He and Grandpa were very close. He'd like a long talk with you about Grandpa's death. And he didn't take kindly to a non-Italian in-law cold-bloodedly murdering my mother, a blood family member."

Steph had learned her lines well. She looked at me in casual shock. "I can't believe I'm saying this."

"Go ahead, you're doing fine."

"Anyway, father," venom dripped from her voice when she said that word, "If you want to stay alive to hear about me getting married to Jerry in a few years, perhaps you should have a long talk with Greg, here."

"You're bluffing."

"Take a look out the back window," I said. Sure, it was all a con, a bluff, but Bradford didn't know that. Stephanie, Wormy, Lee and I worked it out this morning.

When you look out the side of Lee's back window, you can see the residential street that forms the corner where the office building sits. Outside, Greg's partner had two big plain-clothes policemen sitting in a borrowed black Cadillac. He picked them out because they looked like stereo-typical hit men. Big, ugly and mean.

When he sat back down, Bradford was ashen. "Before I say another word, I want my attorney present."

"Good idea," Lee said. "You might want to think about turning State's evidence while you're at it. Who knows? Maybe you'll get a slap on the wrist and a new identity."

"You want me to roll over on the family? You have to be kidding!"

"Think about it, Bradford," I said. "It may be the only way for you to stay alive and out of jail."

I smiled and sat on Lee's desk with a mixture of triumph and relief. The meeting broke up, and when they left, Bradford was sticking very close to Greg and Wormy.

CHAPTER THIRTY-ONE

We had one more thing to do. Get the fat broad who made her bones with children's bodies. Every once in a while the sickly smile that Colleen pasted on her face when the John interrupted us flashed into my brain, and made me a little sick, too.

There's nothing worse than a reformed smoker, drinker, or whore, right? Let me tell you, this reformed call-girl was a bit pissed about what I'd seen in San Francisco.

When I went into the sex business it was with my eyes wide open. These kids didn't have a choice. Willa had too impressive of a reputation just to be running a kiddy-porn house.

There had to be something else to it.

I was pretty sure I knew...but I needed confirmation. So I drafted my new boss.

"You want me to what?" He roared when I told him what I wanted.

"It's not for real, boss." I soothed his ire. "I need to get a girl named Colleen out of Willa's reach, so we can question her."

"So I just go waltzing into a cathouse and procure the services of a what, sixteen, seventeen year old kid? What's the matter with the police breaking into the house?"

"Someone in the cop-shop is dirty, remember?"

"Did you tell me that?"

"Quit trying to weasel out of it. I told you in the club. Anyway, both Greg and I believe there's a sour cop. I have a hunch who it is, but Greg doesn't see it my way."

"Why not?"

"She was his bed-partner sometime before I bounced into his life."

"Oh."

"Please, Lee?"

He sighed and sat back. "I've never gone to a house of prostitution. How do I do it?"

"Well, you can get a phony beard," I smirked. "A lot of men disguise themselves before they walk into a place like that. You knock on the door and I'm sure Willa will answer it. Tell her that you have a friend who recommended you."

"What if she asks who?"

"Say 'John Smith' like it was an inside joke. Half the men who ever use a place like that are named John Smith."

"Then what?"

"Tell her you heard about a kid named Colleen. You want her for an out-call."

"And Willa will just let her go?"

"I think so. I doubt if she'll get too suspicious if you don't want to use the house. That's not uncommon.

Besides, if we figure this right, you'll never have to walk inside."

"That's good."

"Wave a few hundred dollar bills in Willa's face. Make sure they're marked and we can I.D. them in case we have to get on the stand and prove Willa sold Colleen's services. The money will get her undivided attention. She'll probably get Colleen and let her go with you because she has a strong leash on the kid. Colleen won't dare run away."

"What then?"

"Then you drive Colleen around and lose anyone who may be following you. I'll show you how. Afterward, bring her to a place where Greg and I will meet you."

"Why doesn't Greg do the man's part?"

"Because, you chicken," I smiled, "Greg is a former vice cop. Any madam worthy of the name knows every vice-fuzz by name, description and any other means of identification you can think of. There aren't too many men six foot six running around. If she smells cop, it's slam the door time."

"Okay. Assume we have Colleen. What are you going to ask her?"

"Nothing much. Just who is supplying the livestock."

CHAPTER THIRTY-TWO

Not that I was any expert, but we spent a good hour in Lee's Continental over in San Francisco, taking corners, planning an escape path, so he could lose the bad guys. After awhile he began to remember playing bicycle ditch as a kid. He refused to admit he played ditch with a car.

Now we know all California kids play ditch with their cars. The single key about playing ditch was getting two full corners on the car chasing you.

Once you had a two-corner lead, the odds of the followers picking the right corners to turn was high, and got higher with each new turn the lead car made. Just for good measure, Renny and I would each drive a rented blocking car.

When the time came, I parked my rented Ford... ugh... down the block and watched Lee go to the front door. The conversation at the door took a good ten minutes, but it was successful, as Lee took Colleen's arm and led her to the Continental.

They took off and sure enough, the same car that chased me that night pulled out of the driveway and settled in behind him. It was another Ford, older than the one I was driving.

Lee wouldn't try to lose the two guys until they were in a residential neighborhood. Downtown traffic and long city blocks made the idea of gaining two corners impossible.

I drove straight to Renny and told her what kind of car we were going to block. She nervously waved and waited while I took up my pre-planned position a few blocks away.

Lee's Continental wasn't a sports car by any stretch of the imagination. We figured that 'Hey Clyde' had to be a better driver than Lee. So when Lee finally screeched around my corner, I'd pull slowly out behind him and dawdle, slowing Hey Clyde long enough to allow Lee to gain the first corner.

He did. Lee came around the corner with a vengeance, the lumbering lead-sled diving around like a whale in a fish tank. I pulled out like a little old lady and cringed as Hey Clyde skidded around the corner and almost slammed into my trunk.

You Sombitch bellowed loud aspersions as to my present endeavor and sex…accusing me of doing something to myself that just cannot be done alone…not if you want to have any fun…and gave me the finger when they roared around me, which I gleefully returned.

I had slowed them for no more than five or ten seconds. It was enough. Lee had a full block lead. In two more corners, Renny would do the same thing.

I crossed my fingers that all would be as planned and drove to my last place. Lee would still be driving hard, but not hard enough to produce loud tire squeals in case the two goons had enough brains to slow down and listen.

I would block and run one more time, if they had somehow followed Lee around ten turns. If not, I would meet Lee and Colleen with Greg at a Daly City restaurant with a back-alley covered parking lot.

When Lee passed me again, I pulled out and drove sedately. No goons. We pulled it off!

Not too shabby for a girl P.I. on her first case, hah?

The escape didn't take real driving skill. Just planning.

And it worked like a charm. When I got to the restaurant in Daly City, Lee was already there, and Colleen and Steph were having a giggling, tearful reunion. We added our client at the last minute, to prove to Colleen that we were the good guys.

"Hi Kelly!" she greeted me enthusiastically.

"Tracy. My real name is Tracy Cunningham. However, I am a for-real Mick. How was the ride?"

"God," she smiled, "I was never so scared in my life. I thought I was going to be killed by this maniac!"

She grinned in Lee's direction. "I never thought you'd actually get me free of that toilet! I figured all that stuff about helping me was so much bullshit, designed to get information."

"A lot of it was. I'm not a cop, I'm a Private Investigator. The ink on my apprentice license isn't dry yet. If you haven't been formally introduced, this 'John' is my boss, Mr. Brooks. That tall handsome dude is my boyfriend, Sergeant Greg Phillips, San Francisco P.D."

"I'm glad to meet you all," she smiled. "And my real name is Della Sanderson. My buddies call me Del."

"Del, we have one basic question. Where do the kids that Willa has in her clutches come from?"

"Drifters, mostly," she said. "A friend of a friend of mine told me about the place. When I decided to split, I came to Willa's."

"Now the prime question. Where did you go to school?"

"Dumas High, in South San Francisco."

"Damn! That's not the answer!"

"Huh?"

"I was hoping I could make a connection with you and Lincoln High in San Rafael."

"Nope. Never went there, but I know a lot of kids who did."

"I wouldn't say a lot," Stephanie said. "I only saw a couple of kids from Lincoln."

"Dan... Stephanie, you were gone for almost two years. I'm one of the old-timers in that place. There had to be ten different girls who attended Lincoln, one time or another."

"We know the girl who called herself Sandy Reed did. Did she happen to mention how she found Willa's?"

"She said a counselor told her it was a good boarding house for girls."

"Bing-Effing-Go!"

"What?" Greg said in shock.

"I knew it!" I shouted with glee. "I knew there had to be a connection someplace!"

"What is going on?" Greg asked.

"It's still a one-hundred percent guess."

"Out with it." Lee said. "Your guesses have a habit of becoming fact."

"Since I first came into this, little things have come to light. Like the number of kids from one school. Like the only way to get out of Willa's is to turn twenty-one and be kicked out for being too old and used, or you disappear in the night. The only person I know who got out any other way is Stephanie."

"Don't forget Stacy," she added sadly.

"Yes. We still have that murder, don't we? Anyway, all those things can add up to white slavery."

"What?" Lee's face darkened perceptibly.

"Willa was too big in the sex trades to go underground for two years and re-surface as a kiddy-porn madam. I'm sure the house makes good bread, but that's not the prime income producer. If she had certain girls targeted and selected for their physical beauty, she could sell them overseas to all sorts of cretin-type people. A clean, scrubbed all American girl of tender years can bring something like one fifty to two hundred grand at the auction block."

"How does this connect with Lincoln?"

"Wait a sec," I asked Colleen, "What did the girls who disappeared look like?"

"Just like you said. The ones I know of were cute, peppery, California girls. One black teenybopper, who was a doll, a couple of Chinese girls, but mostly blonde, blue-eyed kids. Something like you were."

"Did they all go to Lincoln?"

"I don't know. A couple of them were too young for High School."

"Did those kids say they went to school in Marin, by any chance?"

"One bubble-gummer did."

"Lincoln Senior El?"

"Now that you say it, I think so."

"Greg, someone at the school is steering selected kids to Willa. They are probably all cute but incorrigible kids whose parents have given up on them. They're undoubtedly listed as runaways and never heard from again."

"I believe you." He turned to Colleen and asked, "Will you testify that you saw a girl die in Willa's place?"

"Will you protect me?"

"Bet your life, kid."

"If I testify, I will be, won't I?'" She thought about it for a few moments, then said, "Yes. And if you can give the other girls protection, I know I can get some more kids to get on the stand."

"Good enough for me. I'll call in and get a hit squad."

"Can you trust the police?" Lee asked.

"The ones I'm thinking of, yes." Greg looked me in the eye and said, "And Terry Frankfurter is one I trust. I asked her about your questions. She simply did not know of a connection between A.J. Martucchi and Charles Bradford. Simple answer, Trace."

"You believe her?"

"Absolutely." I didn't have to ask. It was written in his eyes.

"Well, I'm glad it wasn't her. I still don't like her, but I'm glad your friend is clean."

Dammit nose! You better not start growin'!

EPILOGUE

When Lee had presented Stephanie with her first allowance check, she agreed with him that the evidence should be presented to the police forthwith, and not try to make herself queen of the local underworld.

Over the years, A.J. and 'Harry' had set up several small legal enterprises that were being operated in trust for Steph. She and her future husband wouldn't be filthy rich, just very wealthy.

All of which she would receive, legally and taxes paid, when she turned twenty-five. Until that age, A.J. had planned for her support. It was sitting in a bank account, simply waiting for her to ask for help. The key was she had to ask.

The only good thing that Greg had to report was that they had found the rat in the nest who was co-operating with Black Willa. I was in the right church, but wrong pew when it came to ol' Hot Dog being the dirty cop.

Internal Affairs had found a young police woman assigned to vice who was being blackmailed herself.

Anytime anything hinting about Willa's activities was uncovered, she made sure that it was squashed right now. Della Sanderson found enough girls who were willing to testify about the beating death of Stacy Reese, AKA Sandy Reed, to make an impervious case against Black Willa and her two goons.

Funny. I just realized that Black Willa sounded a lot like Black Widow. Wonder if she had a red hourglass tattooed on her fat belly?

I never saw Bradford again. He was arrested by the Feds the moment they were informed that he wanted to make a deal.

I would get my first paycheck in a week. When Steph found out about her trust, she insisted that Harry draw up a check comprising ten percent of her total worth.

My check would be an obscene amount. I told her that it was way too much. She said it was a finder's fee, and if I didn't accept it, she would call that Godfather back east.

"I think," she giggled. "this is what we call an offer you can't refuse."

It was five o'clock, and I hadn't seen or heard from Greg since all this came to light in Daly City. Happy about the outcome of everything, I drove over to his place. I had called Wormy and knew Greg was home.

Just like the movies, I rang other apartments to get the front door opened, so Greg wouldn't find out it was me until I was face-to-face with him. I knocked and chewed on the inside of my cheek, the main sign I'm nervous.

He opened the door and looked down at me. He was dressed... or not dressed... to stay home. He was wearing only royal blue corduroy shorts and a Golden State Warrior's tank-top and looked good enough to eat without ketchup.

I felt a pang of fear. The handsome face I loved didn't register happiness. Or anger. Or anything. He was completely emotionless.

"Hi. Come in."

"Hi." I walked past him and sat in the couch. "Don't tell me, lemme play detective," I said.

"You're pissed."

He sat on the other end. That left a lot of distance between us. "I always knew you were a good P.I."

"My father says the only good P.I.s are dead P.I.s." He didn't crack a smile.

"I'm beginning to see why."

"Greg, I'm sorry for beating you to the punch, but I'm not sorry that I was smart enough to figure things out. I'm sorry I fibbed to you and was working the case behind your back, but you asked for it."

"How do you figure that..."

"All that bullshit about me staying out of the case? Weren't you just parroting my Dad? Weren't you just parroting the whole Male Chauvinist Line? Keep the little woman home, plump, pleased and pregnant?"

He snorted. "Love the alliteration."

"Rather liked it myself. Well?"

"Trace, is there something wrong with me wanting my woman to be safe?"

"Am I your woman?"

"You were. Maybe you still are."

"If I have anything to say about it, I still am. "There's not a thing wrong with wanting me to be safe and sound unless it interferes with my ability to be a real human being. I want you just as safe and sound, too. What do you think I think when you get up in the morning and hustle off to work?

"In the back of my... and every cop's Significant Other's mind... God, I hate that term, is a fear that when you get out of bed and give me that last peck and pat on the ass goodbye, that may be the last kiss and pat I ever get from you.

"Don't you think I have a fear that I suppress, just like millions of other girlfriends, wives and husbands of bluecoats, that one day Wormy may walk up my sidewalk with some really bad news?"

"I suppose you have a point."

"Greg, I know damn well you have a superior intellect in that head. Maybe sometimes the air may be a bit thin up there where it normally resides, which may cause oxygen starvation, which leads to brain-fade, but I see nothing terminal."

He was trying not to smile. "What are you getting at?"

"Among other things you are a good friend of mine, right?"

"Right."

"There are times when we're friends, not lovers? Times when we play games?"

"Yes."

"We compete, right? We have honest contests of skill and intelligence?"

"Yes."

"We have real discussions about things that have nothing whatsoever to do with lovemaking?"

"Yes." It was getting very hard for him not to smile. He was still fighting it.

"Gregory Phillips, do you realize that means, horror of horrors, you are friends with a female? A lowly woman? A not-equal?"

"Not-equal?"

"If I'm not the same as you, aren't a mature enough adult to do what I do best, than I'm not equal to you, am I? Honestly now. Am I inferior to you?"

He leered and glanced at the bedroom. "Only in there, Kitten, and that's usually by your choice."

"What about other places?"

"That's silly. Of course we're equals," he admitted. "What would happen if we went to a restaurant and they said they'd serve you, but they wouldn't serve me because I was a woman? Would that make you mad?"

"Of course it would."

I grinned. "Now we're gettin' someplace. We're contemporaries?"

"Yes."

"Buddies?"

"Yes."

"Chums?"

"Yes."

"Sometimes competitors?"

"Yes."

"Lovers?"

"Yes."

"Still?"

"Yes."

I reached over and felt his hand. "I'm sorry I hurt you, friend."

He tugged on it a little. "I accept your apology, friend. C'mere."

We completely eliminated the air gap between us for almost an hour.

Early in the morning, I allowed that there were two places I was inferior.

Cooking in the kitchen and in bed.

And while in Greg's bed, I may have voluntarily assumed the inferior female position, making him superior, but according to him, I was the most superior inferior he ever had the pleasure of knowing.

The End

TRACY'S RULES FOR TVPIS

1. Do not thou goeth undercover, for thou wilt be uncovered.
2. If thee discoverth a body, thee will surely picketh up the weapon of death.
3. If thou handleth the weapon of death, the lord high sheriff will discovereth thee.
4. In battle, the besteth marksman in the world cannot hiteth the broadside of a castle.
5. In ye's trusty steed, thou will followeth a person "discreetly" while being the steed immediately behindeth thy target.
6. When thou approacheth a suspect on foot, thou will always identify thyself to the subject from too fareth away, so he will runneth away quickly.
7. During a chase afoot, if thou getth close to the target, at next cut, thou will have losteth all ground gained.
8. At least onceth a year thou will be frameth for murder most foul.
   8a. If thou beest a lord high sheriff, at least onceth a year, thy squad, division, office, whathevereth, will beest under suspicion for being dirty.
9. There iseth no lasting romantic interesth for TVPIths.
10. Even if she is more fleet of foot, a woman cannot runneth by herself. She must be draggeth by the hand.